Anna told me I would understand about boys one day.

She said that everything would change and I would look at them differently, assess their bodies and their words, the way their eyes moved when they talked to me. She said I'd not only want to answer them but that I'd learn how, knowing which words to use, how to give meaning to a pause.

Then a man took her.

A man took her before I learned any of these things. He took her and kept her for a while, put things inside of her. Of course the obvious thing, but also some others, like he was curious if they'd fit. Then he got bored. Then he got creative.

Then my sister was gone and I thought: *I understand about boys now.*

And she was right. Everything did change. I look at them differently and I assess their bodies and watch their eyes and weigh their words.

But not in the way she meant.

THE FEMALE OF THE SPECIES

MINDY McGINNIS

KATHERINE TEGEN BOOKS
An Imprint of HarperCollins Publishers

Katherine Tegen Books is an imprint of HarperCollins Publishers.

Library of Congress Control Number: 2016932089
ISBN 978-0-06-232090-2

Typography by Erin Fitzsimmons
19 20 21   PC/LSCH   10 9 8 7 6 5
❖
First paperback edition, 2017

For the victims

1. ALEX

This is how I kill someone.

I learn his habits, I know his schedule. It is not difficult. His life consists of quick stops to the dollar store for the bare minimum of things required to keep this ragged cycle going, his hat pulled down over his eyes so as not to be recognized.

But he is. It's a small town.

I watch these little exchanges. They evolve in seconds, from *I get paid to smile at you* to the facial muscles going lax when recognition hits, the price scanner making a feeble attempt to break the silence by making a *beep-beep* when his food goes past.

I know this pattern but watch it anyway. The bread, the cheese, the wine, and the crackers that sometimes he will crumble and put out for the birds—a tiny crack of kindness that makes him all the more hateful. Because if there's a version of him that feeds birds as winter descends, then there is a decency that he chose to overlook when he did other things. Other things that also fed the birds. And the hawks. And the raccoons. And the coyotes. All the animals that took mouthfuls of my sister, destroying any chance of proving he killed her.

But I'm not a court, and I don't need proof.

I know this road, the one that leads out of town. He'll take a right where the bridge has been out for a decade, then follow the gravel that shoots to the left, each path becoming more decrepit than the last. From two lanes to one, from paved to gravel, and then just dirt. Dirt leading into the woods.

I know all these things because I've seen them every day for months. I'm just a girl trying to get in shape this summer, shedding the last baby fat as my womanhood emerges. How clean I look. How fresh and hopeful and one with the outdoors as I strain to make it up the hill, and then exuberant as I fly down the other side, hair streaming behind, enjoying my earned reward. This is what people think when they see me.

The few people who live out here wave as I go past, awkwardly at first, but later in recognition. As the days get hotter, one elderly lady waits at the end of her driveway every day with a glass pitcher of lemonade. She knows exactly what time I will pass her house, and my drink is always cold, the ice cubes clinking against my teeth.

I do this at first so that it won't be odd that I'm there on *that* day. I've come to like it, the way my legs have become all muscle and how my hair smells like wind hours later. I like the lemonade, too. I almost look forward to seeing the old lady. But I never let it distract me.

Because this is not how I get in shape and make new friends.

This is how I kill someone.

And it's a simple process, really. His hand hesitates for a second when he sees me pause at the end of his driveway. Yes, he's one of the people who wave. He sits on his porch most of the day, a middle-aged man who might be handsome if you don't look closely into his eyes and identify what lurks there. Every day the sun rises and the wine bottle empties and he sits there wondering where his life went wrong until it sets again.

I know exactly where. I'll explain that to him.

He's lonely. So when I stop for the first time ever, I almost feel bad when his face lights up. Almost. Because immediately following that pure smile of a human being who craves the company of another human being, his eyes flick down to my tank top, where my breasts heave up and down as I catch my breath. And we're not two human beings anymore.

We're a male and a female.

Alone in the woods.

And I lie, say that I'm winded, need to sit down for a minute. And part of him knows he shouldn't do this. The part that crumbles up crackers and feeds them to birds knows that he shouldn't bring me out of the sun into the darkness of his house. But another part *wants* to.

And it's much stronger.

I go, smiling when he holds the screen door open for me. It makes my nose scrunch up and draws attention to my freckles, which everyone says make me so cute. They have no idea.

I walk inside, into the cool shadows, pretending not to hear when he flicks the lock on the screen door. Then I turn around, and tell him who I am.

This is how I kill someone.

And I don't feel bad about it.

2. JACK

The thing about Alex Craft is, you forget she's there.

I didn't give her much thought until we were freshmen, chomping at the bit to help with search parties for her sister. We enjoyed pretending to be adults, the feeling that we were actually doing something, even though most of us forgot to check the batteries on our flashlights and Park had a baggie in his pocket that stopped our searching cold once we were out of sight of the real adults.

Branley actually packed a snack, like we were going camping or something. To be fair, after the baggie was empty, we were totally thrilled and she was our hero, just like she wanted. She sat on my lap that night, happy to squirm right where she knew I liked it. And I didn't stop her. I've never stopped Branley. Still haven't learned how.

So our hero was the girl who brought Doritos to chase our weed, and a few yards away from where we sat, an actual hero found the body. Parts of it, anyway. We didn't even notice the gathering flashlights until the girl Park was with made a noise when he got her in just the right place, and they swung toward us.

I've thought about it a lot in the three years since, how we must've looked in that glare. Branley's "Find Anna" shirt shoved up over her tits, my pants around my ankles, all of us with red-rimmed eyes and big *oh shit* looks on our faces.

The guy out in front was all rugged-looking, dirty beard and a hat, a loose jacket. The kind of guy who I thought would laugh and tell us to keep on going while he kept the light on us. But he never even glanced at Branley or Park's girl while they yanked their clothes in place. Instead he looked right at me and said, "Get the fuck out of here, douchebags."

I was so busy tucking it all back in I thought everybody was pissed because of us, that their faces were set hard and their lights were pointing at the ground because they didn't want to know—for sure—what we'd been doing. But that wasn't it.

Her hand was sticking up out of the dirt, stripped to

the bone, the gnawed-on skin peeled back to the wrist. I froze in the act of pulling up my zipper. I didn't know then that once the area was cordoned off, parts of Anna Craft would be found all over the place. I thought it was a shallow grave she'd tried to dig herself out of, with me a few yards away doing my best to pound a different girl down into the ground.

"What?" Branley had said, eyes on my face as always, completely missing that they'd found what we were supposed to be looking for.

I left her. I did exactly what that guy said and turned around and got the fuck out of there. I ran because one of the faces in that circle of light was Alex Craft, a girl I'd gone to school with my whole life, a girl who sometimes you don't see. I saw her then, as she reached down to touch her sister's dirt-streaked fingers, like a kid digging up a toy that got mired in the sandbox. And I haven't been able to unsee her since.

This is what I think about when she brushes past me on the first day of our senior year, her dark hair swinging as she walks, face still wearing the hard mask I saw that night, like it's permanently set.

I wonder if she heard that guy call me a douchebag.

And I want to know if she agrees.

Because I sure as hell do.

3. PEEKAY

I have a name, but everyone just calls me Peekay because I'm the PK—Preacher's Kid. I'm thinking about this because my name—or at least my nickname—should be somewhere in the pic Sara just sent me, a screencap she snatched off my boyfriend's phone while he was passed out at a party. A screencap of increasingly dirty sexting that should alternate between *Adam* and *Peekay* but instead says *Adam* and *Branley*.

I toss my phone into the passenger seat and focus on not crying while I wait for the woman from the animal shelter to arrive and unlock the building. My leg is bouncing up and down while I burn off my anger, the car keys jangling against my knee. I yank them out of the ignition when I spot the beaded key chain that says "Peekay & Adam 4-Ever." It's made out of letters and footballs and hearts, the paint rubbed away in spots from years of friction as it passed in and out of my jeans pocket.

Years.

"Fucker," I say, and break the black cord that holds them all together, sending letters and hearts and footballs all over my car.

I'm not supposed to say that word, because I'm a preacher's kid. But I'm also not supposed to drink beer or know what a dick smells like, so language is the least of my sins. My phone makes a noise at me, one that used to make me dive for it in the middle of the night, breathless and happy. A noise that used to send my stomach up in my throat. Except now that organ is definitely going another way, and I get out of my car so I don't have to look at the screen all lit up with his name, hearts on either side of it. Some beads roll out behind me and one crunches under my foot as I get out.

It's the "&."

More pieces fall out onto the gravel and I hear another car. I tuck my hands up into the sleeves of my hoodie because it's colder than it's supposed to be today (thanks, Ohio) and I'm ready to get inside the shelter and start my Senior Year Experience.

On my grade card it will say SYE—Animal Shelter

Volunteer, and that will probably be followed by a capital A, nicely aligned with all the others. I have a very different idea about what constitutes a Senior Year Experience, and Adam was supposed to be a part of that. Until now.

I stomp my foot, telling myself I'm doing it to keep warm, and that the little heart charm that has now been ground into a fine powder had nothing to do with it. The other car pulls up next to mine, but it's not the lady from the shelter. It's another student, and it takes me a second to place her as she gets out of the car.

Actually, that's kind of a lie. I know exactly who she is, I just can't remember her *name*. So I'm standing there, my fists balled up in fabric and my feet smacking against the ground, when I say, "Hey, Anna. You volunteering here for SYE?"

She looks at me for a second before I realize what I just did.

"I'm Alex," she says.

"I know, right. Yeah, I totally know," I say, my words falling out all over each other. "It's just—"

"It's just that when you look at me all you think about is my older sister, so your brain offers that name instead."

"Yeah," I say, more than a little set back by her factual presentation, like I'm a science fair judge instead of a girl who just put her foot in her mouth.

"Yeah," she echoes back at me, then moves toward the shelter. Which, it turns out, was unlocked.

I watch her walk away from me, back rigid, and I think it's going to be a long Senior Year Experience. Then I hear my phone again, insistently making its Adam noise, and I think about those texts between him and Branley Jacobs and that word slips out of me again.

"Fucker."

It's cold enough that it makes a fog in front of my mouth when I say it, and even though I brushed good this morning I can smell stale beer. So there's the word and the beer, all hanging there together in the air, and my dad would probably be really disappointed in me right now. Also because I know what a dick smells like. Or what Adam's does, anyway.

But just his.

4. ALEX

It's easier to like animals than people, and there's a reason for that.

When animals make a stupid mistake, you laugh at them. A cat misjudges a leap. A dog looks overly quizzical about a simple object. These are funny things. But when a person doesn't understand something, if they miscalculate and hit the brakes too late, blame is assigned. They are stupid. They are wrong. Teachers and cops are there to sort it out, with a trail of paperwork to illustrate the stupidity. The faults. The evidence and incidents of these things. We have entire systems in place to help decide who is what.

Sometimes the systems don't work.

Families spend their weekend afternoons at animal

shelters, even when they're not looking for a pet. They come to see the unwanted and unloved. The cats and dogs who don't understand why they are these things. They are petted and combed, walked and fed, cooed over and kissed. Then they go back in their cages and sometimes tears are shed. Fuzzy faces peering through bars can be unbearable for many.

Change the face to a human one and the reaction changes.

The reason why is because people should know better.

But our logic is skewed in this respect. A dog that bites is a dead dog. First day at the shelter and I already saw one put to sleep, which in itself is a misleading phrase. Sleep implies that you have the option of waking up. Once their bodies pass unconsciousness to something deeper where systems start to fail, they revolt a little bit, put up a fight on a molecular level. They kick. They cry. They don't want to go. And this happens because their jaws closed over a human hand, ever so briefly. Maybe even just the once.

But people, they get chances. They get the benefit of the doubt. Even though they have the higher logic functioning and *they knew* when they did it THEY KNEW it was a bad thing.

The shelter is running a neuter-and-spay clinic next month. One of my jobs this morning is to get the mail, fighting the urge to throw a rock at a speeding car when the driver wolf-whistles at me. The mailbox is full of applications for the clinic, most of them for dogs but a handful of cats as well. Rhonda, the lady who runs the shelter, has me sort them out, dogs and cats, male and female.

Rhonda snorts when she sees all the male dogs on the roster. "People don't learn," she says.

"What do you mean?" I ask.

"Everyone thinks if you fix a male dog it will lower his aggression, but most of the biters are female. It's basic instinct to protect their own womb. You see it in all animals—the female of the species is more deadly than the male."

"Except humans," the other girl volunteering says.

The phone rings. I answer, saying, "Tri-County Animal Shelter, this is Alex," instead of saying to the girl, "You wouldn't be in a position to know."

Which is what had been on the tip of my tongue.

Rhonda gets a call about a stray out on the county line, so she takes the pound truck and tells us to "hold down the fort." There's not much to hold down at this particular fort for the moment. The mornings are filled with volunteer dog-walkers and wives who like to pet cats but "aren't allowed" to have one at home. All of those people have slowly seeped out. The other girl and I are waiting out the last fifteen minutes, me at the desk pretending to sort through spay-and-neuter applications so that I don't have to make conversation, her on her hands and knees poking her fingers through the cage our lone bunny resides in, which we dragged out to the waiting room hoping that someone would cave and take her home.

The front door swings open, slamming against the wall hard enough to knock down three "Lost Cat" posters and an informational pamphlet about Lyme disease. A woman with a red face and eyebrows that are permanently frowned into a meeting position above her nose comes in, talking before she even looks at me.

"Someone just tossed a bag of puppies out down on 9," she says.

"County Road 9?" I ask for clarification, mostly because I know it will annoy her and because I don't like how she's talking to me. Or rather not talking to me, just shouting words in my direction, already half turned toward the door to leave.

"Yes, County Road 9," she snaps. "What'd you think I meant?"

The other girl pulls her fingers out of the bunny cage and stands up but doesn't approach us. She hovers in the background like if I need support she might actually say something but I shouldn't count on it. This annoys me as well, so now I'm happy with no one in the room.

"Where at on 9?" I ask, pulling out a slip of paper to write it down.

"Right before the curve," the lady says. "He slowed down a bit and chucked the bag out the window."

"How do you know it was puppies?" I ask.

"Excuse me?" she says, the brows finally separating a little as they fly upward.

"How do you know the bag has puppies in it?"

"I had to swerve to miss it," she says, her voice losing a bit of its edge. "I could see it in the way that it rolled, you know? Like there was something inside trying to get out."

"Could've been kittens," I say.

"What does it matter?" the lady half yells at me. "I came here to the shelter to tell you there's a bag of kittens or puppies or whatever lying in the ditch on 9 and you're not doing anything about it."

"Why didn't you stop?" I ask, feeling my internal gear switch from argumentative to combative smoothly, a well-oiled machine.

"What?" She's fuming now, her breath coming in shallow gasps that aren't giving her brain enough oxygen.

"You swerved to miss the bag. You care enough to

report it. So why didn't you stop and do something yourself?"

"My kids are in the minivan," she says. "I didn't want them to see anything they shouldn't. Look, I'm doing everything I can. I feel sorry for those puppies—"

"I'm sure they appreciate your pity," I say.

She's done playing nice. I see her own gears switching and know that I've pushed too far, called out a sanctimonious would-be do-gooder who isn't going to fold under my logic.

"Who is your supervisor?" she asks, glancing around the room as if suddenly realizing she's the only adult here.

"God," I say.

5. PEEKAY

"God?" I close the passenger door of Alex's car and she kind of half smiles as she starts it. The shelter is locked up, the sign flipped to "Closed," a heavy cloud of dust marring the air from the lady in the minivan, who tore down the driveway like we'd loosed a biter on her. Alex left a message on Rhonda's phone telling her we were checking into a "tossed bag that is moving" out on 9— not specifying puppies or kittens.

"Technically it's true," she says, in answer to my question.

"So you believe in God?" I want to kick myself as soon as I ask it, because first of all it's not the best icebreaker in the world, and secondly I just firmly filled in all the cracks of the preacher's-kid mold I'm trying to crawl out of.

But Alex shoots back with a question I'm not expecting. "Do you?"

I don't think anyone has ever asked me that before. It's assumed, like the fact that I don't own any naughty underwear or am tattoo-free.

"Yeah," I say, and that's actually the truth. I don't like being a PK, but I'm not a liar, either.

"Why?"

I feel my imaginary ruff going up, like a dog trying to make itself look bigger. I don't know Alex, I don't know if I like her, and I don't feel like defending something as big as my belief in God during our first conversation. I'm about to say something along those lines to her, even though it'll be the pared-down version—*fuck off*—but I bite my tongue. All the shitty things I could possibly say back up in my brain because it sounded like an honest question, not a single-syllable word laced with derision, which is what I'm used to. And I guess if I'm going to be working with Alex at the shelter, we have to speak to each other at some point. Might as well cut the shit.

I take a second to put together a real answer, not some blow-off recitation of "Jesus Loves Me" where I tell her it's "because the Bible tells me so." I know I've got something to say, but I want to get the words right, so I look out the window as Alex drives toward 9.

We hit the one light in town on a green and head

north, going past three bars and two pizza places before we get to the dead zone—a couple of paved streets with real signs (Fifth and Sixth) but nothing on them except dead-end drives. The town planners got a little overexcited in the nineties about what they thought the new calculator plant could bring to the community. Ended up all it had to offer was a broken lease and a big empty building two years in.

Oh, and like a lifetime supply of free calculators for the school. But then someone programmed them all to spell BOOBS when they powered on (58008, upside down) and they got tossed into a school auction. In a terrible twist of fate, a church the next town over bought them for their school-supply drive and apparently a bunch of fifth graders got more than they bargained for the first day of math class. But none of that musing is getting me any closer to giving Alex an answer about why I believe in God, and she's kind of giving me the side-eye while she drives.

"I guess it's because sometimes when I'm really upset, if I quiet down and let myself be still, I can feel . . . *something.*" Tears well up in my eyes even as I say it, because Lord knows I've been really upset lately and that feeling of comfort surrounding me for no reason I can put a finger on . . . well, yeah. It makes a girl cry. Even one who's trying to shed the PK stigma.

But in the end it's still a shit answer.

So I'm surprised when Alex nods like she totally gets it.

"You feel it too?" I ask.

She shrugs. "No, not like that. But things have a way of falling into place for me when I need them to."

"Cool," I say, and our big soul-baring is over.

Alex turns onto 9 and we spot the bag at the same time. It's an industrial-strength black garbage bag, visible heat waves rolling off it. Alex pulls over and puts her hazards on—although why she bothers, I don't know. We're surrounded by cornfields waiting for harvest and haven't seen another vehicle since we passed the last bar in town. We both get out of the car.

I know before we get to it that there's no hope. The bag's not moving, which is part of it. But there's also the reek of urine in the air and the slight metal tang of fresh blood. I don't even know if I want to see inside, but Alex doesn't hesitate. She opens it without flinching, both smells amped by about a thousand when she does.

I look away.

I hear the rustle of the bag while Alex checks to make sure they're actually dead, and then the zip sound of her lacing the drawstrings up tight and double knotting them.

"Three puppies," she says. "Two broken necks and an asphyxiation."

I look up and down the road, the only sound the dry corn stalks rustling against one another and the persistent, regular ticking of Alex's hazard lights. "No chance anybody saw him out here," I say.

"No," Alex says, taking the bag to her trunk and laying it in gently. She snaps the lid shut. "But at least that lady felt sorry for them."

We head back to the shelter, Alex in silence, me fuming. I've got my mouth clamped shut tight, all my breath coming in and out of my nose in short little bursts. All I can think about is that truck flying down the road, the hands that would've put their sleek little bodies in the bag before tossing it out like so much garbage.

A puppy feels like life and love. Their entire bodies are soft—fur, skin, the pads of their feet new and delicate. They radiate warmth in the way science can explain, but it goes further than that. The heat of affection pours out of their eyes and makes their little butts wiggle like crazy as soon as they see a person—they don't even care who. They're love, encapsulated. And someone touched that, put it in a bag, and killed it.

We come to a four-way stop in the middle of nowhere, corn stubble on one side of us, a collapsing barn on the other. It's one of those places that have stop signs on all the corners for no apparent reason, because never in the history of the county have there been four cars here at the same time. But there is another right now, an elderly lady in her Buick. She waves at us to go ahead and Alex waves back, her fingers a casual up-flick on top of the steering wheel.

My breath is catching in my chest, my mind still thinking of puppies wriggling together, trying to draw comfort from one another in the overheated trash bag, the little whining noises they would've made to signal to the guy driving that they were scared. Their mystification that he didn't care. And the sound it would've made when the bag hit the road. For one second I wonder what I would've done if there had been a truck sitting at the intersection, and I let myself follow the thought.

I imagine a rusted-out truck, a guy wearing a T-shirt with ripped-out sleeves. I think about how he'd roll down his window, a casual question on his face until I open the door, drag him out, and kick him in the gut over and over and over until he's making the same noises those puppies probably were.

It's a fantasy, and I know it. I'm a tiny thing—five foot four—and on the days I have to bring more than two textbooks home I struggle lifting my backpack. I'm not big. I'm not strong. I'm not intimidating. I will never kick the shit out of anyone, and even if I had the chance I wouldn't do it.

But it kinda feels good to think about it.

6. **JACK**

I'm the guy who other people want to be.

I see it in their looks when I sink a three-pointer, hear it in the collective roar from the stands when I score the game-winning touchdown and do a series of backflips—and fuck the ref for throwing an "excessive celebration" penalty flag, anyway. I can do those things and look good before, during, and after, knowing the whole time that I'll have at least one tit shot texted to me that night. And then on Monday I can go to any one of my classes and deliver a speech, nail an exam, or speak in a foreign language the entire time without blinking because I am the whole package. I get girls, I get trophies, and I most definitely am going to get to be valedictorian.

Except . . . I'm not.

Alex Craft is.

I'm sitting next to her in the guidance counselor's office with my mouth hanging open just enough that I've probably disqualified myself from salutatorian as well.

"I don't understand," I say for the third time. "I've got a 4.0."

"So does Alex," the guidance counselor says. "And she's taken more weighted classes than you have."

"But I want . . ." I close my mouth then, aware it's more than a want, it's a *need*.

If I can't get a scholarship, I won't be going to college. I'll be another senior who says they're taking a year off first, and then ends up trying to pay for my kid's college from behind a burger grill, wondering what the fuck happened. And then my kid'll do the same thing and when I retire I can cede my spot in the drive-through to my grandkid. I can keep my body in shape anywhere, but my brain is going to rot in this shitty little town because I'm too poor to get out of here without a free ride.

I'm so focused on me, I'm not sure I've heard her right when Alex says, "You should just give it to him."

Alex, who could write a book about things that aren't fair. That guy in the woods had it right three years ago—I'm a douchebag.

Miss Reynolds's eyebrows come together. "Class rank is not given, Alex. It's earned."

"It's nonsensical for me to have it. I'm not going to college."

Now the guidance counselor's mouth tightens as she says, "We've talked about this and—"

"Why wouldn't you go to college?" I interrupt Miss Reynolds, turning to look—really look—at Alex. I don't think I've ever been this close to her, and when she turns her head, I see how green her eyes are.

She shrugs. "I can't conceive of myself outside this place."

"Oookaaaayyyy," I say, glancing at the guidance counselor. She smiles at me encouragingly, but her eyebrows are still stuck together in concern.

"It's very simple," Alex says patiently, dividing her words between the two of us. "We've both earned it. He wants it. Give it to him."

The way she says this makes it seem so easy that I know I'm wearing a *yeah, see?* look on my face. But the guidance counselor sighs and shakes her head.

"I can't just arbitrarily decide who is the valedictorian."

"You're misinterpreting where 'arbitrary' fits in this conversation," Alex says.

Miss Reynolds closes her eyes and pinches the bridge

of her nose. I get the feeling she's had many, many conversations with Alex that end this way. When she looks up, she's got her professional face back on.

"A lot of things can change before the end of the year," she says. "And, Jack, you need to remember that being salutatorian is nothing to sneeze at."

Which to me sounds like: *Alex is very unlikely to make any mistakes, so you need to start adjusting to the new reality.*

Alex and I walk out of the office together and I find myself in an awkward situation that only people from small towns can appreciate. I know Alex Craft. I know her in the sense that I could pick her out of my class photos from kindergarten on. I know her because people don't leave this place and our parents know each other—hell, I'm pretty sure my mom dated her dad. I know her because everyone knows everybody here, and Alex especially because her sister is the only reason a news crew has been in this town, ever.

I know Alex Craft. And I have nothing to say to her.

But I want to find some words that will make her look at me again, because I liked the way her green eyes stood out among all those freckles. And the part of me that goes to AP English digs that she's smart, while the part of me that slaughters freshmen with dodgeballs is kinda turned on by the idea that I'm competing against her for something.

And she's walking away from me.

I know how to do this. I know the things to say to people that will keep them at arm's length while reinforcing how cool I am. I know how to speed up or slow down to give them the idea that you're really not into talking to them and the distance between the two of you grows even though you're the only ones in the hallway. I know how to make a joke about taking a shit and duck into the bathroom for a few minutes until they're gone.

Instead I take a few extra inches in my stride until I'm keeping pace with Alex. I see her eyes flick in my direction for a nanosecond when she picks me up in her peripheral, but she doesn't slow down.

"Crazy, huh?" I say.

"Excuse me?"

"The valedictorian thing. Crazy."

She stops at her locker, gaze going to the hallway clock instead of me. "I don't know that it's crazy so much as an indication that we're both intelligent people."

"But you're *more* intelligent."

Alex spins her combination lock. "Not necessarily. I've never been quite clear how such a thing is determined."

"They take your GPA and—"

"I know how the school does it," she says, snapping her locker open. "I mean in general."

"Oh," I say, because I can't really think of anything else.

The bell rings. The sound slices through the hall, scattering all the words I'm trying so hard to accumulate between us. She jumps as if she wasn't expecting it, her hands curling into fists.

"Are you okay?" I ask.

"No," she says immediately, the unexpectedness of the question prompting an honest answer.

"Can I"—*help? Have your number? Touch your arm? Get you to look at me again?*—all of these things are utterly lost as my name comes rolling down the hallway in Park's drawl.

"JAAAAAAACK," he's calling for me, more than a little obnoxious as he turns the corner to find me at Alex's locker. The halls are filling up and there's no reason for him to think that I've actually been talking to her. Except she's finally looking at me again, waiting for me to finish whatever this sentence is going to turn into.

And I can't come up with a single goddamn word. My mouth is hanging open and it's like she's the hook and I'm a fish and I can't do anything but flop around when Park pushes his body against mine so that we're touching from toes to forehead and all I can think is *Jesus, really? Right now? This is the moment he chooses to pull out a joke from seventh grade?*

"Jack, baby," he says. "I missed you so much." He

clenches my head in his hands and covers my mouth with his thumbs and fake kisses me so hard I swear I'll have bruising tomorrow. "And you, girl," he says to Alex after pulling away from me. "I could just eat you up."

He's going for her with a big dumb grin on his face, absolutely certain that she will have no problem with him smashing his fingers into her lips and his face up to hers. Her expression doesn't change; that slightly confused look that had been directed at me as I struggled with words now turns to Park as the fist that never unclenched finds a target.

She drops her shoulder to gain some momentum as she takes a jab at his crotch, one bony knuckle protruding on purpose for maximum effect as if she wants to pop his testicles like water balloons.

And he goes down like a box of rocks.

7. PEEKAY

We are having a funeral for Park's balls.

That's how it seems, anyway.

After Alex brought him to his knees in the hallway and walked away like she'd done nothing more than litter, Park curled up into the fetal position. He pulled the hood of his sweatshirt up over his head so that nobody could see his face while he recovered his masculinity, and everyone gave him a wide berth. The hallway was totally silent except for the occasional *What happened?* followed by an explanation, followed by the kind of respectful silence we reserve for male groin injuries.

Jack tried to talk to him but got only grunts in response, and everybody decided to leave him there and went to class. Mr. Franklin walked past a few minutes ago, and I imagine he'll say a lot of understanding things that end in "buddy" for a while until he can coax Park up off the floor.

Miss Hendricks wasn't quite sure what to do because she isn't equipped to offer support to Park, and not forceful enough to make us stop talking about it. So instead of discussing *Crime and Punishment*—which Alex is calmly sitting in her seat reading—we're talking about the fact that Park was dick-punched.

The guys are laughing their asses off. They keep reenacting it and attempting to fist-bump Alex, but she couldn't be less interested. The girls are split into two camps: the ones who have on very straight faces and keep saying that Park could be *seriously injured*, and those who find it genuinely amusing every time one of the boys involved in the instant replay pretends to reinflate their balls by blowing on their thumbs.

I'm part of this last group.

Branley, who everyone knows is a Friend to All Penises, isn't making much of an effort to control her volume, and her natural soprano is grating on my nerves.

"What if he can't have kids now?" she asks, a perfect little pout following up her intense concern for Park's man parts. "That's just *crazy*." More emphasis than necessary is put on this last word, and she glances at Alex as she says it, who turns a page of Dostoyevsky.

A little burn of resentment starts down in my belly

and I try to quash it, fast. I don't know if it's because Alex and I have established a kind of companionable silence after incinerating three dead puppies, or if it has more to do with the fact that Branley now traipses around holding Adam's hand.

But I really want her to shut up.

Seeing the two of them together hasn't been easy. I finally answered a call from DickFace (he's been renamed in my phone, all heart emoticons removed) about a week ago. I guess it was our official breakup, even though he'd been sharing one chair with Branley at lunch ever since Sara sent me that screencap.

"Babe," he'd explained, unable to drop the endearment even as he dumped me, "it's *Branley Jacobs*. I have a shot at *Branley Jacobs*. I can't pass that up."

I guess he expected some sort of congratulations from me as he climbed the social ladder, stepping on the skull of the preacher's kid so that he could jam his face up the skirt of the blond cheerleader. And he seems pretty happy. So, whatever. Fuck him.

"Fuck her," Sara says as she flops into the chair next to mine.

"Right?" I agree, but can't stop my eyes from going back to Branley as she keeps using words like *vicious* and *dangerous*.

Branley is kind of perfect. One of those girls who wear matte foundation and always look like a porcelain doll, except I think if you spread a doll's legs as far as hers go, they would break. I can say this with some accuracy because of the pics she sent my boyfriend.

Ex-boyfriend.

I concentrate on that (*ex-boyfriend ex-boyfriend ex-boyfriend*) and flip open my own copy of *Crime and Punishment* as I try to distract myself from a visual I accidentally created. A picture of Branley's perfectly molded, heart-shaped face, breaking into shards under my fist. I clench my fists and my teeth, warping a classic paperback and shredding my own enamel at the same time.

Miss Hendricks finally gets everyone in their seats and Branley passes my desk, leaving the scent of strawberry-vanilla shampoo in her wake. She tosses her phone into her open backpack on the floor, and I can't help but glance at it.

I expected to see a selfie background, something coyly posed and angled for maximum cheekbone effect, probably shot from above to make sure the cleavage gets its due. Instead it's her little sister holding a vanilla ice-cream cone while a clearly well-trained Saint Bernard stares longingly, dual slobber chains caught in midwobble.

Nice. I want to punch a Saint Bernard owner, the most patient people on earth.

Good job being the preacher's kid, Peekay. Good fucking job.

8. **ALEX**

We use objects to navigate spaces, making a map in our heads as neurons fire, pathways so well-worn we don't even know we reference them as we move from one location to the next, the same pattern. Every day.

There are things in place to help us, signs in certain colors and shapes. Arrows pointing. Symbols indicating. Making your own framework is more entertaining, more personal. Less constricting.

The blue house she would've seen last.

The tree that has bloomed three times since then.

The dirt road that used to be gravel, the gravel road that is now paved, the paved road that is disintegrating back into gravel.

Here in this building I have the dent in the locker

where I broke my wrist after hearing a rape joke, dropped as casually as pocket lint.

A ceiling tile still knocked askew two years after I took a vicious kick at thin air and my shoe flew off. No one has noticed it.

The residually sticky spot on the wall outside the science classrooms where the anatomy classes hang their posters with double-sided tape every year, the obligatory genitalia comically large. Nothing hangs there now but a thread of my own hair, torn out.

No one sees me do these things. Until today.

Now there is a new place, a place where a boy came at my face with his hands, his mouth open, tongue out. A place where he fell, pale-faced. A place where his tears pooled afterward. It is a place where I did not mean to, but it happened.

I use my markers as I go from place to place. Seeing evidence of my small rebellions, spots where my wrath was allowed to vent and has impacted the world around me, no longer safely encapsulated inside. My life is made of these tiny maps, my paths always steady as I move inside a constricted area, the only one I should ever be allowed to know.

My violence is everywhere here.

And I like it.

9. **PEEKAY**

If I were to uncoil my trumpet, I'd have four and a half feet of brass pipe. This fact was on repeat in my head at last night's football game, because I was seriously considering dismantling my instrument so that I could wrap it around Branley's swan-white neck and strangle her. I also considered just sticking all four feet into the ground right when her squad threw her up in the air so that when she came down she'd be impaled on it.

I played out both scenarios in my head, picturing the cheerleaders screeching as I choked their poster child, the other bandies trying to stop me. Maybe one of the trombone players would hook me with their slide. I imagined the stunned silence that would emanate from the bleachers after the homecoming queen had a trumpet

bell explode from her chest when she came down from
a toss, her perfect smile slipping into confusion, Adam
running from the sidelines, his football spikes clicking against the track. He'd hold her while she died and
maybe one of the other trumpet players would do a riff
on "Taps."

And then I spotted her little sister in the stands, two
blond pigtails poking from either side of her head, a
popcorn kernel stuck on her chin as she cheered along
with Branley, who she probably thinks is perfect. I
reminded myself there's a Saint Bernard with big woe-
ful eyes who loves Branley, so of course I did none of
those things. Instead, I wallowed in my rage and missed
a quarter turn on the thirty-yard line that threw off
the entire trumpet section during the halftime show, so
that's karma for you.

Anger makes you tired, but guilt keeps you from falling asleep. So I hit my alarm twice this morning, even
though it's Saturday and my SYE is as good as a class
and I need to get my ass out of bed.

I'm still the first one at the shelter, and there's a
dump.

It's a mutt, part retriever (maybe), part shepherd
(maybe). Definitely all pain and anger. Rhonda told
me this has been happening more lately with the shitty
economy. People can't afford their pets but they can't

pay the surrender fee either, so they tie their dog to the fence at night and drive away.

Once someone didn't even cough up the money for a chain, instead just chucking the poor dog in the trash. Rhonda found that one. She had to climb into the empty Dumpster while Alex and I leaned over the side standing on chairs, Rhonda's arms wobbling as she tried to get the terrified dog to us and we tried to get him over the edge without losing our balance.

But today is something new. Someone apparently tossed this dog *over* the fence, and I'm guessing he didn't land right because he's holding one paw up in the air and showing teeth at me as I twirl the combination lock on the gate. His fur has a fine coating of early November frost, which can't feel good.

"It's okay," I say quietly. "I'm here now."

He doesn't seem convinced that everything is okay, and when I get a closer look at him, I understand why. Someone really did not give a shit about this dog. One of his eyes is crusted completely shut, and both his ears are sprouting growths.

"Not a lot of love, huh, buddy?" I say, and he lunges at me through the fence, teeth clicking against the wire. The wave of stench that follows him makes me back off more than the snarl. I'm sitting on the concrete step with my hand over my nose when Alex pulls up.

"What?" she asks as she gets out, using one word to encompass me, the dog, and the locked door.

"Rhonda's not here yet," I say through the sleeve of my sweatshirt. "Somebody dumped this guy. I think they threw him over the fence. He's got a broken leg and smells something awful."

Alex walks toward the fence and he goes for her.

"You might want to leave him alone," I say. "Unless you think you can punch him in the dick through the fence."

The words pop out before I realize it, but Alex doesn't seem to care. She digs into her pockets and pulls out a set of keys. "Rhonda gave me these last week," she explains. "She said we're familiar enough with the morning routine to handle it alone. She'll come at open hours."

"Fair enough," I say, accepting the duplicate that Alex hands me. We walk into the front office. My heart dips a little every time. There's a single desk with a phone, a computer someone gave us when they upgraded, and a line of metal folding chairs the church donated a few years ago. That's the sum of our only weapons in the battle to help unwanted animals across three counties find homes—and the phone is a rotary phone. Sometimes I'm really glad that the door separating the office and the kennels is solid and heavy as hell. I don't want them to see how hopeless it all is.

Alex flips the lock behind her and we glance at each other in the oddly private space of a public area before the lights are turned on.

"I would never punch a dog in the dick," she says.

I bust out laughing. She's so intense, her mouth in the firmest, flattest line I've ever seen, serious as my dad on Easter morning.

I've never heard her say anything normal. Two months of working with Alex Craft and I've learned that she doesn't say "Huh?" She says, "I'm sorry, could you repeat that?" Alex says, "Were you able to scoop the litter pans this morning?" Not, "Did you get the cat shit?"

So when she says "I would never punch a dog in the dick" with the same gravity as a newscaster on 9/11, I laugh hysterically. And I think maybe, just maybe, there's the slightest upturn of a smile on the corner of her lips as she turns the lights on.

"What do you think about the dump?"

"I suppose we should wait for Rhonda," she says. "Unless you think we can get him to come in through the outside run and into one of the caged kennels."

"We can try. He might bite, though."

She shakes her head. "He's scared, not mean. I'll stay inside and open the run gate; you see if you can steer him in the right direction from outside."

"Deal." I head outside, grabbing a pair of gloves from the staff shelf as I do. They're heavy, but I know if he wanted to, that dog could have it off my hand, skin included. And once he bites me—scared or mean—he's dead.

He backs into a corner when I go to the gate, front leg dragging. There's a continuous low growl as I walk in, swinging it shut behind me.

"Hey, buddy," I say quietly, going down in a crouch so that he doesn't think I'm trying to intimidate him. "We're going to get you inside, okay? It'll be warmer, and there'll be food and . . ." I'm trying to think of something else enticing when a voice pipes up behind me.

"And surgery, by the looks of it," Rhonda says.

"I wasn't going to tell him that part." Just then Alex opens the run from inside and he turns toward it, teeth on display. Alex backs out of his sight and the warmth emanating from the building is enough to coax him to follow.

"You shouldn't be in there." Rhonda pulls the lock off and opens the gate. "He's mad and hurt and feels cornered. Never know what a threatened animal will do."

"Sorry," I say as I slip outside. "We just thought we should try to get him in if we could."

"Nice idea, but he hurts either of you girls, he gets

put down, and I doubt the school sends me any more volunteers."

I follow her into the office, stripping off the gloves. We're heading back to the kennels when the barking starts. First thing in the morning is always the worst, which is why I prefer the cat room. Alex doesn't seem to mind the clamor of a dozen dogs all waking up hungry, sick of being caged, and desperate for attention. The cats just stretch languidly, take jaw-cracking yawns, and then look at you like, "Oh, have you come to feed me? Splendid."

If the dogs like Alex, then they love Rhonda. I swear they know the second she walks in the door. They don't have to see her or even hear her, they just get so spontaneously happy some of them literally lose their shit.

Alex has convinced the dump to follow her from the outside run to a kennel. She's making all the right noises to reassure him, but the cinderblock walls aren't overly inviting even on a good day. And that dog is not having a good day.

Alex is down in a crouch with her hip holding the kennel door open when the other dogs explode at the sight of Rhonda. The dump, who had taken his freak-out from an eight down to about a two, snarls and shoots forward into the kennel. Alex swings the cage door shut, and it all would've been very nicely handled except for the fact that she's in there with him.

"Get out of there," Rhonda says.

Alex shakes her head and slides down to the concrete floor, her jeans soaking up the bleach water she'd sprayed around earlier. "Don't want to startle him," Alex says tightly.

And while she has a point—the dog's ruff is up as high as he can get it, his teeth out for more than show, and he's climbed onto the cot so that he's got some height on her—I hear something more in Alex's voice. Even though we've exchanged only a handful of words, I know her tone. And I'm pretty sure that dog bit her when he ran past and she's trying to hide it.

"You probably shouldn't make any sudden movements," I say. "Maybe just let him get calmed down and we'll get you out of there."

Alex looks at me and nods, while Rhonda eyes the dog warily. He's still growling, but the snarl is out of his tone. "All right," she says. "But—"

The doorbell from the front office chimes, sending everybody into a fresh peal of barking. "Christ," Rhonda mutters, backing away from the kennel door. "Stay here in case he gets it in his head to rip hers off."

I nod even though I'm unsure what to do if Alex is decapitated, and drop down to my knees to talk to her through the kennel door. "He get you?"

"Right in my butt," she says, and I start giggling again even though it's not funny.

"How bad?" I ask.

"I'm bleeding." Alex lifts her rear off the floor for a second and we share an awkward moment of me investigating her ass through a wire fence.

"Your jeans are ripped, but you're not bleeding too bad. If Rhonda finds out—"

"I know."

We look at each other through the wire for a second as the dog relaxes onto its back legs, a whimper escaping as his dangling paw bumps the side of the cot.

"I've got my yoga bag in the car," I say. "I'll bring it in, tell Rhonda your clothes are all wet. You can clean yourself up in the bathroom."

Alex gives me a quick once-over and I know what she's thinking. Her legs are probably as long as my whole body.

"Wear high-waters or have a wet ass all day. Your choice," I say.

Alex considers this for a second. "I'll wear your clothes. But first, would you do me a favor?"

"Sure."

"Sneak me a tranquilizer for him. If he's unreasonable when the vet gets here, it won't go well."

It wouldn't be hard. The key to the meds hangs on

the wall right next to the cabinet, a silent testimony to how much Rhonda trusts her volunteers.

Hard? No.

Totally legal? Er . . . I'm not clear on that.

But the exhausted sound that escapes the dump as he settles onto his cot, followed by the pathetic scraping of his tongue over his paw in an attempt to get to a hurt he can't understand, undoes me.

"Be right back," I say.

It's quick and easy. I sneak the pill to Alex wrapped in a slice of ham I pilfered out of my own lunch. When I hand it to her through the wire, our fingers touch briefly, slippery with grease, and I think: *This is how you become friends with Alex Craft.*

"Dogs are really good at taking the treat and spitting out the pill," I say, watching through the fence as the dump chows down. "Make sure he gets the whole thing."

"She," Alex says.

"What?"

"It's a girl," she says, reaching a tentative hand out to the dump, who growls again, low and threatening.

"Either way, it has teeth," I say. "Watch it."

"It's okay, girl," Alex says, her voice entirely different than when she speaks to me or Rhonda. It's melodious and gentle, with an undercurrent of emotion I wouldn't have dreamed her capable of. "I won't hurt you," she says, and the dog hesitantly sniffs the ham. It disappears in a few seconds, hunger outweighing caution.

The dump bows her head, watching Alex's hand come nearer until it rests on her crown and they both relax, the tension slipping out of the cage until the only thing I can hear is them breathing, in unison.

10. JACK

It has been two weeks since I talked to Alex, two weeks since she dropped my best friend to the ground at my feet. Two weeks that I've wished every girl I saw, talked to, or touched was her. But my dad likes to say that you can shit in one hand and wish in the other and see which one gets full first. And he's totally right.

I've told myself to forget Alex, which shouldn't be all that hard since we've only shared a few sentences, only held gazes for as long as a lightning bug can hold a burn. And I've been doing okay at taking my own advice, with a little bit of Branley's help one weekend when her parents were out of town and Adam wasn't answering his phone. I definitely did *not* have Alex on my mind when Adam realized he'd missed her calls and I had to run out the back, sweat sticking my T-shirt to my shoulder blades, Branley trying to finger-comb the sex-bump out of her hair before she answered the door.

So I've done a good job of clearing my mind of this girl that I've got no business thinking about anyway when she appears out of the rain. I'm coming around the bend of the sharpest curve in the whole county when I see someone walking, shoulders hunched, and I remember passing a car that had slid off the road a ways back.

I slow down so I don't hit them, but I stop because I see that the person is unmistakably female. I would stop anyway—just to be clear—but there's more of an incentive when the rain has plastered her already tight clothing to a very fit body. I swing alongside, roll down the passenger window, and say, "Need some help?"

I don't realize it's Alex until she raises her head, dark hair hanging in wet sheets on either side of her face. She looks at me carefully, as if she's trying to remember who I am (it hurts more than I want to admit), and then there's the phantom of a smile.

"Jack?"

She says it quietly, as if she's either unsure that's my name, or like she's been waiting for a chance to talk to me and can't quite comprehend that I'm actually in front of her. I hope like hell it's the second option, because that's exactly how *I* feel.

"Yeah," I say. "You okay?"

I realize the second they're out of my mouth those words are both the last thing I said to her two weeks ago, and the single most asinine thing I can say to anyone who is drenched and walking away from a broken-down vehicle. I reach across my passenger seat and pop the door. "Want a ride home?"

Alex chews her bottom lip for a second, and it kills me because I know she's wondering if she can get in the car with me and not end up in a hole in the woods like her sister. I don't say anything. It's her call.

She releases her lip, leaving behind two little white indents, and says, "That would be ni—" She stops, searching for a different word. "Convenient."

When she gets in the passenger seat, I smell rain and girl and a hint of chemicals.

I pull away, all the conversations I'd imagined us having since we talked last leaking out of my brain completely. So I say, "Were you swimming?"

"No. Why would I be?"

"Nothing, it's just . . . you smell like the pool, or chlorine, or . . . something."

"It's bleach. I'm doing my SYE at the animal shelter and we clean out the cages on Saturdays. Turn right here."

I brake and look for the road, aware that she hasn't

given me her address or any real directions to her house. "Here?"

She nods, but is quiet after that. I clear my throat.

"Doesn't Peekay volunteer at the shelter, too?"

Alex wrinkles her nose, sending her freckles into a huddle just on the bridge. "That's not her real name, is it? I always wondered."

"It's what we call her. PK because she's the preacher's kid, you know?"

Alex nods and looks down at herself. "These are her clothes. That's why they're so tight on me."

There are about a thousand sex jokes Park would trot out right now about girls wearing other girls' clothes and naughty overnights. I'm so glad he's not here. But it makes sense to me suddenly why I was so surprised to see Alex's face on the trim silhouette that emerged from the rain.

She's slipped out of the conscious thought of just about every guy around because she doesn't make herself visible. Other girls push the dress code, showing a solid few inches of cleavage or leggings that hug so tight you don't need an imagination. The cheerleaders' skirts are short enough you can easily pinpoint where leg makes the curvy transition into ass.

But Alex is different, remarkable because her clothes are utterly nondescript. She wears jeans that give no clue

what's underneath and solid-color shirts that are all func-
tion, not fashion, like they've done their job of keeping
the wearer from being naked and that's all that can be
expected. I notice these things because in a sea of flesh,
all I can look at is Alex's hair swinging as she walks.

It's been like that since I saw her face the night I
ran away from a dead body in the woods, shame tearing
through the high of weed and sex to punch me so hard
that I had to stop to catch my breath fifty feet away
from that circle of flashlights. Three years I've been trying to find the right things to say to this girl sitting
in my passenger seat, and all that pops out of my idiot
mouth is:

"Well, you look nice in Peekay's clothes."

"I . . . thank you," she says awkwardly, like the words
don't quite fit around her tongue. "Turn left."

"You really do." I plow ahead. "I didn't know you
were so fit."

It's an incredibly stupid thing to say, but it's also the
only thing on my mind. She's put together in a way that
seems a little dangerous, all whip-thin and muscle. On
a guy that build means he can kick your ass, but he can
also lean against a wall and you don't see him until he
wants to fuck with you.

I don't know what it means on a girl, but I know I
like it.

"I run a lot," Alex says. "I like to be outside. Turn left again. It's the third house."

It's pretty much the only one. The other two are abandoned farmhouses with rotting barns splitting like old shoes, ancient bales of straw hanging out of busted haymows. But Alex's house is nice and shiny, the kind that you pick out of a catalog and someone builds in two weeks. They're expensive and they look good, but it's good skin with a folding skeleton, a house that will collapse in forty years while the farmhouses down the road with no windows and sagging porches will stand against the elements for another century.

I pull into the driveway, but she stays in the car and looks at me for a second longer than necessary. My heart goes up into my throat.

"Thank you," she says again, this time thinking through each syllable so it comes out a little more smoothly. "That was ni—"

"Convenient," I interrupt with her word from before and she smiles, the hint of a blush flushing her cheeks.

"I'm sorry," she says, and those words flow out easily, like she says them a lot. "I'm not used to . . ."

"Talking to boys?" I supply.

"Yes."

"Well, get used to it," I say, and before I even think about what I'm doing, I give her a punch on the arm.

Which, it turns out, might have been the best thing I could do because she busts out laughing and punches me back.

And it kinda hurts.

11. ALEX

Sometimes I forget for one second and it hurts.

It's a different kind of pain than the constant, the weight that hangs from my heart. It swings from twine embedded so deeply that my aorta has grown around it. Blood pulses past rope in the chambers of my heart, dragging away tiny fibers until my whole body is suffused and pain is all I am and ever can be.

But sometimes it swings just right and there's a moment of suspension when I can't feel it. The rope goes slack and the laws of physics give me one second of relief. I can laugh and smile and feel something else. But those same laws undo me, and when it swings back there's a sharp tug on my heart to remind me that I forgot.

Anna told me I would understand about boys one day.

She said that everything would change and I would look at them differently, assess their bodies and their words, the way their eyes moved when they talked to me. She said I'd not only want to answer them but that I'd learn how, knowing which words to use, how to give meaning to a pause.

Then a man took her.

A man took her before I learned any of these things. He took her and kept her for a while, put things inside of her. Of course the obvious thing, but also some others, like he was curious if they'd fit. Then he got bored. Then he got creative.

Then my sister was gone and I thought: *I understand about boys now.*

And she was right. Everything did change. I look at them differently and I assess their bodies and watch their eyes and weigh their words.

But not in the way she meant.

I remember the night Anna left, a casual *see you later* tossed over her shoulder as I sat in the living room with a book. I grunted in response, having told her a million times before not to talk to me when I was reading. She usually kept chattering until I'd raise my eyes and say, "I'm *trying* to read," to which she'd mock sympathy and say, "Oh, honey, I thought you knew how. This is so sad."

It was a tired joke, one she used every time but somehow made me smile anyway. She didn't trot it out that night, instead making for the back door like she couldn't get out of the house fast enough, which I totally understood. She and Mom had had it out earlier, a real rip-roarer that had centered over whether or not I should go to a month-long poetry camp. Mom was all for it, seeing an opportunity to get me far away from her under the guise of good parenting.

Anna said I shouldn't go, that sending me out into the world alone was like letting a wolf loose, and her, my keeper, nowhere near. I was mad at her when she left, even though a part of me knew she was right.

Then she was gone, and I unlocked the cage myself.

The first time that I acted on my rage it could have gone very badly, but fate played along with me and I had my way. I've learned things since then, watched videos with instructors who teach you where to punch, what to pull, things that pop. I'm living my life waiting for the man who comes for me like one did for Anna, with hungry eyes behind the wheel and rope in the trunk.

I'm ready.

But I don't know how much longer I can wait.

12. PEEKAY

When I get to school on Friday morning there's a cop car in the lot, which results in a lot of people hitting the brakes so that they're actually going twenty in the school zone and more than a few pretending to clean bags of chips and scratch-off lottery cards out of their passenger seats and casually walking to the Dumpster as if there isn't pot in the gas-station bag they're carrying. I cram a couple of empty beer bottles under my driver's seat with my heel while pretending to check my phone for texts after I park.

Sara meets me in the hall with a simple, "What the fuck?"

"I don't know," I say. I haven't actually seen the cop anywhere, even though half the student body found a reason to walk past the fishbowl of the office and glance in to see if anybody was standing there in cuffs. The secretary spots me and waves me in, making my heart go up so far into my throat my eyes probably bulge a bit.

"What's up, Karen?" I ask, trying to ignore Sara miming at me through the window to run for it. The secretary goes to my church so I'm allowed to call her by her first name, which I admit I kind of lean on for a second, like maybe if I'm really nice to her she'll hide me under her desk when the cop comes to quiz me about where I was and what I was doing last night. Answer: at Sara's, pretty sloshed.

"Hey, sweetie pie," she says. "The copier at the church is broken again so I ran off the bulletins here. Could you get these to your dad?"

My mouth twitches when she holds up her own bag from the gas station, straining against the huge stack of paper inside. "Don't tell anybody," she stage-whispers at me when I take it. "Technically I'm using school supplies for the church."

"I doubt that fast-tracks you to hell," I say before I can reconsider my language.

She laughs a little, her rhinestone-encrusted glasses moving up on her face about an inch as her nose crinkles.

"Hey, Karen," I say, since we're being conspiratorial. "What's with the cop car?"

"Drug assembly," she says. "You know . . ." She holds her fingers up to her mouth, and totally surprises me by using the right indication for pot instead of a cigarette. "We'll be on a one-hour-delay schedule; everyone will go to the auditorium first thing. The principal will make an announcement soon, but you've got a hot tip so you can get a good seat."

I tell Sara what's up as we head to our lockers, the promised announcement drawing groans from the kids in the hall.

"Why can't you have connections that can get us a hot tip for good seats to a Reds game?" Sara asks.

"I'll see if they have a Lutheran night or something coming up," I tell her, and she elbows me.

"What's in the bag?"

I lean in a little closer to her than necessary when I answer. Carrying around church bulletins at school is not going to break me out of the preacher's-kid label anytime soon. Sara's trying not to laugh at me when Branley's very bronzed, perfectly smooth shoulder knocks into mine hard enough to send the bag flying out of my hands, a hundred copies of the Lord's Prayer and next week's hymn numbers spreading out in a fan down the hall.

"Sorry," Branley says. She's on her knees restacking bulletins before she even looks up to see who she obliterated with her bony knob. Her eyes meet mine as I start scraping piles of paper into the bag, not caring that a bunch are getting bent.

"Oh," she says, her hands freezing. "Sorry," she mutters again, before her similarly tanned friend Lila pulls her to her feet and they head off toward the auditorium. Sara helps me with what's left and we're the last kids in the hall. Someone is tapping the microphone in the auditorium, the *knock-knock* sound filling our ears as we turn the corner to the double doors. Branley and Lila are standing in the doorway, heads craning as they look around the darkened room for the rest of the in-crowd.

"What's going on?" I didn't hear Alex come up behind me, so I jump when she asks, drawing the attention of the teachers lining the back wall.

"C'mon, girls, let's go," Miss Hendricks says, shepherding me, Sara, Alex, Branley, and Lila up to the front row—the only place there are five seats left.

"Good seats, *sweet*," Sara hisses in my ear.

"Shut up," I say, settling in with Sara on one side of me and Alex on the other. At least I didn't end up next to Branley, both of us trying not to share an armrest or keep our legs from touching the entire time.

The principal takes the podium and tells us about how a member of the local police is here to give an important presentation, and reminds us that we're representing our school. He trots out a few more stock phrases that none of us even hears anymore. We politely clap as the officer comes out, a few girls paying more attention once we get a good look at him.

He's got the clean-cut thing going on, a good jawline, and the kind of body that makes me wonder if they actually rented him from somewhere. But he's wearing a gun and walks like he's taking each step really seriously, so I'm pretty sure he's a legit cop. He takes the microphone off the podium and walks to the middle of the stage so we can see his whole body. No dumbass, this one.

"Hey, I'm Marilee Nolan's brother," he says, instead of introducing himself as Officer Nolan, which is smart since we were all going to surreptitiously text one another until we figured out why he looked familiar anyway. Over in the right wing Marilee buries her face in her hands, which I totally get because I feel the same way every graduation when my dad blesses the senior class.

"I graduated from here eight years ago," he says. "Back then the rough kids smoked pot and the National Honor Society kids drank. Now the NHS kids are smoking pot and the rough kids are on heroin."

There are a couple of giggles. Sara leans over to whisper in my ear, "And the preacher's kid drinks," to which I say "Damn straight" and give her a fist bump.

"Here's the thing, guys," Nolan goes on. "I'm

supposed to come in here and talk to you about drugs, but I'm guessing most of you already know plenty."

It's really quiet in the auditorium. Nolan doesn't have notes; the big screen is pulled down and there's a laptop on the podium, but he's not showing us pictures of meth teeth or heroin sores like we expected. He's just talking to us. And we're listening.

"I know a lot of you drink," he says, and Marilee's head goes a little farther down into her hands. My cheeks are burning for her because this is way worse than Dad saying a prayer over a bunch of teenagers. "I know because I did it and I know because I find all the Natty Light cans out on 27."

There are more than a few concerned glances shared at that point. Drinking out on County Road 27 was definitely something we thought flew under the radar.

"So you're drinking, no big deal," Nolan says. "Except maybe it is, not because you're under twenty-one and it's illegal, but because of what happens next."

I expect the slides to start up then. Pictures of ruined kidneys or maybe a car crash where someone went through a windshield. But the screen stays blank and Nolan's eyes land on the front row instead.

"What happens next is you're more likely to be a victim of sexual assault," he says, and I feel Alex tense beside me. "Girls, one in three of you." He points right at me, Alex, Sara, Branley, and Lila. "There are five right here, so let's be generous and say it's just one. Which one of you will it be?"

From the left a boy yells, "Please say it's Branley," followed by a chorus of laughter.

"Let me guess, she's the hot one, right?" Nolan says, smiling along with them. "Guess what—one of you is the one who's going to do it."

That shuts it down, fast.

"It's a small town," he goes on. "Ninety percent of rapes are acquaintance rapes—that means you know your attacker, girls. And guys, that means you know the girl you damaged physically, emotionally, and mentally. One in six of you boys is going to be sexually assaulted too, by the way."

And that really kills the room.

"Boys are also more likely to OD than girls," Nolan says, his eyes off us and narrowing in on Jack Fisher and his friends. "You're also twice as likely to die in a car crash, a full quarter of which was your own damn fault because you were drinking at the time."

The principal clears his throat at the use of the word *damn*, which I think is kind of ridiculous considering it's the least alarming thing we've heard since Nolan opened his mouth.

"And here's the thing," he says. "We can't do anything

about that unless you report it. We can't stop your friends from driving drunk and killing themselves or someone else unless we know they're behind that wheel ahead of time. Girls, we can't prosecute that guy who spiked your drink unless you tell us it happened.

"And you don't want to, I get it. It's a small town. The person behind the wheel is your buddy. The person who touched you is your best friend's cousin, is your parent's coworker, is someone everybody trusts so no one is going to believe you. But I'll believe you."

The room is so quiet I swear you can hear people weighing their options.

"The truth will always out," Nolan says, his gaze heavy on the crowd. "And I and the rest of the department will see justice served."

"What about Comstock?" a boy yells out. "You guys never found out who did him in."

There's a spatter of laughter and some murmured agreements, but Nolan rolls with it, absorbing the slam. "I know, right? Only two murders ever committed in this town and we haven't solved either of them."

Sara leans in to me. "I thought Comstock was arrested for . . ." She trails off, nodding toward Alex instead of finishing her sentence.

I shake my head. "He was arrested but never charged, not enough evidence. They had to release him, and that's when—" I draw my finger across my throat, although there was more to it than that. A lot more.

"Yep," Nolan goes on. "Pretty funny, right? The cops can't put a guy away so someone else takes care of it, serves justice on their own terms."

"Hell yes" comes a call from the audience.

"Kinda cool." Nolan nods. "Until you actually think about it. I'm assuming I don't have to tell you what happened to Comstock."

He doesn't; it's the stuff of slumber-party talk. The kind of party where nobody sleeps well.

"Think about it for a second," he says. "There's someone out there who can do *that*. They're loose. They're among us. And they'll do it again. Hilarious, right?"

Yeah, nobody's laughing. We're all pillars of cement in our chairs. Except Alex, who I notice is lounged back, looking at Nolan the same way dogs do when they take each other's measure. I guess hearing someone say they don't heartily agree with what happened to Comstock might be kind of hard to take.

The screen behind Nolan suddenly lights up, the only thing on it an email address and phone number.

"That's my info," Nolan says. "I knew if I said come up and get business cards half of the people who wanted to wouldn't, and half of those who did would toss them five minutes later. So get out your phones and take a pic. Everybody. Right now."

We do. All of us. There's a wave of movement across the auditorium and a bunch of camera clicks in stereo. I'm willing to bet some of the girls are going to use Nolan's number for reasons other than reporting under-age drinking and sex crimes, but it's cool that we've got this moment, everyone with their phones in the air.

Except Alex. I look over at her and she shrugs.

"I don't have a phone," she says.

"I'll email it to you," I tell her, and she shrugs again.

I think about reaching over and taking her hand, or rubbing her shoulder. Something to show my solidarity with her over the fact that right now everyone in this room is thinking about her dead sister.

But I don't, because much like a strange dog, I'm not sure if she'll bite me when I do.

13. **ALEX**

We all walk out of the auditorium into the bright lights of the hall, blinking. It's a harsh awakening that breaks the spell the cop managed to weave, quieting constantly running mouths and forever-lit-up phones. In the anonymous dark, the air was heavy with thoughts, the blond girl sitting next to me fighting to breathe normally when a boy suggested she'd be the one raped of the five of us who were called out. Out here in the light it's harder for her to hide how badly that upset her. Her face is tight, her smile stretched too thin, and she pretends to have a wayward hair in her eye that explains the pooling tears.

The light is taking a toll on all of us, the deeply personal thoughts brought on by darkness whisked away as someone makes a joke, and then another, and soon all

anyone wants to know is what's for lunch. Not who will
be a victim and who a perpetrator. A hand clamps on my
arm and I jerk away immediately, down and with a twist
so that they can't keep their grip.

"Whoa, hey, sorry," a male voice says. Jack is right in
front of me, and I have to focus on stringing together
the right words in order to seem normal.

"Are you okay?" he asks when I don't say anything.

"You're always asking me that," I say, and part of me
wonders if that's because he instinctively knows I am
definitely not.

"No, I mean . . ." He brushes his hand through his
hair. "That assembly. It was pretty fucked-up. Sorry."

I don't know if he's saying that he's sorry that he
swore, or that he's sorry I had to sit through that, or if
he's sorry that he scared me when he grabbed my arm.
I'm cradling the wrist that he touched, holding it against
my chest because where our skin met burns so badly I'm
sure it's blistering, and I don't want him to see how hard
my heart is beating.

"Did I hurt you?" he asks, eyes on my hands.

"No," I say. "I'm . . ." I stop talking because I don't
know what I am.

"Good, because I wouldn't do that—hurt someone,
I mean." His eyes have moved up to mine, and they're
so honest I have to wonder what mine look like to him.

"You or anybody else," he adds.

"You can't know that." I say the first thing that comes to my mind, a reactionary cog setting another in motion. "It's impossible to know what any one of us will do in a given situation. Especially intense ones."

His friends are gathering at the end of the hall, looking back at us. The blond girl calls his name and he waves at them to go on, drawing a pout from her as the second-period bell rings. He walks with me to class like it's a normal thing, and I let it feel that way too, for a moment.

"Alex Craft," he says. "I think every situation with you is an intense one."

I feel a smile on my face, muscles that haven't twisted in that manner since I talked to him last shaking with the oddity of it. An answering smile echoes on Jack's face, and I can see laugh lines forming around his lips, a life only starting but already well lived.

"Anyway," he goes on. "I don't want you to be upset about what that cop was saying, about the person who . . . well, you know. About there being a killer out there, and that they'll do it again."

I settle for smiling as we part instead of answering. Because the only words I have are:

The cop is right.

And it doesn't upset me at all.

14. PEEKAY

"Best. Assembly. Ever," Sara says as she gets in my passenger seat. Her basketball conditioning was canceled, so she's bumming a ride—and probably dinner—off me. "People were either going to cry or start punching each other," she says. "Loved it."

"I felt bad for Alex," I say.

"What's her deal, anyway?"

"I don't know," I tell her honestly, flipping off the car full of junior boys who are riding my ass. "I'm not sure she so much has a deal as she just minds her own business."

"Uh, yeah, small town. No such thing," Sara says. "Take it from the lesbian contingent of one."

"You're not the only lesbian in town," I tell her for the hundredth time.

"Do me a solid and let me know when you spot another one," she says as I pull into my driveway. Sara cranes her head to look at the bell tower, as always. I'm so used to growing up next to the church I don't even see it anymore, don't think about the massive graveyard that I live next to, either. Giving people directions to my house has always been easy—drive out of town on the state route until you're in the middle of nowhere and suddenly there's a huge church. I live next to it. Easy to locate, sure. Easy to pretend not to be the preacher's kid when you use the steeple as a navigational point? Not so much.

I grab the bag of bulletins from the backseat and we go inside. Mom and Dad are sitting at the dining room table, trying to look like they haven't been waiting on me, which immediately sends out warning signals.

"What?" I ask before I even put the bulletins down.

"Sara," Mom says, walking toward her for a hug. "Good to see you."

Sara hugs her back but repeats my question when she steps away. "Yeah, sorry, Peekay's parents, but definitely *what*?"

My dad doesn't go in for a hug on either of us, but gives us both an awkward smile. "We heard you had an assembly today."

Sara and I both make half-vomit noises. "Was there

some kind of parental alert call system that kicked in?"
I ask.

"Do I need to go?" Sara asks.

"No, it's probably best if you hear this too," my dad
says as he ushers us into the living room, my mom
following with glasses full of iced tea that have been
poured for a while now because they're sweating like
crazy. Mom and Dad sit on the couch, Sara and I take
the love seat, and we all look at each other.

"So what did you think about the assembly?" Mom
finally asks.

"Uh . . ." I share a glance with Sara, who makes her
eyes really big and takes a huge sip of iced tea. Lots of
help there. "It was kind of scary, you know."

Dad surprises me by saying, "Good."

He goes on: "Sorry, honey. The truth is often alarming. I've been fielding phone calls all day from parents,
and I've been telling them the same thing. I understand
you were one of the girls the officer pointed to when he
mentioned rape statistics?"

"Yeah," I say, the one word catching in my suddenly
dry throat. "Me and Sara both. Were people pissed off
about that?"

"Some," Dad says. "Apparently Branley Jacobs's
mom called the school and gave the principal an earful
over it."

"I think Branley was kind of upset," Sara says. "Somebody made a joke and . . ." She stirs her tea. "I don't know if she was crying or anything like that, but she sure wasn't laughing."

"How did you feel about it, honey?" Mom asks me.

"I don't know," I tell her. "I wasn't, like, pissed off or anything, but it was weird. I mean, we hear numbers like that shit—oops, sorry. We hear statistics like that all the time, but when he actually pointed at five of us . . ."

"It made it real," my dad says, nodding.

"Yeah, like, really real."

"That's what your father said to the parents who have been calling," Mom says. "If we have to hit you over the head with a sledgehammer to make you be careful, then I'll be the first one in line at the hardware store."

"I don't want you to walk around scared," Dad says, eyes sliding over to Sara. "Either of you. But things aren't good around here. There's never been a lot of money in this county, but times are tighter than ever and poverty breeds desperation. People look for escape in different ways: through drugs, through alcohol, and through sex."

My hands leave my glass to cover my face.

"I'm sorry, honey, but it's true," Dad says.

"You were doing great until you said *sex*," I tell him, my words muffled by my fingers. "Now I can't look at you."

"For the record, me neither" comes Sara's similarly muted voice beside me.

"We'll keep talking, but you don't have to look at us, okay?" Dad says.

I nod, and I feel Sara doing the same thing beside me.

"I don't know how much you know," Dad says, giving me a little pause where I can feel free to volunteer all my sins if I feel so inclined.

I don't.

"There's been an influx of heroin in the county."

"Bad heroin," Mom clarifies, and I know Sara is trying just as hard as I am not to laugh at the idea that apparently she classifies some heroin as *good*.

"A handful of people overdosed last week," Dad goes on. "It's out there, along with meth—which in some ways is even more dangerous, because people are trying to make it themselves."

"Cook it," Mom corrects, and I have to wonder if they went to some kind of seminar or something where buzzwords were printed on PowerPoint slides in italics.

"We're not stupid; we know you drink," Mom says, and I am so damn grateful my head is already down. "We know what it's like growing up here, honey; we did it too. But neither one of us was ever the preacher's kid."

"And I know that's not easy for you," Dad adds. "I want you to have a normal high school experience without that defining you. But you're also my daughter, and

I'm just a dad who wants his girl to be safe."

"I am safe, Dad," I say, and part of me wants to keep my face covered and part of me wants him to know that I didn't start crying until this moment, and embarrassment has shit to do with it.

"Sara." Dad clears his throat. "This applies to you too. Just because you're not interested in boys doesn't mean they're not interested in you."

"Oh, sweet baby Jesus," Sara says into her hands.

"Girls," Dad says. "If either one of you is ever in a situation you're not entirely comfortable with—call me. I don't care what time it is. I don't care who is there or what is going on. You call me and I will come get you."

I'm totally crying now, and I don't even care. I look up at my dad and he's crying too; my mom's got her hand on his knee like she's the only thing keeping him attached to the world.

"Baby girl," Dad says. "There's nothing you can ever do that will make you unwelcome in my house."

I nod, a few tears falling into my lap when I do. Sara's still got her face covered. Mom takes my glass to refill it and Dad goes to get some tissues. Sara looks over at me and wipes her eyes.

"You've got the best parents in the fucking world," she says.

15. ALEX

It's dark when I get home, even though the sun is still up.

Our windows stay closed, our curtains drawn. It's easier for Mom to ignore the outside world this way: out of sight, out of mind, the only thing perpetually in her line of vision a bottle of scotch. I put myself in her way accidentally, our paths crossing in the kitchen as I get a glass of water. She looks up at the clock, confused.

"You're home?"

"School lets out at three, Mom."

Her eyes thin out as she squints at the clock, the shakily applied eyeliner she puts on only for herself crimping together as she does.

"It's three-thirty," I supply.

"Oh." She busies herself for a few minutes, trying to make it seem like she came into the kitchen for
something other than to refill her glass. I wait her out
patiently, sipping my water and crunching ice between
my teeth.

"How was school?"

I imagine this question is asked all over the world,
every day, receiving everything from flippant answers
to in-depth reckonings. But it's hardly ever asked here,
in this house. The last time I answered this question I
was wearing a Hello Kitty book bag and the heels of my
shoes lit up when I walked.

I pulverize some ice with my molars while I think. I
could tell her, I suppose. Let her know that Anna was on
the minds of everyone today. Something that rightfully
belongs to only us resurrected once again as a caution-
ary fairy tale, a warning to all the Little Red Riding
Hoods that there are wolves in the forest.

I could tell her, but I don't. Because I know why the
curtains are drawn and the windows are shut. Nothing is ours; nothing is sacred. The one thing we shared
was pulled into pieces, memorialized and mythologized
so that everyone could participate in it. When she was
missing, Anna's picture was tacked in so many places
around town it's what I see when I think of her, not her
actual face. I see that picture next to a lost cat poster

and a lawn-mowing service advertisement.

I learned later they did find that cat.

"School was fine," I say, and dump the rest of my water in the sink.

16. PEEKAY

We're cleaning cat ears.

Rhonda doesn't require us to come in on Sundays, but somebody has to feed the animals. Yesterday Alex and I helped five cats and two dogs find homes, one of them being the newly spayed dump, who was pretty cute once she got cleaned up. We agreed we probably could have placed a couple more cats if their ears were nice and pink inside like in the wet-food commercials. We told Rhonda to take a much-deserved break today and we'd come in, feed everybody, and make our cats a little more like the ones you see on TV.

So I skipped church to clean cat ears. Normally that wouldn't fly, but since we had a half-mortifying, half-heartwarming family moment Friday, Dad was okay with it.

It's kind of a gross job. A lot of these guys come in here with ear mites. They get this nasty black buildup that has its own special smell if it's been sitting in their ear canals a while. It doesn't matter how much I wash my hands; I can still smell it hours later, like an onion.

And cats don't exactly love having their ears cleaned, so it takes two people. Alex has this weird hypnotic effect on them. I wrap them up in towels, bundled tight like cat burritos in my arms, and then Alex talks to them, low and soft. I don't know if she relaxes them or if it's more like utter defeat because they know they've come up against an unstoppable force with a Q-tip, but they go limp after a few minutes. When she's done, she'll nod at me and I let them go. They stalk off with their ears down and their tails in the air, trying to regain whatever dignity we took from them.

It's a close work environment. Alex leans over the cats while I've got them tucked under my arm like a football. She smells like cold air and the late-evening showers that are two degrees away from being snow.

"What are you wearing?" I ask.

She grunts something that might be a question, her usual word choice lost in concentration as she digs into a tom's ear.

"Perfume? Body spray? You smell good," I clarify as her confusion deepens.

"I suppose it could be my shampoo," she says as she squirts medicine into the tom's ear, massaging it down into the canal. Inexplicably, he purrs.

"It was raining earlier, and I jogged here. Wet hair smells," she adds, as if this statement is nothing odd. "He's done."

I unwrap the tom and he jumps down, leaving us empty-handed and looking at each other. "What do you mean you jogged here? It was almost snowing this morning."

"My car is in the ditch," she says, like it's been casually misplaced.

"Are you okay? Did you get hurt?"

"It was last weekend. I'm fine."

"Okay . . ." I look at her for a second, unsure how much I get to pry now that we've shared lunch meat through a fence. I don't ask why she didn't get her mom to bring her, because I consider other people's parents an out-of-bounds topic. I've been picked on enough about mine.

"Do you want a ride home or something?" I ask slowly, not sure if I'm even supposed to offer. If Alex says no, then it's a very clear statement: she'd rather run home in cold weather than have our friendship move any further.

She puts the unused Q-tips back in the box one at a time while she deliberates. "Yes, that would be nice."

"Cool."

"What's your name?"

"What?"

She's said my name before. I know it. I remember because it came out funny, like she was stumbling a little with it. But Alex licks her lips as if they've gotten dry from this new experience of talking so much and repeats herself.

"What's your name?"

"Peekay."

Alex shakes her head and sprays down the counter, sending fluff from every disgruntled cat we've worked on today flying into the air. Tiny black, gray, white, and ginger hairs settle onto the floor before she tries again.

"That's not your name. It's what people call you."

"It's my nickname," I say, an edge of defensiveness sneaking into my tone. "It stands for—"

"I'm aware of what it stands for. I'd like to know your name."

Alex holds eye contact, almost always. Even when she says insignificant things like "Is it my turn to clean the toilet or yours?" it's like the fate of the world hangs in the balance. So when she's staring me down over a stainless steel table asking me what my name is, I feel a weird bump in my throat . . . like maybe it actually is important.

I clear my throat to make room for the answer.
"Claire. My name is Claire."

Her smile breaks out, ear to ear, infectious as hell.
"That's a lovely name. I would go by that, if I were you."

I drop my eyes. "People have always just called me
Peekay."

And I let them. Even though maybe in the beginning it wasn't meant to be nice. Maybe in the beginning
there was a taunt underneath it, an edge born on the
playground that supposedly matured into affection. But
maybe it didn't. Maybe it was a constant affirmation of
who I'm supposed to be, said into my face every day to
remind me of my place. Maybe when I sucked Adam's
dick and he said my name at the end it wasn't because he
wanted *me* but because he just got a blow job from the—

"Preacher's kid," Alex says.

"Yeah," I say, feeling that stupid bump again. "I'm
the preacher's kid."

"I'm the girl with the dead sister."

"I'm sorry about that," I say quickly, and she cocks
her head exactly like one of the dogs. "The first day
when I called you . . ."

"Anna." She waves it off. "It's understandable. Sometimes it's how I perceive myself, too."

I laugh a little, and the bubble in my throat pops.
"Why do you talk so funny?"

Alex doesn't hesitate. The answer is right on her lips, like she's had it prepped in anticipation.

"I read a lot. I don't have a lot of experience in conversation, so my turn of phrase is different from . . ."

"Pretty much everybody else, yeah," I finish. "Don't you pick it up, though? Like in the hallways or whatever?"

"I try not to listen."

I can dig that. I've overheard things I definitely wish I hadn't. I suddenly remember Branley, her shiny, waxed legs stretched out in front of her while she talked about Alex loud enough to be heard, shooting snide glances and waiting for her to take the bait. And Alex reading Dostoyevsky like it was nothing, her own world blossoming around her.

Her own world. Population: I.

When we get in my car, I jack the heater up, the stale air blowing out of the vents and fanning Alex's hair away from her face. She gives me directions to her house and I flip off her car, resting in the ditch, when we pass it. She actually laughs at that. It's funny to hear such a natural sound when her conversation comes out so stilted. As soon as I think it, I hear my mom's Sunday school teacher voice in my head, about how a smile is the same in every language. I guess that goes for laughing with the socially awkward, too.

I sneak a glance at her when I pull into the driveway. We kept the conversation on the drive to shelter talk— who we hoped would get adopted next, and Rhonda's creative non-swearing insults (*friend-eater* is my current favorite; Alex likes *sweater-unraveler*). I put the car in park and open my center console to grab the last senior picture I have.

It's an awkward pose, the one I liked least. I'm leaning against the stone wall at the local park, my mouth stuck in a grimace that suggests I'm at the end of my shoot and patience at the same time. Mom loved this one, a traditional shot that she ordered more of than necessary, the pose I pawned off on freshmen who asked if they could have one.

"Hey, want one of my pictures?" I ask impulsively, and Alex pauses, her hand ready to unlock the passenger door. She thinks about it a second, as if accepting it might mean taking an irreversible step. And maybe for her it kind of is.

"Yes," she says.

I take a pen off the dash—turquoise ink—and am about to scribble "Peekay" and our graduation year on the back, but I stop. Instead I twist the pen in my fingers for a second, the unfamiliarity of writing my given name making my hand awkward. It actually takes concentration for me to write it in cursive, the handwriting shaky and childish. But Alex smiles when she accepts it and nods when I tell her I'll see her in school on Monday.

And the truth is, I'm kinda looking forward to it.

17. **JACK**

I'm in bed with Branley again.

She dragged me upstairs even though I was so drunk I didn't think it would be worth her effort. But the girl knows me, and while the party music from downstairs pumps so loud I can feel it vibrating the floor in Park's bedroom, Branley climbs on top and does what she wants. She's over-the-top with a push-up bra and her hair a wild mess while she makes noises straight out of low-budget porn.

I'm man enough to know I shouldn't let her do this shit to me, but enough of a boy to be completely turned on.

She shrieks dramatically and falls forward, heavy and panting onto my chest. I let my eyes slide closed as her breathing evens out, and the dark clouds of unconsciousness gather in my brain. I'm fading, but I know that my mouth is hanging open and I might have just snored a little when Branley starts drawing little circles on my chest with her finger.

"Tickles," I mutter, shoving her hand away.

"Fine." She rolls onto the other pillow. I don't need to look to know she's pouting.

I'm supposed to do something now. Reach out. Tell her I'm sorry. Touch her hair. Instead I ask her where her boyfriend is.

"What?" She sits up, her necklace pooling in her cleavage. "Why?"

I shake my head, and can't pinpoint exactly when it stops moving.

"I said, WHY?" Branley shoves me.

Jesus Christ.

"Because maybe we shouldn't be doing this, okay?" The words smell like everything I've drunk, mixed with stomach acid. "How do you not get that?"

An easy smile—a Branley smile—slides across her face. "But this is what we do."

"Maybe not anymore."

She leans in, the necklace swinging away from her chest and slipping down to touch mine. "As long as there's a *maybe*," she whispers, and then her mouth isn't talking anymore, and all I can think is *Why'd you say maybe, dumbass?*

But I know why. It's because I'm addicted to her and have been ever since we discovered things together in junior high, all sloppy and confused in the backseat of her brother's car. She's gotten a lot better since then, and I'm still a drunk idiot fumbling in the dark.

And it is dark. And I am drunk.

It's so dark that Branley's hair isn't catching much light when her face hovers near me. It could be any color as it cascades around us. Not the blond I'm so used to seeing splayed across the pillow, but dark, like the strands that were left behind on my passenger seat. I'm so drunk that when I touch skin all I have to do is imagine freckles and they might as well be there.

And then they are. They just are. And I pull her down to me and roll onto her, wishing the smell of rain and cold air into the room with the misfiring of a synapse. We're skin to skin, and I'm into this with an urgency that didn't exist before and she's making noises I've never heard. Never heard because they've always been practiced and perfect, and I've taken her by surprise. She's loving it and I am too. But I'm not just in it for the fuck right now. I want this. I want her. I want to see the smile that flashed ever so briefly at me in the hall the other day. I want—

"Alex." Her name slips through my teeth as I collapse, utterly spent and crushing her.

Crushing *Branley*.

"What. The. Fuck."

"I'm sorry. I'm sorry, Bran. I'm so, so, sorry."

And I am, because that was shitty as hell. Branley shoves me away and rips through the covers looking for her clothes. How could it be so dark in here a few minutes ago I could let *that* happen, but now be damningly light? Light enough to see that she's crying.

"Branley, wait," I say, reaching for her hands, trying to stop her as she struggles into her jeans.

But she's saying only one word, over and over. "No, no, no, no, NO. You don't do that to me. I'm *Branley Jacobs*! Do you understand that? *Branley Jacobs!*" She says her own name the way most of the guys do, a mix of How the Hell Can That Even Exist and Can I Make It Mine?

"Guys fuck other girls and think of me," she says. "*Not* the other way around. You're an asshole, Jack Fisher. A real fucking asshole."

She slams the door so hard I feel the reverberations in my spine. I collapse back onto the bed, and for the first time in a long time, Branley has my undivided attention.

Because I think she might be right.

18. **ALEX**

I never thought it would be Jack Fisher.

In third grade, our class went on a field trip to the state park. We were at the end of a hike, the last hundred feet or so impossibly angled and difficult. Most of the kids and all the teachers were taking the stairs, gripping on to the rails, holding hands and saying encouraging things to one another about almost being there. I left the trail, not wanting to move at their pace. I climbed the hill on my own, reaching for tree branches and pulling myself forward, feeling a deep burn in my calves and loving the half second of panic every time I slipped a little.

I passed Jack and Branley as they picked their way up the stairs, him carrying her little plastic bag of whatever she'd bought for herself at the gift shop. I remember the slightest trace of impatience on his face as he offered Branley an arm, pulling her up where a step had been washed out. Our gazes met as I moved past them, ripped hands and filthy knees making my own way, and I saw a flash of envy, quickly stifled. And I knew that he'd rather be off the path with me, moving quickly, tearing his clothes.

But he stayed where he was, and I heard another boy's voice behind me. "It ain't easy but it sure is faster," he said, just as he lost his foothold. My arm shot out and he grabbed for me instinctively, and I steadied him until he got a firm grip on a tree trunk. We climbed up together, passing our classmates and ignoring the adults who yelled at us that we were going to break our necks. Sweat dripped off our foreheads, cutting clean tracks through the dirt on our faces, but we beat everyone to the top, breaking out of the shade and into the light.

We looked at each other and he said, "I have a tree frog in my pocket; don't tell anyone." I promised I wouldn't and we huddled together in the back of the bus on the way home, marveling over the little creature.

We fell into the habit of meeting each other outside at recess, climbing trees and wading in mud puddles, not worried about getting dirty. His name was Mike and he came to school dirty anyway. Mike was gone the next year. I stood on the playground on the first day of fourth grade, looking for the only person I called my friend, and he wasn't there.

I think he was the first boy I ever noticed.

And now Jack Fisher has my attention. Jack, who I always thought was like everyone else, loud and boring. Jack, who is more intelligent than I gave him credit for. Jack, who looks like he has something he desperately wants to say to me, and doesn't know how. Jack, who wouldn't leave the trail to follow me when we were little.

Maybe now he will.

19. PEEKAY

It's like Adam and Branley got married over the weekend and now we all get to watch the honeymoon.

"She'll be pregnant by fourth period at this rate," Sara says, tossing her books onto the desk. "I mean, I don't know if you saw, but he had her pressed up against—"

"I saw," I say a little too sharply. Everyone in the room looks at me, and I realize how nasty I must have sounded, because I even have Alex's attention.

I lower my voice. "Sorry," I tell Sara. "It's just not cool."

She nods and touches my hand, but I hardly feel it. I might as well still be out in the hallway, watching Branley drape herself all over my boyfriend (*ex-boyfriend, dammit*). Adam was always casual with me. Some hand-holding at lunch, a peck on the cheek in between classes, a tossed "See you, babe" as we walked out of school.

Branley he can't get enough of. Branley he touches constantly. Branley he won't be separated from. Branley—

—walks into the classroom reapplying her lipstick because it's all been kissed off by my boyfriend.

And I'm going for her. There's no logic involved, no weighing of pros and cons or thought of consequences. I smack the lipstick out of her hand just as it reaches her lips and she yelps in surprise.

Violence in real life is not the streamlined performance art of movies. It's not sexy. It's awkward and confusing. Branley just looks at me, like maybe there's been some kind of mistake, some weird blip in physics that made my hand hit hers and makeup fly across the room.

"What was that?" she asks, and I see a smear of glittery pink across her front teeth where the lipstick dug in a little. Her eyes are wide, totally clueless. She's waiting for me to say something, and the entire class is listening. But I don't have the words, and Branley's glance shifts over my shoulder to someone else.

Alex's voice is in my ear. "You should stop now," she says quietly.

"I don't want to," I say, eyes still on Branley, who looks concerned.

"What did I do?" she asks, and now Jack Fisher is with her, one hand on her elbow. Park immediately joins them, loyal as hell.

"Leave it alone, Bran," Jack says, and tries to pull her away, but she's still locked on me.

"What did I do to you?"

"You took my boyfriend," I say, hating the childishness of the words the second they leave my mouth, the fact that the word *boyfriend* makes tears come to my eyes.

Branley's face changes then, the honest confusion replaced with a smug mask, the one she wears so well. "No, sweetie," she says. "I didn't take him. He left you."

I swing. It's so simple I don't understand why I never did it before. My fist is on an arc that will break her perfect nose when it's stopped in midair, my elbow locked with Alex's, her strength so superior to mine that her arm is like a steel pipe and mine the pipe cleaner.

"Get your shit under control, Preacher's Kid," Park says, and I lunge at him before the last syllable is out of his mouth. Alex spins me into the wall, the knuckles of her fist in my spine pinning me in place like a butterfly.

"You need to calm down, Claire." It's the same voice she uses on the cats at the shelter, the one that makes them melt a little bit. I kind of get their reaction, because I understand that if I'm unable to do it on my own, she will make me.

I take a shaky breath. "Okay," I say. "Okay."

Alex relaxes her grip and I turn to see Branley nestled behind Jack, her boobs pushed up against his back. Sara rustles around in the corner and picks up Branley's lipstick. "Here," she says, handing it over as if restoring it makes everything better. Branley takes it as Miss Hendricks walks into the room, the bustle of the hall dying behind her.

"What's going on?" she asks, eyes narrowing at the sight of the tears that finally spill over onto my cheeks.

"Peekay lost her shit," Park says.

"*Parker Castle*," she screeches at him, but he only shrugs. She narrows in on me. "What happened?"

"Nothing, it's fine," Branley says suddenly. "Don't worry about it."

"I'm the one who decides what's worth worrying about," Miss Hendricks snaps back, but Branley walks away, leaning into Jack more than necessary.

My breaths are coming deep and heavy now, the tears running down my cheeks freely. Sara has one hand on my shoulder, and Alex stands on my other side in what feels like support, but I'm pretty sure she'd gladly faceplant me right into the tiles if I flipped again.

"I think I need to go to the guidance office," I say.

Hendricks nods. "One of you go with her."

"I will," Alex volunteers, and I swear there's the tiniest

bit of relief on Sara's face when she does.

We're halfway to Miss Reynolds's office before I get my breath to stop hitching in my chest and it occurs to me to wipe my face. "Bathroom," I say, ducking in because a cold sink and some running water sounds a hell of a lot more comforting than trying to decipher what kind of judgment Miss Reynolds's eyebrows are delivering. Alex leans against the wall, eyeing me in the mirror while I splash my face.

A flush of embarrassment rises up my neck and into my cheeks, underscoring the hot tear tracks. "I'm sorry," I say.

"Why?"

I watch the water sweeping away the salt on my face, the drops collecting on my chin as I lean my forehead against the mirror. "Because that's not me," I say, closing my eyes. "I don't hit people. That's not who I am."

And Alex's voice in the darkness. "Wrong. That's *exactly* who you were in that specific moment. That was Claire at her most basic, unaltered by expectations."

I open my eyes, the blue of my irises so much more intense now that I've been crying. "But you stopped me."

"Venting your primal self in an emotional moment can be more than your socially constructed self can handle after the fact," Alex says, her eyes gliding over me. "Look at you. Your hands are shaking. Your voice is weak. And your conscience is reasserting itself."

I heave a sigh and pull back from the mirror, my forehead leaving a smear behind. "Yeah," I admit. "It totally is."

All I did was smack Branley's hand a little, dent her makeup, and give her a lesson on what her new lipstick tastes like. And I feel like shit.

I turn to face Alex, resting my back against the sink. "Thanks for stopping me."

"Of course," she says, as if restraining people is part of her routine. Her eyebrows come together as she scrutinizes the wall above my shoulder.

"Is Marilee Nolan a bitch?" she asks.

"What?"

Alex nods at the wall behind me. "Right there, it says *Marilee Nolan is a bitch.* Is she?"

"No, I don't know. Not really. I don't think so," I say. But whoever wrote that had a red Sharpie and a lot of conviction.

"We should erase it," Alex says.

"That's permanent marker."

"Nothing is permanent." Alex pumps the towel dispenser half a dozen times and I find myself playing janitor with her, our knuckles scraping against the cinderblock wall as we wet fistful after fistful of cheap towels.

"I stopped you because it's easier to fantasize about

violence than actually perform it," she says a few minutes later. "Most people consider things they wouldn't do in real life, and there's enough visceral satisfaction in the thought to alleviate the emotion. In reality, hurting another person on purpose is not a simple task, and not everyone is up to it."

I remember how I wanted to find the guy who threw out the sack of puppies and kick him bloody, how many times I've considered punching Branley in the face. But when I actually tried, it all went the wrong way, like a carefully scripted scene I imagined ahead of time falling apart because nobody else knew their lines. Of all the times I imagined smashing her nose until it bled and shredding her pouty lips on her perfect white teeth, I never factored in that look of complete incomprehension on her face when I did it. Now that I can't unsee it, the absolute innocence in her eyes when I was bent on hurting her is its own revenge, and I feel gut punched even though Branley never raised a finger.

"It's not restricted to violence," Alex continues, still scrubbing at the wall. "People fantasize about sex with someone they can't attain, or what they would do with the money if they won the lottery. It's wish fulfillment, a break from reality."

"A way to escape," I say, thinking about my dad's words the other day.

Alex nods. "Until it becomes your new prison, and you either live in the daydream or make it reality. And in your case, that would mean going against who you actually are, inside. A good person."

I toss my last handful of paper towel, now stained pink, into the trash and get myself a fresh one from the dispenser. I wet it and press it against my still-hot face. She's right. My new friend with a good vocabulary knows me better than I know myself.

"We should go to the office," I say. "Talk to Miss Reynolds."

Alex follows me into the hallway and we walk the rest of the way in our special kind of silence, the one that doesn't need to be broken for us to be comfortable. I get into the guidance office just as Reynolds is hanging up her phone, probably getting a call from Hendricks saying I'm on my way. I don't know why I'm here. I don't need her anymore.

Alex made the bathroom more productive than the guidance office, more honest than my father's confessional. But I say the right words, tell the truth like I'm supposed to, and promise to apologize to Branley, who is reportedly *being very mature* about the entire thing.

When I'm done, I find Alex waiting for me in the hallway. She's pressed against the wall underneath the sign for the girls' bathroom that someone drew on—an erect penis with eyes glaring up her plastic skirt.

I didn't expect Alex to be there. I am the preacher's kid. My friends are on the debate team and Quiz Bowl. My friends are in marching band. My friends are in class right now because that's where they're supposed to be. Except Alex isn't.

And I'm pretty damn sure that she's my friend.

20. **JACK**

It's definitely a girl-fight day. First Peekay went after Branley; now Alex and Branley are vying for space in my head. It's a good thing I have a job where your mind can be elsewhere. In fact, it's better that way.

Because I kill things for a living.

It's raining. The holding pens smell like wet shit and anxiety. The living cows might not know what the coppery tinge to the air is, but they do know it's nothing good. Another one comes down the chute toward me and I put my bolt gun right on its fuzzy forehead, the spot a kid would kiss if this were a stuffed animal being tucked in at night. I pull the trigger and it drops, fifteen hundred pounds of unconscious steaks and hamburger hitting the ground with a meaty *thump*.

I hook a chain around a back leg and this one is hoisted away from me, tongue lolling. Depending on which line it goes down it might see my dad in a few moments, pupils reflecting his face right before he slits its throat and the brightness fades. He did that job before the animal rights groups said they had to stun them first. He says the pigs would scream like women while they hung and you had to spin them to get their throat pointed at you right. He wore earplugs then.

Now he wears earbuds, says the screaming was almost better because you didn't hear the skin tearing, the blood dripping onto the concrete. I know for a fact that his playlist is straight classical music. He just stands there all day, a huge guy with a blood-spattered beard wearing a rubber apron, holding a knife, pumping Bach into his ears so he can go somewhere else in his head. Nicest guy you'll ever meet.

Dad got me this job when I turned eighteen, told me this was the best way to earn money for college and appreciate it at the same time. And I sure as hell do, because there's another cow already coming down the chute, looking at me with big, confused eyes that won't close, not even when I pull the trigger. I don't know how my dad has done this for so many years, but I know why—so that I don't have to. I love the shit out of him and have grown too old to say it, so when he pulled some strings to get me a shift after school that would overlap with his for one hour I said yes.

Yes because even that little bit of money will help get me through college. Yes because when he asked he expected me to say no. Yes because I don't think I'm better than him, not by a long shot. Yes because when he's leaving he walks past me and claps me on the shoulder without speaking. Yes because my dad is a good guy, and I want to be one too.

So I shoot the next cow and try to let the impact noise jolt Alex and Branley out of my head, but they won't go. They're stuck there, revolving around each other while I try to sort out what's what.

When Branley faced down Peekay I was right next to her because that's where I've always been. In fifth grade it was me and Park across from Jimmy Owens when he knocked her into the gravel on the playground because she wouldn't lift up her skirt and show him her panties. She's got tiny white scars on her knees from that, places the gravel dug deep and turned her skin to ground meat. I look at them sometimes, and I can still hear her crying.

But I remember a time before that when she didn't wear skirts, before she realized that she was cute as hell and it could go a long way. I remember hunting for crawdads with Branley wearing jeans rolled up to her skinny knees, mud smeared on her cheeks, sweat making her hair dark. I remember when Branley was my best friend and we didn't understand why people smiled at us when we held hands. And now my hands have been everywhere on her, and she doesn't dish out a smile unless she wants something.

"Goddammit," I say to a new cow before I shoot her.

I don't even know Alex, I remind myself. There's no reason why I'm so fascinated by her, but I just *am*. I can't get her out of my head. All my memories of Branley can't compete against a few minutes of conversation with Alex, awkward and stilted, both of us weighing every word like we're testing out a new language on each other. And we kind of are, I guess. We use the same consonant and vowel sounds but have never said them to each other before, and somehow that makes them all new again.

I've been with enough girls to know that one body is as good as another when the lights go out. Discovering women is far from a new thing to me, but the outline of Alex's taut arm when she held back Peekay was like a damn aphrodisiac. I want to know about *her*. I want to know what she looks like with tousled hair. I want to know what the scar on her wrist is from. I understand now why my mom always asks me if I'm *interested* in any girls as opposed to if I *like* them.

I like Branley. I've always liked Branley.

I'm interested in Alex.

She's buried in my head so deep I'm still thinking about her as I drive home, and when my headlights bounce off the same ditched car I saw yesterday, I hit the brakes. It's pitch black but I see enough to know it's her car, and that it hasn't budged an inch. I take the curve slow, thumbs drumming on the steering wheel in thought.

Alex hadn't offered me her number, and I was so focused on keeping a conversation going I didn't think to ask. Driving to her house to tell her the car is still in the ditch seems pretty pointless, since I bet she already knows. What I'd also bet is she has no idea how to get it out and isn't the type to ask for help. I call for Dad the second I walk in the back door, kicking off my blood-slicked boots to sit next to his in the mudroom.

"In here," my mom calls from the living room.

They both look so comfortable I hate to ask. Mom's curled up on the couch with a book. Dad's hair is still wet from a shower and he's got his recliner up, a football game on the TV.

"Hey, Dad, can I get a favor?"

"What's that?" he asks, eyes flicking from the screen to me.

"Friend of mine went in the ditch, and her car's still there."

"Oh, *her* car," my mom says, over the sound of Dad's ancient recliner squealing in protest as he flips it down.

"How bad?" Dad asks.

"Barely in the ditch, right on the north side of the curve."

"Are you interested in this girl, honey?" Mom asks, eyeing me over the pages of her book.

I take a deep breath instead of waving her off like I usually do. "Yes. I'm definitely interested."

Mom raises her eyebrows at Dad. "I guess you better get going, then."

It's the work of one truck, one chain, five minutes, and then I'm in Alex's car with Dad following me. I drive it to her place while trying to formulate the perfect thing to say when she answers the door.

Except her mom does.

She's all poise and coolness, a drink in her hand and a question on her face when she looks at me. She's like something out of a magazine with drawn-on eyebrows . . . one of them arching a little more severely than necessary as I continue to say nothing.

"Hi," I finally manage. "Is, um . . . is Alex home?" She looks confused for a split second, and I wonder if I somehow drove to the wrong house in the dark.

"Mom?" Alex's voice calls from somewhere inside. "Was that the door?"

"Yes," her mom says cautiously, still eyeing me. "It's for you."

And then Alex is there, standing beside her in the doorway. They're shoulder to shoulder and staring at me as I stand awkwardly on a welcome mat with very little wear and tear. I remember the shriek of the hinges when the front door was opened, sticking for a moment in the frame so that it had to be yanked. The long pause inside a dead house right after I rang the doorbell.

No one comes here.

Alex shakes off her bewilderment first. "Hello, Jack."

Not *hi, hey, what's up*. She says *hello*. And she says my name, to me, which is something people don't usually do in conversation. It feels so intimate I nearly blush.

Her mom goes into motion, like a robot that just now went into start-up. "Yes, hello. Are you going to introduce us, Alex?"

"Mom, this is my friend Jack Fisher." Alex says it automatically, as prompted. The word *friend* comes out awkwardly, one her tongue and lips haven't practiced enough.

I'm thinking about her tongue and lips when I should be shaking the hand her mom is holding out, waiting patiently for me to divert my attention from Alex's mouth. Her hand limp in mine, a greeting as warm as the wind biting my back.

"I got your car out of the ditch," I say, eyes back on Alex so quickly it's like she's a magnet. Her glance goes over my shoulder to the driveway where my dad sits in the truck, lights dim, engine idling.

"I was going to call, but I don't have your number," I add, hoping the hint is enough.

Her mom has faded away, a pale figure receding back into the house.

"I don't have a phone," Alex says.

"Maybe you should get one."

Her eyes are on mine, and it's like there's no such thing as casual flirting with this girl. Every word she speaks is intense as hell and thoroughly investigated before she lets it out of her mouth.

"Maybe I should," she says.

And I kinda feel like I just won the world.

21. **ALEX**

You learn how to pretend when you live in this house.

We're both so good at it now we don't know how to do anything else. Pretend that I'm okay. Pretend the scotch bottle is as full as it was yesterday. Pretend that Anna's permanently closed door might open again. Pretend that mine doesn't exist. Pretend other families live like this.

It's the only thing we do well together.

It wasn't always this way. I remember my father. I remember marking the calendar, putting smiley-face stickers on the day when he would get home from his run. I remember Mom's mood changing as we got closer to it, her face reflecting the sticker.

Dad would come home. The rumble of a semi in the

night and the flash of lights trailing across my bedroom walls, slipping downstairs in my footed pajamas, unable to mask the *swish-swish* noise of them as I came down the stairs, Anna behind me. We never got in trouble, no matter how late it was. He'd scoop us up and hug us, toss us in the air so high Mom would squeal a bit. The house would smell like gas and takeout and nobody cared.

Then things changed. Mom seemed to prefer the days in between the smiley faces on the calendar, her face stretching into a tight mask as we got closer to the next one, the muscles creating the best parody of it that they were able. We were bigger and harder to toss in the air, and Dad just kind of looked at us when we ran to him, unsure what to do with something not shaped like a steering wheel.

So we stopped running to him.

And then a sticker day came and he didn't. It faded, the color creeping back from the edges until only the teeth were yellowed. Mom never took the calendar down. It hung on the refrigerator, a silent testament to his failure, a constant reminder whenever we wanted a drink.

It was her litany when Anna was still alive, her echoed refrain any time my sister pointed out tangles in my hair or toenails grown too long.

"At least I'm *here*," she would say, stomping away from

the argument so that her footfalls shook the house, asserting the simple fact of her presence.

Every day that passed brought my real face out from under the baby fat, the elongating cheekbones too much like his, the eyes reminding her of another pair that couldn't bear to look at her anymore.

Dad's things are still here; his clothes hang limply in his closet, his tools unused in the garage. The only thing of his not covered with dust is a punching bag, because I've kept it in perpetual motion since he left, the rage my small fists vented growing into an actual threat now that I'm older.

When I'm throwing punches is the only time I remember him clearly, all the hours I stood nearby, my own face crunched in fierceness like his, my feet mimicking his movements. I went out there alone only once, after Mom had tossed something I was reading into the garbage disposal after I ignored her instructions to clean my room. Pages had flown in the air, shredded words floated between us, and I wanted to cross the distance with my knuckles, wipe the smirk off my mother's face.

But I knew better, and I ran to the garage to do all the things I wanted to do to her to the punching bag instead, screaming, punching, slapping, kicking, sweating, crying, heaving. I was red-faced and out of air when Dad found me resting on the tailgate of his truck, one sleeve of my shirt dried stiff from wiping tears. He sat next to me, his weight pushing the truck bed down, my little feet that much closer to the ground. He rested his hand on my head and sighed, and I saw that he was crying too.

I didn't understand then, but I do now. Anna never forgave him for leaving, for the absence that the checks—bigger every month once he owned his company—didn't fill. But I know it was the better alternative, just like I know why he cried that day he found me in the garage.

There are parts of yourself that you hate; parts that you know other people wouldn't understand. And he knew his own worst elements had been passed on to me, this unwieldy wrath that burns through my brain, turning reason into ash. So I can't be angry with him for leaving when I understand too well the reason. If he'd stayed, he would've killed our mother, eventually. Maybe when we were kids, maybe when we were older, maybe once we had left. But either way, it was a foregone conclusion. We could either have a mother and money coming in, or we could have a cold grave and a father in jail.

And while I know he made the right decision for Anna, I don't know about me. I want to tell him all these things that I have done. Whether he would be disgusted or proud, I do not know. But at least I would have someone to tell, someone who knows me.

It's the deepest part of who I am, a fundamental part of myself that has been shared with no one, the essence of who I am, the core of understanding me—and I'm the only one who knows.

If Mom has guessed, she is neither proud nor disgusted. With Anna gone we listen for footfalls, each of us avoiding the other with an intense concentration. Occasionally we cross paths by accident, our bubbles of personal space like a Venn diagram, becoming darker where they overlap.

Dad left.

Anna is gone.

I have never been here.

22. PEEKAY

When Alex walks into the church with me it gets still so fast it's like there's been a trachea rapture.

This is not a quiet kind of church, so the little bubble of silence that surrounds us gains notice as it expands. It turns heads, exposing faces that still at the sight of Alex Craft. Here. In the old church in the woods.

I hadn't even thought about it when I brought her with me. Alex is within shouting distance of her sister's last resting place . . . all of them. Alex isn't Anna's little sister to me anymore; she's Alex, my friend. So when she came over and I told her we were going to a party, it never occurred to me I was also dragging her back to the woods where her sister died.

Sara shoves a beer into my hand, the cold glass

clinking against one of my rings. "Good to see you in church, Preacher's Kid," she says, her breath sugar-laced, lips tinged red with her own drink.

"Cheers," I say, clinking my bottle against hers.

I step over a piece of the roof that has collapsed since the last party. The conversation starts up again, the anomaly of Alex's presence fading fast while everyone chases their own goals for the night, whether it's at the bottom of a bottle or in someone else's pants. Alex follows me, her eyes combing the crowd of our classmates as I do the same.

It's already dark, but someone was thinking ahead tonight. Everyone has to raise their voices to be heard over the hum of a generator, loud and persistent, lighting the strings of lights thrown around the walls and feeding the space heaters. There are fires too, made in the places where the stone floor has been torn up, exposing the black earth underneath. The whole place smells like fire and ash, sweat and vomit, rain and rot.

We love it.

I bet our parents loved it too, when they were our age. Once some of us made a game of trying to find them in the graffiti, names and dates mixed in an obscene smear, a town history more colorful and honest than the stories on paper. I found my mom, her name paired with Park's father, and then I stopped looking. I knew my dad didn't write on the walls of any church, collapsed and broken or not. But I don't doubt that he came here.

Sometimes after I've had a few beers I think about their parents—our grandparents—and then back further, to people who loved this place for a different reason. People who pulled rocks out of the ground to make the walls, cutting timber for a roof that has now rotted mostly away. The supports still in place are stained black from ashes of the generations that followed, our hands hard at work to tear it back down.

There are only five pews left, the rest cut up for fire over the years. Those that remain are high-value real estate, the only place to sit before you find somebody to sneak into the woods with. Branley has set up court at one, her eyes already artificially bright, her voice loud and brassy while Adam sprawls next to her, one arm thrown possessively around her shoulders. I flinch at the sight and look away to find Jack Fisher coming toward us, a beer in each hand, happier to see me than he's ever been in his life.

But he walks right past me, gives a bottle to Alex and takes her other hand, leading her over to a pile of rubble where the less fortunate sit once the real seats are taken. I take another swig of beer and my eyes slide back over to Adam. He's looking at me. I jerk away, following Alex and Jack. I perch next to her on a rock, trying to find a spot to put my ass so that I'm not in pain.

"I bought a phone," Alex says to Jack. Her words come out smoothly, her voice more accustomed to use from hours of us talking at the shelter, sentences shared over dog shampoos, punctuated by the *snip* of the nail clipper.

"Here's my number," she adds, with a note of confidence she wouldn't learn even in years of conversation with me.

Jack snatches the piece of paper she hands him like he's afraid it'll evaporate, punching the numbers in. He raises his phone to snap a pic of her, then puts it back down, cautious.

"Is it okay if I take your picture?"

She smiles hesitantly, but her arm goes around my shoulders, barely resting on my skin. I lean in, surprised at the contact, and what's left of my beer sloshes onto my pants. "Shit," I say, just as Jack takes the pic.

"Oh, nice," he says, laughing a little as he turns the screen toward us.

I'm staring at my lap, my lips pursed right on the *i* in *shit*, mild annoyance stamped on my features like my own crotch offended me somehow. Alex's arm dangles awkwardly near my neck, as if she's not quite sure how to touch someone. She's not smiling, just looking into the camera with the dead stare that makes feral cats reconsider their choices.

"God," I mutter. "Redo."

Jack shakes his head. "It's perfect." He stands to put his phone in his back pocket and leans toward both of us, his breath heavy with beer in a way that makes me feel relaxed instead of repulsed.

"Park and I tried to chase off a couple of tweakers when we brought in the generator," he says, head jerking toward a dark corner where there's a circle of guys I don't know. "Just be aware of them."

"I am," Alex said.

They're older than us, their features vaguely familiar, like they're either somebody's brothers or graduated when we were still puckering our faces at the taste of alcohol. One of them is good-looking in a grungy way, lanky blond hair back in a ponytail, dark circles under his eyes that could be makeup, could be something else. The gauge in one of his ears is connected to his nose ring with a chain. He catches me looking and tips me a wink. I glance back down at my bottle.

"I'm empty."

"Here." Alex switches out our bottles, hers heavy and cold, mine light and warm from my grip.

"I'll get you another one," Jack says.

"No," she says simply, eyes still on the tweakers.

"I'll get rid of the empty, then," he says, but she shakes her head.

"No."

"I'll go get myself another one, come up with a different line of conversation, then come back and sit next to you," he says, leaning toward her a little too much, taking up more of her personal space than she usually allows.

But she's smiling when she says, "I would like that."

He brings out the million-watt smile that's separated more than a few asses in this room from their panties, but it looks genuine and sweet, like a little kid who found out he's getting exactly what he wanted for Christmas.

"Okay, be right back," he says. "Don't move."

Alex flaps her arms maniacally in response and he busts out laughing, the sound carrying as he heads to the altar, where there's a collection of coolers and a keg.

"Um, hey, friend," I say, nudging her knee with mine. "Part of this whole friendship gig is that you tell me when you like a guy."

Her mouth curls a little bit in a half smile. "Oh, really?"

"Yeah, it's totally a thing," I say, slinging back what turns out is—somehow—the last swallow of the beer Alex gave me. "I need another."

"So who do you like, friend?" she asks, ignoring my request.

"Adam," I say automatically, followed by, "Fuck."

"Why?"

I look at the collection of glass scattered near the bases of the walls, some remnants of long-broken stained-glass windows, most the dull browns and greens of accumulated beer bottles. Even the sharp edges are deceptively beautiful in the flickering firelight and the weak glow of the naked bulbs hooked to the generator. The sea of colors is punctuated by flattened shotgun shells from the hunters who hole up here during deer season, and I spot—for the first time—empty hypodermic needles among them.

"I don't know," I finally answer, bringing my bottle back to my lips even though there's nothing in it. "Force of habit, maybe."

Alex takes the empty from me, carefully balancing it on a slanted rock between my knees. "Remind me," she says. "Which one is he?"

I sigh and rub my eyes. In the past few weeks I've grown accustomed to Alex's ignorance of the names of the people we've grown up with, so now that I'm forcing her out into society she's getting a crash course. But right now my brain is slowing down, my tongue growing heavy. Jack hasn't made it back from the keg yet, his T-shirt snagged on Branley's fingernails, sharp as blackberry thorns. She's left Adam behind, and we look at each other across the sputtering fires, his features smeared in the heat shimmer.

And I don't have the words to identify him anymore. If he's not *my boyfriend*, then I don't know how to differentiate him from the others.

"He's there," I say, pointing at him.

"Oh, him," she says, clearly unimpressed. "I don't understand."

She squints at Adam, as if somehow my attraction will make more sense if he's viewed through a fuzzy lens. And I don't even know if I'm into him anymore, so it's not like I can rant about how hot he is or how his eyes make me melt. Because they did back in seventh grade, but that was a hell of a long time ago. I've gotten so used to thinking of Adam as my boyfriend that his name and face kick in good memories and I'm salivating like one of Pavlov's dogs even when there's no food on the way. So maybe that's all I want anymore, the memories and not actually Adam. The explanation makes sense in my head but I'm a few drinks deep and don't trust my mouth to make sense of it.

Alex watches Adam watching Branley, who watches Jack, who only has eyes for Alex, and I think if there were lines connecting us all it would be a tangled mess.

Jack disengages from Branley, who sulks back to Adam like he's the consolation prize. A couple of sophomores try to escape into the privacy of the woods without anyone noticing, but the tweakers call them out on it.

"Hey, man," the shortest one yells. "Don't let Comstock get her."

"Long as you get her first," the blond says, sticking his fist out for a bump, which the sophomore returns even though the girl gives him a dirty glare. They slide into the shadows, but not before she shoots a furtive glance at Alex, wondering if she heard.

"Sorry about that," Jack says quietly as he joins us, and I don't know if he's talking about the fact that it took him so long to get back, or that someone casually dropped the name of Anna's killer as if he were nothing more than an urban legend. Nothing more than a scary bedtime story to keep girls out of the woods, their pants above their ankles.

He may just be a cheaply bandied-about name now, a capitalized word that makes us shift uncomfortably and drop our voices, but he was a real person only a few years ago. A real person who kept duct tape and a hammer in the trunk of his car, waiting for the right moment. A real person who spread legs and spilled blood.

That blood flows in the veins of the person whose knee is touching mine, and as I finish off the bottle

Jack brought me I wonder if she can smell the blood-saturated dirt, or hear her sister's screams still echoing off of trees.

That's when I realize exactly how drunk I am.

Lately I can't eat much. My throat doesn't want to do anything other than say Adam's name and my stomach only wishes to digest him. I might as well have popped an IV in my arm and hooked up to the keg as soon as I got here. There's no food in my stomach and the alcohol is passing straight through its lining into my blood, soaring through my body to infect my brain, my heart, my organs.

Everyone around me is talking but my mouth doesn't want to participate by doing anything other than wrapping itself around a beer bottle. I want to ask Jack if he'll get me another one but he's entirely lost in Alex, his eyes drinking her up like she's the keg and he's an alcoholic. I know I'm going to have to concentrate in order to stand up and I take a moment to identify the best way to do it, which foot to move first and what rocks to brace my hands against in order to get vertical.

I make it happen, and I'm on a path for the keg when Branley beats me to it, shoulders bare even though it's nearly snowing. She's coated in a sheen of sweat from sitting so close to the fire, her blond curls losing some of their bounce. One of the guys who has taken up a post at the altar tells her she looks like she needs to cool off, and sprays her down with beer.

She shrieks, her white tank top plastered to her chest. Beer is dripping off her and she stamps her foot, sending everything that will shake into a jiggle.

"Holy shit, dude," one of the guys says, staring. "That was . . . not cool."

"Yeah, not cool, man," another agrees, but they all might as well have their hands down their pants.

"Adam!" Branley yells, and he's on his feet to come to her rescue, her jacket in his hand.

I change my course, in no hurry to be near a wet, pissed-off, nearly naked Branley and my loyal—to her, anyway—ex-boyfriend.

I've got an empty bottle in my hand and no one to give it to. Despite the fact that a bum could come out to the church and make a fortune in recycling, I've never had the nerve to just throw mine in a corner. I drove around with bottles rolling in my backseat for a week once because I couldn't bear to litter.

Sara's deep in conversation with some of the other basketball players, something about how the ref lost them their last game. Everyone has settled down into groups for the night, people cuddled around fires they made, or curling up with each other in sleeping bags. I can't even go out into the woods for fresh air and privacy because there are more people out there than in here by now. And they don't want company.

Somebody is taking the bottle from me, and I just stare at his hand for a second. Big knuckles with drying skin, a broad silver band on the middle finger.

"Need a fresh?" he says and my eyes slowly find their way to his face.

It's the blond tweaker. The chain on his face accents his sharp nose, the hollows of his eyes dark in the flickering firelight. This close his skin has the unmistakable rough quality of a long-time user, pocked yet oddly clear. But his eyes are arrestingly blue, and as I look into them recognition dawns.

"You're Ray Parsons," I say. "We were in study hall together my freshman year, third period, cafeteria."

He smiles, the chain resting lightly on his cheek when he does. "Oh yeah?"

"Yeah," I go on, the details coming out with such clarity it's obvious I kind of had a thing for him then. "You sat at the corner table. I'm Peekay. I sat over by the water fountain. You were a senior. You didn't notice me."

"I'm noticing you now, Peekay," he says, dragging his eyes over my body and not even trying to hide it.

I know I look good tonight. I'm not Branley and I never will be. I'm not even Sara, with her athletic build, or Alex, with her green eyes and freckles. But I am small and cute, with a decent rack that I know how to accentuate. I put on a push-up bra tonight, opened my top two buttons, and zipped my down coat right up to the bottom of my cleavage. My tits couldn't be more on display.

And Ray Parsons is definitely window shopping.

I feel a little rush in my stomach. A wave of motion that pushes my heart into my throat and makes my pulse skip. I haven't felt that for anyone but Adam in a long time. Ray Parsons had my attention when I was a freshman. Basketball player, casual smoker, and the guy most likely to pull the fire alarm. He had an edge to him then that might have sliced some of the softer bits away in the past few years, but he's still Ray Parsons and I'm so very alone right now that I don't argue when he hooks a finger through my belt loop and takes me over to his friends.

"Guys, this is Peekay," he says.

They all give me an up-nod and one asks what the hell kind of name is that.

"Nickname for Preacher's Kid," I answer as Ray throws my bottle over his shoulder and heads to the altar.

"Oh yeah?" They're suddenly more interested, eyes going over me like Ray's did now that he's not here anymore.

"You a virgin?" one of them asks.

"Really?" another says. "You gonna ask her that?"

"Yep," I say, not caring.

There's a plastic cup in my hand now and Ray's finger is back in my belt loop, his thumb rubbing up under my coat to press against skin.

"Hey, Ray," one of his friends says, pointing two fingers at me like pistols. "Virgin."

His eyes do their pass again as he says, "Nice."

I don't like his friends, but I'm still more than a little captivated by the image of Ray Parsons, a guy who never glanced at me three years ago, now unable to look away. I lean against him as I drink, not caring that the present version of Ray has slightly greasy hair and an obvious drug problem. I'll make him take a bath. Clean him up in all the ways and finally get the prize I wanted as a freshman.

"I always thought you were cute," I try to say, but my words are tripping over one another, endings running into beginnings and middles being left out completely. My knees give out but I don't go down. Ray's got me pressed against him so that I don't fall, his blue eyes no longer on me but scanning the crowd as he edges us into the shadows.

A hand is on my spine, pushing down into my pants and past my panties, fingers twisting in search. I know it's not Ray because he's practically carrying me now. There's a voice in my ear that says, "Come on, Preacher's Kid. We'll take you to church for real."

They've almost got me out into the darkness, and a nearby fire pops, bringing a brief flash of light as my eyes slide shut. I see a cartilage stud in Ray's ear as my head falls forward onto his shoulder.

And then I'm gone.

23. **JACK**

I'm going to catch hell from Park, but I haven't been able to stay away from Alex all night. He's doing what he does best, playing the room, making every girl there feel like she's the one he's thinking about even if he is talking to somebody else. But I can't even pretend. Yeah, I still notice stuff. I've always thought of Peekay as someone I could borrow decent class notes from, but tonight she's sporting a pair she might've bought from Victoria's Secret but she's wearing them like they grew on her. So it's not like I've gone blind or anything.

I just don't care.

I don't care about any of the other girls because Alex accepts a beer from me, even if she doesn't drink it. I don't care because when I take her hand she lets me, and we're sitting next to each other on the rubble pile. I'd rather be there than on a pew with Branley, or in a sleeping bag with anyone else.

I'm halfway toward being drunk and swimming in her when I go to get Peekay another beer, partially to be a gentleman, but also because Branley has taken it upon herself to transfer all her body heat to Adam (even though she can't be retaining much—put on some clothes, Branley, it's November) and I know that can't be easy for Peekay.

Branley looks perfect, as usual. I've never seen the shirt she's wearing so it's probably new, and I doubt it's got two tiny holes in it like all mine do because I buy everything at the thrift store where they staple the price tags on. Her family can afford real new clothes, not *new to me but it belonged to someone else two weeks ago.*

I pull two beers from my cooler and am headed back from the altar when Branley snags me, her fingernails digging past T-shirt and down into skin.

"Shit, Bran," I say, stumbling back. I bump the altar but it doesn't even shiver. Dad says that thing is the most solid-built piece of furniture in the whole county, which is a good thing because I bet more than a few of us here tonight were conceived on it.

"Seriously?" Branley is up in my face, my spine braced against solid oak. *"Seriously?"*

"Going to need more to go on than that," I tell her, but I'm not stupid.

"Alex Craft?" she says, practically spitting the name. "I thought maybe it was that Alex cheerleader from Twin Rivers, or, God . . . maybe even a *dude*, but Alex *Craft*? Seriously?"

"So, it's more realistic to you that I would want to bang a guy than her?" I say, trying to make it sound like a joke. Trying to ignore the burst of anger in my gut. I don't like the way Alex's name sounds in Branley's mouth, like a poison.

I try to shove past her, but her claws are in me and I'm not going anywhere until she's finished. "It doesn't make sense," Branley insists. "I mean, look at her."

And I do. She's so normal, perched on the crumbled pile of stone. Not like a girl in a magazine, or even Branley, so impossibly gorgeous she would never, ever be crawling around in rubble. Alex has a smudge of dirt across her cheekbone that only accentuates the paleness of the skin under her freckles. She's picking at the label on her empty beer bottle, and I love the fact that she couldn't give less of a shit about her fingernails.

"I am looking at her, Branley," I say. "I can't *not* look at her."

"Whatever," she mutters, releasing me in a huff. I leave her behind me without a second thought, perfectly aware that any number of guys there will be happy to reinflate her ego.

"Jaaaaaaackkkk." My name stretched into as many syllables as possible. Park is done making his rounds, so happy to see me it's like he forgot we were just talking twenty minutes ago.

He sails toward me, arms spread wide, when he sees Alex and hits the brakes so hard that shards of glass spit out from under his shoes. His face goes blank and for the first time in my life I'm seeing Park at a loss for words.

"Hello," Alex says.

His grin is plastered back on. "Hello," he says, his tone almost mocking her but not quite. He bows low. "Please do not crush my balls, madam."

"Don't touch me without my permission and I won't."

"Okay, cool." He joins us on the pile, taking the spot Peekay vacated a few minutes ago. His eyes move in between the two of us. "So is this, like, going to be a thing now?"

"Yes," I say.

"In that case, you need to be my friend," he says to Alex. "Jack and I are a package deal so you're my friend now. Okay?"

Alex looks him up and down, taking her time before she answers. "Yes."

"Sweet." He holds out his fist for a bump. "No hard feelings?"

"Is that even possible?" she asks, her mouth going up in a teasing smile I haven't seen before, her gaze directed at his crotch.

Park howls with laughter, clapping a hand down on Alex's shoulder to keep from rolling off the rocks. "It took *a while*, if you really want to know. I was out of commission. And there was much weeping. All the girls you see here were devastated. Back in business now, though," he adds, tipping her a wink as he finishes off a beer.

He suddenly seems to realize he has his hand on her and he lets go quickly. "Sorry," he says. "And sorry about those asshole tweakers saying Com . . . you know, saying *his* name like it was no big deal. A joke or something."

She nods, accepting the apology. "His name means nothing to me."

"Really?" Branley's friend Lila pokes her head out from her sleeping bag, her short blond hair sticking out in spikes. "Because I couldn't even handle that."

Alex shrugs, a slow rolling movement like a cat unfurling in the sun. "It means nothing to me because it's already been handled."

Lila nods, the words resonating with her.

"I heard his face was beaten in so bad they found

teeth down his throat," a freshman pipes up, his eyes bright with drink.

"No, man," a buddy corrects him. "He chewed off his own lips 'cause he was left there to starve. Needed teeth for that."

"That's all bullshit," someone else says. "It was a clean execution. Head shot."

I feel Alex's hand tense in mine as they keep going, a demented Greek chorus rising up from the fires around us, echoing bits of urban legend that have grown and coalesced, spawning off each other in a town that has so little ugliness to celebrate that the story can't possibly be dark enough to penetrate the truth.

"None of those things are true," Alex says calmly, her words stopping the spray of myth around us. Everyone looks to her, myself included, our faces like little children around the campfire, ready for our story.

"He was drunk," she says slowly. "Incapacitated by a blow to the head." Her words, always careful, come even more cautiously than usual.

"I heard it was his own baseball bat, that he used it to prop the screen door and whoever did it hit him upside the head with it," the freshman says before his buddy smacks him into silence.

"That's possible," Alex acknowledges, and he smacks his friend back. "They put him in one of his own kitchen chairs and bent him forward, chest resting on his own lap. There were a hammer and nails lying out because he was working on the porch railing. They wrapped his arms under his chair and drove nails through the palms, up through the seat to hold him in place."

"Then what?" Lila asks.

"Then he woke up, I imagine," Alex says, and the boys start laughing until Lila kicks at them from under her sleeping bag.

"I mean what killed him, then?" she asks. "You said he wasn't left to starve and you don't die from being nailed into a chair, no matter how bad it hurts."

Alex watches everyone carefully and I squeeze her hand. "You really want to know?" she asks.

"Yes," everyone says in unison, Alex's story the first sermon this place has heard in a long time.

"He was stabbed in the back with a screwdriver, puncturing one of his lungs."

"Holy shit," Park says.

"I heard there were two chairs," the freshman adds. "Like someone sat across from him. They sat there and watched him die."

"That is actually true," Alex says.

"Fuck him, anyway," Lila says. "He deserved it."

"That's why nobody tried too hard to find out who killed him," the freshman says, eager to contribute.

"Everybody knew it was Comstock who killed that girl; they just couldn't prove it 'cause the animals got to her and all the evidence was contaminated."

He says *contaminated* very carefully, drunk tongue enunciating syllables, then plows on. "My mom went to school with Comstock, said he was a nasty son of a bitch. She said he dated this one girl for a while but she broke up with him real fast, said he got off on hurting her, you know? Mom wasn't surprised at all when they questioned him after that girl turned up dead. Had him up at the station for hours, asked him all kinds of stuff but couldn't hold him because they didn't have any proof."

Lila sits up in her sleeping bag and pounds her fist onto his foot. "Would you shut up?"

"What?" He looks around, eyes wide until his friend whispers into his ear, probably explaining *that girl who turned up dead* was Alex's sister.

"We don't have to talk about it anymore," Lila says to Alex.

"I don't mind. But there is something I have to take care of, if you'll excuse me," Alex says politely, and hurls her beer bottle against the far wall. Glass sprays in a shower above the heads of the tweakers, who look like they're finally leaving. They duck instinctively, and Peekay slides to the ground between them, hair spilling out in a fan around her as she hits the stone floor.

"Oh, *hell* no," Adam says as he stands up from the pew, dumping Branley off his lap.

Alex beats him there, Park and me half a second behind, her sober strides cutting a straight path to where Peekay lies. "What are you doing?" she asks, each word heavy and cold.

"You throw a fucking bottle at me?" the guy with the chain asks.

"What are you doing?" Alex asks again, this time spacing each word out, as if to give him the benefit of not understanding her the first time.

"Just having some fun," he says. "You got a problem with it?"

People are up now, shadows thrown from fires reaching long as they gather to see what's going on. Sleeping bags unzip, and couples with messy hair emerge.

"Yes," Alex answers.

"Really, Adam? Just throw me on the ground, that's fine, that's awesome," Branley complains, forcing her way through the crowd until she sees Peekay. "What the hell?"

"She's just drunk," one of the other tweakers says, the lilt of panic in his voice giving away the lie. "She asked us to take her home."

"Oh yeah, where's she live?" Park asks.

"She's not drunk," Branley says, suddenly on her knees, cradling Peekay's head in her lap. "She's totally out. Dead weight." She holds one of Peekay's hands in the air and it drops to the ground heavily. "She was walking around a few minutes ago."

Branley looks up at them, her face set in a fierceness I remember from the night she went ballistic on me. Branley is about to blow.

"You roofied her," she says.

"I'd like your mouth better with my dick in it, bitch," the blond says, and I go for him, but Alex's arm is across my chest.

"No, Jack." She presses me back, pushing me a couple of inches behind her. She looks the guy up and down for a second. "What is your name?"

"What's it matter?"

"It's Ray Parsons," somebody yells from the back.

"Ray Parsons," Alex repeats, and Park shoots me a questioning glance, like he doesn't know if we should take care of this shit now or let Alex do her thing.

But she's shifting her weight, so subtly I doubt anyone else sees her moving. She's back on her heels, torso turned to the side, her hands (long unclenched from mine) open and palms up. Alex is ready to fight, and she looks like she knows what she's doing. I remember Park crumpled on the hallway floor in two seconds flat and

I shake my head at him. Right or wrong, I think she's got this.

"Yeah, I'm Ray Parsons," the blond says. "And you're a fucking bitch who should mind her own business."

"By which you mean I should let you rape my friend," Alex says.

All around us people flinch at the word *rape*, and it's so ridiculous I almost start laughing. Peekay is unconscious, her body flowing like water through Branley's arms as she tries to get her into an upright position. Her shirt is torn open so far I can see her bra. Her jeans are unbuttoned, already pushed a few inches below her underwear. Yet the word *rape* still jolts people, like maybe these guys were just dragging her out to the woods to help Peekay take a piss.

"By which I mean," Ray mimics Alex's words, his temper punching through, "that I think you need to shut the fu—"

Alex's hand shoots out, her finger resting lightly on his lips. "Shhh," she says, almost whispering. "It's my turn now.

"Ray Parsons, you have no soul," she says, her voice gaining volume as she speaks. "You are a bag of skin. You are a pile of bones. Every cell that has ever split inside of you was a waste of energy. Where you walk you leave a vacuum. Your existence should cease."

Ray's mouth hangs open as he formulates a response, the church quieter now than it has ever been, even in prayer. One of his friends finds his voice first, saying exactly the wrong thing.

"What the fuck is wrong with you?"

Alex hooks one of his feet with her ankle, spinning his back to her and punching him right above the ass with enough force that I hear a *crack*. He moans, a soft, defeated sound, and slumps forward, one hand on Ray's knee. I picture the bruise that will be left behind, a pattern of broken blood vessels tracing the path of pain that just streaked through his body.

"What the hell are you doing?" Ray demands as he reaches for his friend.

Alex smiles. "Whatever I want. Just like you."

Her hand flashes out, a pale arc that connects only briefly with Ray's face. There's a ripping sound, like denim giving out at the seams, except it's his cartilage letting go as she swipes his chain off, bringing a chunk of nose and his earlobe with it. It dangles in Alex's hand, fleshy weights on either end as Ray falls to the floor shrieking.

The third guy backpedals with his hands in front of him even though Alex isn't advancing. "What the hell is wrong with you?" he asks over and over. "What the hell is wrong with you?"

Alex fades away from my side, no longer interested in the tweakers. She's on the ground with Branley, the two of them propping up Peekay to get her to her feet.

"You need to get them out of here," Park says to the only guy left standing. "Don't any of you come back, either. If Jack and I ever find you here again . . ." He trails off, any threat he could deliver paling in comparison to what Alex did to them.

But the guy nods, eager to agree. "Okay, okay, man." He hauls Ray to his feet, who's still making noises like a deer that's been hit by a car and hasn't had the luck to bleed out yet.

"Dude," Park says to me, "your girlfriend is, like . . . fucking scary. But also totally awesome. Is it okay if I'm half in love with her right now?"

"Yeah, man. It's cool," I say, my eyes still riveted on three dark drops of blood against the stone floor.

Because I feel exactly the same way. On all counts.

24. **ALEX**

What is wrong with you?

I know this game, have played it often. It's a question asked many times, always in Mom's voice, following my vocalization of something I'm not supposed to say. When I was younger, Anna would turn it into a joke, our version of family prayer at dinnertime, when something I'd said or done came to light over the potatoes and corn.

Like the time I punched Phil Morris at a basketball game after he snapped Anna's bra. Her cheeks had been red with humiliation, the straps still new to her body and the burn of vengeance something she'd never owned. My hands were small, sticky with the remains of a sucker. When I hit him in the gut, it knocked his breath out and left a child-size fist-print on his T-shirt, neon blue with chemical flavoring.

Usually Anna's comebacks to Mom's favorite question were silly, designed to make me laugh. "Let's see . . . what is wrong with you, Alex? Do you have smallpox? Are you allergic to wheat? Are your legs broken? No? Hmm . . . I guess there's nothing wrong with you," she'd finish pointedly.

But when Phil's mom called, there had been no jokes, no diversions. Anna had set her fork down after Mom's diatribe, which ended with her favorite question. "She's defending her sister," she said. "And there's nothing wrong with that."

And there wasn't. And there isn't. And I'll keep doing it.

I'll keep doing it even though she's not here to defend.

Because there are others like him still. Tonight they used words they know, words that don't bother people anymore. They said *bitch*. They told another girl they would put their dicks in her mouth. No one protested because this is our language now. But then I used my words, strung in phrases that cut deep, and people paid attention; people gasped. People didn't know what to think.

My language is shocking.

They would have hurt my friend. They would have

left bruises on her, like the one that will radiate from his coccyx. Theirs would have been thumb-shaped and pressed into her waist where they held her down. Instead of a warm rush down her legs when she first stood in the morning, I drew blood from his face. He'll be mutilated, I know, and some might think me too harsh.

But some men should be marked. I'm fit for that task. And I don't feel bad.

Still, the question remains: *What is wrong with you?* Because something *is*, and I know that. I've tried to find out, looked up the words and the phrases that seemed as if they should fit. Words like *sociopath* and *psychopath*, ones that people like to toss around without knowing what they actually mean. But neither of them fits. They spoke of lack of empathy, disregarding the safety of others—when I am the opposite.

I feel too much.

I wanted to ask Dad, when he showed up for Anna's funeral. I wore high heels for the first time and they kept sticking in the mud, and I felt like the earth itself was stopping me from going to him. He came to me instead, putting a hand on my head just like when I was small. He met my eyes and all the words built up in my throat, every question I had for him wanting to come out at once.

What is wrong with us? Why did you leave me behind? Can I stop being this way?

But before any of them came out he said, "How's my little firecracker?"

Like it was a joke, this thing inside me. A cute quirk for a girl to have, our dark leanings reduced to one word. So I said, "I'm fine."

I'm not fine, and I doubt I ever will be.

The books didn't help me find a word for myself; my father refused to accept the weight of it. And so I made my own.

I am vengeance.

25. PEEKAY

Hands on me. Hands touching. Hands twisting. Hands on all the places I warned our church campers about during the awkward hour of stranger danger, where I said *the places your bathing suit covers* instead of *vagina* or *penis* or *butt*. Trusting little faces turned up toward me in a semicircle as I stammer through the talk, tiny mouths trying not to twist into giggles because they're good kids. Mom and Dad watching from the sidelines, ready to jump in if I flub too badly.

Mom and Dad.

Oh my God.

What will I tell them about the hands that were definitely in places they shouldn't be? Places that even a damn thong would cover. I keep my eyes closed, refusing to acknowledge that the blackness has abated. I don't want to know where I am, or what has happened. They say ignorance is bliss and it has never been truer than now, as I will myself back into unconsciousness. But the darkness that had me before was deep, and my eyelids are nothing in comparison. I grit my teeth and open my eyes.

To the brightness of a new morning.

I'm in a bed I don't know, surrounded by blank walls that lack even the impersonal art of a hotel room. There's a dresser and a desk, and in the corner of the mirror I see my own picture. It's the pose of me leaning against the rock wall at the state park, the cockiest little twist of my head that was a result of the cameraman telling me one too many times to smile, and I kind of felt like twisting his head off like a chicken at that point. It's the last one I held on to, the one I gave to Alex, and as the darkness in my head fades I see her on the floor, curled into a ball, her back to the bed.

She's sleeping, the rise and fall of her breathing deep and rhythmic, her hair wrapped around her hands and tucked under her head as a pillow, because she left both of the real pillows in the bed for me. I lie back, feeling the bump of my phone in my pocket. I've got eight missed calls from my mom, five voice mails and three texts, the last one asking simply ARE YOU SAFE?

I look at Alex, the pattern of her breathing changing as she comes up out of sleep, hearing even the smallest movements I make. And I think, *Yes, I am safe.*

But I slip into Alex's bathroom to be sure, trying to ignore the bump of fear that rises in my throat as my underwear slides down. I'm clean, the smell of man nowhere on me, the unmistakable whiff that varies from guy to guy but always seems to have an edge to it, like chlorine. A sob catches and I sink in relief onto the bathroom floor, propping myself against the toilet only to find the cool tiles against my bare self in stark contrast to a slight burn, a sliver where the fleshiest parts of me have been slightly scraped away.

I know what it is. A fingernail scratch from the guy who had his hand down my pants from behind, so anxious to know what I felt like he couldn't wait for cover of darkness. My brain is like a slide show on fast forward, images flickering so quickly I can't get a grasp on what his face looked like but I do remember in great detail that he had dirty hands and long fingernails, a cake of grime packed under each one.

I gag as I riffle through Alex's cupboards, looking for anything to get me clean. Rubbing alcohol is the first thing my hands find and I dump it directly onto my crotch, the sting and the panic forcing the solids behind the gag up into my throat. I make it back to the toilet in time, the cool porcelain calming against my cheek as I vomit over and over, losing everything I drank and whatever the hell they gave me.

I'm empty, stinking of sterility and vomit at the same time when Alex opens the door, not bothering to knock. I don't care that my panties are around my ankles and there are snot runners hanging out of my nose. I can't feel embarrassment because my brain has room only for revulsion, my entire being shrunk to the tiny area of inflamed skin I can't even see.

"I don't know how anybody can stand it," I say, shaking fingers reaching for the toilet paper roll.

Alex leans against the doorway in a tank top and pajama pants, her arms crossed in front of her, the space between us needing to be filled with words. I blow my nose, wiping the few stray tears.

"All I have is a scratch," I explain. "One little, tiny . . ." I break down again. Because it's not just a little tiny scratch, and I know that. The softest parts of my skin are under a stranger's dirty fingernails, my DNA embedded there along with fast-food grease and his own dandruff. Some of my cells are with him right now and I don't want them to be. I want them back. I want them all right where they belong and I can't even imagine if it were the other way around, if I'd woken up with a miasma of *them* deep inside of me, and the thought sends me retching again, the sound almost drowning out the buzzing of my phone.

Alex nods toward it as I flush. "You okay to get that?"

"Yeah," I say weakly. The word *Mom* splayed across the screen in stark black and white is one of the most terrifying things I've ever seen, but not answering isn't an option.

I pick up.

"I'm okay" is the first thing I say, the most important detail that needs to be made clear before all else.

She just starts sobbing, the sound drawing my own from deep inside of me, from somewhere even the jolt of vomiting hadn't touched. We cry together as Alex leaves, shutting the door behind her.

"I'm okay," I say again, once I can get words out. "I'm safe and I'm with a friend."

"Who?" Mom demands, her relief spent, anger on the rise.

"Alex Craft."

There's a quiet moment of confusion. "The dead girl?"

"Mom—*Alex* Craft."

"You're with a *boy*? Claire, your father—"

"Mom!" I cut through her sentence, Mom when flustered somehow even more hilarious when I'm sitting in a puddle of rubbing alcohol and no underwear. "I am with

Alex Craft—who is not dead and who is in fact a girl."

"Oh, well . . . good," she says. I giggle a little, and she does too, knowing herself well enough to be aware where the hook is and that she's an inch away from flying off it.

"What were you going to say about Dad?"

"Your father went to the church."

"Did he think God would hear him better there or something?" Because I know my dad's first response when I didn't come home at curfew would've been prayer.

"He went to *the* church, Claire."

"Ohhhhhhh . . ." is all I can think of to say. A flush creeps up my cheeks as I picture my dad picking his way through sleeping bags full of bleary teens, probably tucking them in more securely and advising them to drink plenty of fluids in the morning.

"We tried not to be too upset when you didn't come home," Mom goes on. "I was mad but your dad said you were probably there, and that showing up would just make it worse . . . but then . . . Claire, you didn't come home and we didn't know what to do. He went out to the church, and when he didn't find you . . ."

She starts crying again and I close my eyes. "I'm sorry, Mom. I'm so sorry."

"So what happened?" Mom asks; there's a tone of resignation, the sound of a parent who has tried really hard for a long time and realizes that the end of the tunnel doesn't have a light so much as a black hole.

"Some guys put something in my drink," I tell her. "They drugged me and it could've been really bad, but Alex was with me and she . . ." I pause, because I don't know what happened in between me falling onto Ray's shoulder and waking up in Alex's bed. I just know what *didn't* happen.

"She kept me safe," I finish.

"She must be a good friend, then," Mom says, followed by the sound of her nose blowing. "It sounds like we should meet her."

"Yeah, that'd be cool," I say. "Maybe I can get her to come over for dinner tonight?"

"Sure," Mom says, and I'm just pulling my jeans back on when she adds, "Oh, and Claire?"

"Yeah?"

"You're grounded."

Alex tells me what she did after I get a shower, scrubbing so hard it hurts. We're eating salads—she made two without comment, slicing hard-boiled eggs into some greens and tossing cheese on top, sticking a fork in everything and handing it to me like feeding me was a common occurrence. Her mom passes through the kitchen briefly, slightly puzzled by the sight of me.

She refills a glass, using her shoulders to hide what she pours. I wait for her to leave before I respond, my eyes on the crumbly boiled yolk of my egg.

"That's . . ." I trail off, aware that I was about to say *crazy*, along with words like *you shouldn't have done that*. It's a reflex, something that's been ingrained in me. Do no harm. Be nice. You catch more flies with honey than vinegar.

But what if I don't want to catch the flies? What if I'd rather see them swatted?

"Thank you," I say instead.

She nods as she polishes off her salad, finally meeting my eyes. She hadn't been looking at me while she explained, as if all her concentration was required to eat. "I wasn't sure how you'd feel about it," she says.

I don't answer because I'm still sorting that out myself. I know what my parents would say, that violence is never the answer; all conflict can be resolved peacefully. But my mom doesn't have a fingernail scratch in her crotch, and my dad doesn't know what it feels like to be carried away by three guys.

"They were so thrilled when I said I'm a virgin," I blurt out. "I'm so fucking stupid."

I start crying again, and Alex hands me a napkin. "You're not stupid," she says. "You simply don't assume that people mean you harm."

"Yeah, well." I blow my noise loudly. "Last night that equaled being stupid."

"No, it means you're normal," Alex says, gathering up my bowl when it's clear I'm more interested in crying than eating. "Believe me when I say it's better."

"Why me, then?" I ask. "Why not Branley? She's way hotter and was just as drunk as I was."

Alex shakes her head as she sits back down. "Physical attractiveness has nothing to do with it. You were alone, isolated, and weak. The three of them had been watching girls all night, waiting for someone to separate from a group. It happened to be you, but it could've been anyone. Opportunity is what matters, nothing else."

I look down at my chest, the push-up bra jamming my cleavage almost to my chin. She follows my gaze.

"I'm telling you, Claire. It doesn't matter. What you were wearing. What you look like. Nothing. Watch the nature channel. Predators go for the easy prey."

I think of Branley, gorgeous and soaked in beer, but surrounded by admirers. Then there was me, drunk and sulking, wandering around and practically begging for attention. Easy prey, indeed.

"She actually helped, you know," Alex says.

"Who?"

"The blond girl, Branley. She was the one who got you up off the floor. She buttoned your shirt back up, and made sure Sara had your phone when we carried you out to the car."

"Oh," I say.

"I know you want to hate her," Alex says. "But I don't think she deserves it."

"Wait till she bangs your boyfriend," I mutter.

"Judging by both their behavior, I'm pretty sure she already has," Alex says. "But he wasn't my boyfriend before, so it doesn't matter."

"What exactly did I miss? Is he your boyfriend *now*?" I ask.

"I don't know," Alex says, the same mild puzzlement that her mother wore earlier now crossing her face. "How do you establish that?"

"You ask, plainly," I say, ready to take my turn as coach. "And with Jack Fisher, you need to be clear that monogamy is part of the deal. He gets around, and I swear if he hurts you, it'll be my turn to kick some ass." I shake a fist in her face to make my point.

"Your thumb goes on the outside," she says.

26. **JACK**

My dad was right.

Skin makes a sound when it tears, one that burrows down into your subconscious and makes a home in the gray matter of your brain. It won't slip away easily and can't be replaced. Instead it takes precedence over everything else, so that the sound of Mom stripping the plastic off slices of cheese as she packs my lunch for work has me cocking my head, thinking, *No . . . that's not quite it.*

I've spent twenty-four hours simultaneously trying to forget the sound of Ray Parsons's ear coming away from his head and comparing everything else I hear to it. I've done that about as much as I've tapped my finger against my phone, debating about whether or not I'm going to call Alex. Every time I tap on her profile the pic of her and Peekay pops up and I suddenly have no problem remembering *exactly* what skin tearing sounds like, and how Ray's voice came out awkwardly, words bubbling through blood.

"Penny for your thoughts," Mom says as she puts my lunch in the fridge, ready for me to grab in the morning when I head out. It's like I'm five. I don't know if I love it or hate it.

"You'd be overpaying," I say, an old joke that stopped being funny a long time ago. Mom could fake laugh and rub my arm casually, walk away feeling like she's got a great relationship with her son. But she's not like that.

"Girl problems?" It's a question, but there's more of a statement in it than anything. She pulls out a barstool on the other side of the counter and rests her chin on her fist.

"Don't wanna talk about it," I say, which is only half true.

"Okay," she says brightly. "We can just stare at each other, then."

"Mom . . . ," I say, the inflection so much different than it was ten years ago. All the annoyance of my life is buried in that syllable, just like it used to be the one word that could fix everything.

"Jack," she interrupts me. "I'm not stupid."

"I know."

"No, Jack, you don't. I am not stupid and I was a teenager once too, right here in this same town. I know what alcohol smells like. I know what pot smells like. I've smelled them both on you, and I can't even keep track of how many different girls' perfumes—"

"*Mom* . . ."

"Oh, shut it. You're lucky I said *perfume*."

I shut it.

"You're not out there breaking new ground and making discoveries, Jack. You're living the same life your father and I did twenty years ago. But I never had the look on my face that you did just now, and it worries me. I'm your mother and I'm asking you what's going on."

I spin my phone in a circle, the black screen reflecting our faces as we have a stare-down. And Mom's not blinking.

"How much do you know about Alex Craft?" I finally ask.

She definitely blinks then. "Alex Craft? The girl—"

"—with the dead sister," I finish. "Yeah, her."

Mom straightens up on her chair, back into full-on parent mode. "Well, I guess I don't know much more than that. She had an older sister who . . . died."

Died. Like she had an unexpected heart attack or something. But I'm not going to get into semantics when my mom is clearly trying so hard to keep her face open and blank. And it's totally not working.

"What else?"

She goes doe-eyed. "What?"

"I'm not stupid either, Mom. And I know you pretty well. So what are you not saying? Is it weird because you dated her dad?"

I thought she'd blush, maybe swat that little fact away and change the subject. But instead she busts out laughing. "God, no. It's a small town, kid. I probably dated the dads of half the girls you've—"

"—borrowed perfume from?" I cut in before she can finish with something that'll make me blush instead.

She puts her hands up. "Fair enough."

"So what's the deal? Why when I said Alex Craft's name did your forehead wrinkles get a lot deeper? *Is* it because you dated her dad?"

Mom ignores the jab, her gaze traveling to the well-worn path on the kitchen linoleum that needs to be replaced. Dad priced new flooring last year, and even though it wasn't expensive, my mom didn't get a new kitchen floor.

"Nick Craft is not a bad person," Mom says in a way that makes me think it's something she's repeated more than once. "He split when those girls were little, left a lot of tongues wagging behind him. People said it was because he made out good with his trucking company and wanted to go live it up. But I knew him, and if that's the truth, then the man was a far cry from the boy I grew up with. Nick wouldn't have left without a good reason, and whatever it is—that's between him and his wife."

I think about the cardboard cutout of a woman standing in the doorway, chewing her lip in confusion when I ask if her daughter's home. "She's different," I say.

Mom shrugs. "He married outside the county."

It's something you can't miss if you're raised here. Most of us don't have money, but that doesn't take away a certain element of pride that goes along with being part of this place, right down to the literal sense that your ancestors actually are in the dirt that grew the crops that you'll have for dinner. When I've gone out with a girl more than once or twice, Mom and Dad have filled me in on her biological heritage, maybe just to reassure themselves that we're not related.

But if you step outside the county line it's like you're taking your chances, rolling the dice to see what kind of inheritance you might be marrying into. *Not from here* is one of the most damning insults that can be tossed, carrying with it the eternal question mark of what an outsider might be carrying inside of them, a mental or biological dark passenger that will rear up and bite your ass thirty years down the road. And I realize maybe that's what I'm actually asking.

"How do you ever really know someone, Mom?"

She smiles then, real slow. So slow that there are tears pooling in her eyes before the edges of her lips have made it up into her cheeks.

"Honey, you just don't. You can love someone down to their core and they can love you right back just as hard, and if you traded diaries you'd learn things you never suspected. There's a part of everyone deep down inside of them not meant for you. And the sooner you learn that, the easier your life is gonna be."

I swallow hard. "So how do you try?"

She stops my phone in midspin, pointing it toward me. "You start by calling her, I guess."

And right then my phone rings. Alex's face fills the screen and my heart leaps into my throat, my pulse so loud in my ears that it drowns out the sound of skin tearing.

27. ALEX

It's very odd to me that a string of numbers can put me in contact with a specific person. I told myself that I bought a phone because Claire might need to call me about the shelter. And while her name was the first entry, it still felt like an incomplete action until Jack was in there too. It feels heavier in my pocket now. Like a loaded weapon. One that might backfire on me.

Branley also put her number into my phone when we were taking Claire home, along with strict instructions to report back to her. I shot her a quick answer (*she's fine*) shortly after my friend stripped down and vomited. It's not true. Claire is not fine.

I now have three people in my phone. I can call them at any time, invading their lives with a series of numbers, like spinning the combination on their locker and suddenly being in their space. It's so intensely personal it almost feels profane. I haven't taken advantage of this permission yet, because they will know it is me calling. Which means they can choose not to answer.

This is what bothers me.

Jack can choose not to let me in, and I will know by the time his voice mail picks up that the decision has been made, and I will know why. Part of me will understand. Part of me knows that I should have never been admitted, that I should not be walking among these people. People who are able to make friends easily because they don't first assume everyone is a threat. People who can get through a party without tearing a man's face off.

I am a wolf that my sister kept in a cage, until her hand was removed. I have been out, curious as I wake up from a lethargic solitude, self-enforced because I know I don't belong here. It's not safe for me to be out, but they rattled my cage. First Claire and then Jack. And now I'm awake, deviating from the paths I created in order to remain stable. I'm out, and awake, and afraid I won't be easily put back in.

It's not the sheep that call to me, but the other wolves. I want to run with them, so that I may tear out their throats when they threaten my flock. But I can't return to the sheep with blood on my breath; they will shy away from me.

Even when I was a child they knew.

I remember the only family reunion my mother ever took us to, the first and last time we met our cousins from her side. One of my male cousins had taken my doll and stripped her, taunting me with her naked body high above his head while I tried to reach, red-faced and shouting. Anna put an end to it before I was pushed too far, snatching it back and redressing her, assuring me everything was okay.

But everything was not okay.

I waited until everyone was asleep, our pleasantly warm child bodies relaxed in the blue light of the television, the dull undertones of the adults' conversation reaching us from the outside deck. My cousin was out cold, his head thrown back against the couch, a snore emanating from him.

Until I punched him in the throat.

Lights came on and accusations flew once he had his breath, the adults bringing a cloud of alcohol fumes and confusion in with them as he tried to explain what had happened, the pointing finger always returning to me. One woman kept insisting it wasn't possible. I was too little. Too cute.

But the other children knew, with their survival

instincts still fresh on them, not tempered by assumptions. Anna knew. My parents knew, an understanding shared in a glance that carried over into a long, silent car ride home, my fully dressed doll belted in safely by my side, the wolf in me satiated.

We never went to another reunion.

And so I'm waiting for another rejection, another affirmation that I don't belong among these people. That it's not safe for me to be here. The wolf in me is expecting it.

But another part of me will die a little bit when that happens. The part that enjoyed the easy familiarity of borrowing Claire's ill-fitting clothes. The part that likes the way Jack's eyes stay on me, even in a crowded room.

I've spent an hour staring at my phone, trying to decide which of those is the better part. Which of those is really me. And if there's any way that I can be both.

When he answers it's like the better half of me explodes into a thousand pieces of light, hope spreading through me to touch places that can't recall the feeling.

"Hey," he says, and I love the casualness of his tone, like this isn't the first time I've ever called him, like there's no reason for either one of us to be nervous. And suddenly I'm not.

I don't have many words inside me. All I know is that I like being with him and I want to be exactly that right now, and I can think of only one way to make that a reality.

"Do you like to run?" I ask.

"I don't know," he says. "In every sport I play running is a punishment, so it's kinda hard to *like* it. I mean, I would run if something was chasing me, though."

"Would you run if I was chasing you?" I ask, because I'm still trying to create this scenario where we're together, and I don't do many things that I can invite other people to do with me.

"If you were chasing me I would definitely *not* run," he says, and I'm laughing because this is so much easier than I expected.

"How about if we were running side by side?" I ask.

"That I can do."

28. JACK

We are running.

When Alex asked if I'd meet her at the track, I said yes without caring about the temperature, or that it's supposed to snow, or that it was going to be dark in just a few hours—a fact Mom yelled after me as I rushed out the door, grabbing my coat. Alex was leaning against her car when I got to the school and we took a few laps without talking, our legs finding the same stride perfectly comfortable as we looped once, twice, and then again, our footfalls still the only sound passing between us.

When she breaks away from the track and shoots for a path into the woods I go with her, keeping the quiet intact. The path meets a gravel road and she follows it, me taking a wider stride for the beat of a second to draw alongside her. The road arcs slightly under our feet, the rise not visible to the eye but felt in the burn of my calves. I toss a glance sideways but she is lost in movement, brow furrowed and cheeks a blazing red from the cold.

The woods suddenly fall away on our right and she nudges my shoulder with her own, the first contact we've had the whole time. I follow her unspoken instruction, taking the grass-covered drive that leads to the last thing I expected to see.

A graveyard.

Alex stops, puts her hands on top of her head, and breathes in deeply. "Sorry," she finally heaves.

"I can keep up," I say, even though I'm sucking more wind than she is.

"No." She waves one hand at the stones in front of us. "Sorry that I didn't warn you I use a graveyard as a turnaround."

I shrug. "It's fine." Our words are weightless, none of them carrying any of the importance they have in the past.

"Rest for a minute?" she asks, walking toward a bench. I nod and follow her, sitting near her but not next to her. The inches of air in between us could be filled with concrete. The sun is sinking and the last bits of warmth are leaving the air, letting the cold in. I scratch my nose, suddenly bothered by it.

"Sorry," I say. "My nose itches."

"It's okay."

"Doesn't it mean someone is talking about you if your nose itches?"

"No." She shakes her head. "That's if your ears are ringing."

"That's it. My dad always said if you pull on your earlobe the person talking about you will bite their tongue."

Alex stiffens and I realize that I just said *earlobe*, and now we're both picturing large red drops of Ray Parsons's blood on the dusty floor of the church, his chain hanging from her hand.

"I hate that we're talking about stupid things," she says, kicking the toe of her shoe into the little pockets of snow scattered in the grass.

I grab her hand, breaking the wall between us and linking our freezing fingers. "I hate it too," I say.

She looks at me for a second, her eyes roaming over my face in search of something. "I'm sorry if I scared you the other night."

"You don't scare me."

Her mouth pulls to the side like she's about to argue, but I stop her with a question. "Why'd you call me?"

"Because I wanted to see you." It comes out quick and honest, and she looks a little confused about how easy it was, or maybe that it's the truth.

"I wanted to see you too," I say.

I don't know which one of us leans in first, or if we've both been covering the distance while we talk. But we're talking and then we're kissing like it's how a run is supposed to end, and it's electric and fluid and totally normal all at the same time. I pull her into my lap and she wraps her legs around my waist as if she knows exactly what she's doing, even though she's clearly an inexperienced kisser.

Which I'm thrilled about. I can tell I'm the first guy to kiss her, the first guy to bury his hands in her hair and crush her against him, torso to torso. And while making out isn't part of my usual run, I'm all for it becoming a habit. Because I'm definitely running with Alex again. I'm definitely going to hold her hand in the cold and cross all the space between us until we can't be any closer.

I don't realize until later, when I'm lying in bed with lips swollen from kissing, replaying every second, that she didn't say she was sorry for tearing into Parsons.

She said she was sorry if it scared me.

29. PEEKAY

Sara is looking at me like maybe I might break, spontaneously shatter on my own bed, and then she'll have to explain to my mom and dad why she needs to borrow the Dustbuster.

"You're sure you're okay?"

"Yeah, I actually am," I tell her.

I'm not, but I can't explain that to her. I love Sara, but something was taken from me at the church, something that she can't relate to. Every time I walk outside I think maybe someone is going to grab me. I take a sip of a glass of water I got out of my own tap and swish it around in my mouth first, like maybe it's a threat. And I'm starting to understand why Alex always walks on the balls of her feet, why her back muscles are always tensed, like a cat ready to spring.

She knows. She gets it. So that's why I'm going to tell Sara that I'm okay and leave it at that.

"So . . ." Sara looks down at my quilt, tracing the pattern with her finger. "Should we call that Nolan guy, do you think?"

She's not the first person to bring it up. Five or six girls sent me their pics of the cop's cell and email, even though I still have my own. I've looked at it a couple of times, wondered how I would phrase that email, or what I would say on the phone. Mom and Dad want me to press charges, but I told them I don't remember anything, or who the guy was. Which is totally a lie, but it's not like it's the first one I've told them.

Just the biggest.

"I don't know," I tell Sara. "He'll ask questions. He'll want to know who was there so he can talk to them, and then I'm giving him a list of people who were out at the church partying. I don't think anyone will thank me for that."

"Yeah, but wasn't that kind of what he said at the assembly?" she says. "You're too scared about ratting out your friends to report a crime so it doesn't happen and he just gets away with it."

"He hardly got away with it," I point out, and Sara looks away from me.

"I'm kinda wondering if we should report that, too,"
she says.

"What?"

Sara starts tugging on the fringe of my quilt, like
unraveling it will help piece this conversation together.
"Alex is . . . I know that you've gotten to know her working at the shelter and all that, but . . . have you ever seen
the way she watches people? It's not normal, okay?"

"No," I shoot back. "Not okay. Maybe if you had a
sister that was torn into pieces by another person you
might not be normal either. And maybe I'm glad she
watches people because if she *didn't*, I'd be sitting in a
clinic choking down morning-after pills right now."

"Fine," Sara says. "But she tore part of a guy's face
off like it was nothing. You didn't see that, Peekay. I did.
Girl didn't even flinch."

"I wish I did see it," I say, and Sara shudders.

"No, man, you don't. I'm not saying he didn't deserve
it, but . . . God, I don't know." She looks up at the
ceiling, tears sitting in her eyes. "It was fucking awful.
He kept screaming like he couldn't stop. You remember
that time your cat caught that mouse and he played with
it for like an hour before killing it?"

"Yeah," I say. "We tried to take it away from him so
he freaked out and actually bit down."

The noises that mouse made as it died were impossibly

loud, a panicked sound of incomprehensible pain that faded as my cat ran off to the field with it twisting in his mouth, still trying to free itself even though it was obviously too late.

"Ray sounded like that mouse," Sara says. "I couldn't hear that coming from a human being and not feel like something bad just went down. Something wrong."

I think about Alex's bathroom and pouring rubbing alcohol on my crotch. I probably sounded a lot like that mouse, too.

"I don't want to talk about this anymore," I say. Because it doesn't matter how much we talk about it; we're not going to agree, and I don't know if there is a right answer anyway.

"Fine," Sara says, but it's not, and I know it. We sit together in silence a little longer, pretending everything is fine.

30. PEEKAY

I'm sitting in Branley's driveway, counting out the beats for the new marching band routine because that's easier than going up and knocking on her door. I may be grounded, but when I told Mom and Dad that I had some apologizing to do, that seemed to lift the ban momentarily. I drove into town with the playlist for the fresh show on repeat, and I'm sure I am going to be stuck walking in four-four time for the rest of my life if I don't get out of this car in two seconds.

Branley lives in one of the old houses in town, the ones that people built expecting their great-grandchildren's grandchildren to live in. It's all brick and has a porch that looks like someone should be sitting on it reading a classic novel at all times. Even once I'm in front of the door I don't take the final step of knocking until I force myself. I'm not the hot girl. I'm not the smart girl. I might not even be the funny girl. I'm just the preacher's kid. But I do have my pride, and this is one crow pie I'm not looking forward to eating.

Branley's little sister answers the door. She's got chocolate in her eyebrows, which seems like an accomplishment, and a freshly painted rainbow on her cheek that smooshes together when she smiles at me.

"Hi," I say. "Is your sister home?"

"Bran," she yells over her shoulder, before bounding away. "For you."

"Coming," I hear Branley yell, and then the door is pulled open wider. It takes a second for me to recognize her. It's a Saturday afternoon and she's fresh-faced—no makeup, no eyeliner, no layers of mascara that make her look like she's auditioning for manga porn. Her usually smoothed and perfected hair is up in a sloppy ponytail, her typically designer-clad body wearing nothing more revealing than a sweatshirt and pajama pants. And she's got face paint splattered on her fingers from decorating her little sister's cheek.

But she looks like a million bucks. Like the girl next door who will play touch football, then slam a beer and doll up a little bit to go out to dinner. Why can't she just have one obtrusively large pimple right in the middle of her face like everyone else?

"Hi," she says cautiously.

"Hey," I say. "Can I talk to you?"

"Um, yeah, sure," she says, but she doesn't open the door any farther, so I don't ask if I can come in. She's like the people who will feed a stray cat all summer but not let them in their house when winter comes.

Those cats die, by the way.

"Okay, well . . . Alex said that the other night out at the church that you helped her"—*no, that's not right*— "that you helped *me*. And I wanted to thank you for that. So . . . thank you."

"You're welcome," Branley says.

"I was kind of surprised, honestly," I admit, when she doesn't add anything else. "After I . . . well, after what happened in Hendricks's room."

"When you almost punched me?"

"Yeah." I drop my eyes. "Sorry about that."

"It's okay," she says. "You're not the first girl who's wanted to punch me."

I doubt I'll be the last either, but I don't say that.

"It wouldn't have mattered who it was, just so you know," Branley continues. "It could've been your friend Sara, or one of my friends, or some chick I don't even know. I would've helped. My cousin went to college last year and . . ." She lets the sentence die, the awkwardness between us growing thicker. "I would've helped," she says again.

I think about how I felt that night, watching Branley with her perfect body on display for the boys to ogle and the girls to envy. I wonder if I'd seen her being carried out if I'd have interfered, and I just don't know.

"So your friend Alex . . ."

"What about her?"

Branley watches me closely before going on, one hand on the doorframe, her finger tapping as she thinks. "You know what she did after you passed out?"

"Yeah."

"That's all you're going to say?"

"I also know what those guys were going to do to me."

"I think she's crazy," Branley says.

I feel my blood kick up a notch, my heart skipping a couple beats when I think of Alex, unquestioning in her own bathroom doorway as I lay crying in my underwear. "She's not crazy," I say, keeping my tone as level as I can.

And then I spot the edge of a hickey peeking out of Branley's sweatshirt, perched precariously right on the edge of her collarbone. The same place Adam always liked to leave them on me.

"You just don't like her because she's got Jack," I add,

throwing some of the hurt that just bloomed in my belly onto her.

Her eyebrows shoot up, the relaxed girl-next-door face sliding away as every muscle she has tenses and the Branley I know comes out. Eyes half slit, a little color high on the cheeks, nose a centimeter too far in the air for the commoners to try to approach.

"Why would I care about that?" she asks. "I have Adam."

It's a challenge, and she's got her chin stuck out, begging for me to crunch it back into her teeth. And I want to. I want to pop that perfect jawline out of place and tear some of her hair out by the roots and inspect them to see if that's natural color she's flaunting or if there's some chemical assistance at work. But that's not who I am, and I know that playing the fantasy out in my head and actually doing it are two very different things.

And it's also not why I came here. I unclench my fists.

"Hey, you know what, Branley?" I say, and her eyebrows go up even farther, waiting for whatever cut I've got next, her own response probably lined up and ready to fire as soon as I finish.

"You're really pretty," I say, and her perfect mask falls in a pile of confusion.

"Seriously," I go on. "I always thought your looks were all in the makeup, like you try too hard or whatever. But you don't need it. You're naturally really good-looking."

"I . . ." She just kind of stands in the doorway, mouth hanging open as if I'd informed her I'm pregnant with the next Jesus. "Thank you," she finally says, eyes slipping back into slits as if expecting a backhand tacked onto the compliment.

"That's all. Thank you for the other night," I add quickly as I head for the porch steps, back toward the safety of my car and the predictability of four-four time. I've cracked the driver's side door when Branley calls my name and I turn to see her standing on the porch, barefoot, arms huddled against the cold.

"I'll see you Monday," she says, her words sapped of all energy by the time they cross the distance between us, the frigid bite of the air stealing any intended warmth.

But she still said them.

"Yeah, see you in school," I say.

And maybe on Monday I won't feel like punching her.

And maybe she won't try to make me.

31. ALEX

I have a boyfriend.

I have said the word aloud only once, at Anna's grave. I went to tell her because she's someone who should know. Claire knows; Jack knows. My circles don't extend farther, so I stalled at the end of my run, picking my way through the monuments until I found hers.

I haven't been back since the funeral, since the day my dad called me a *firecracker* and reduced my wrath into an adorable nickname. I know that the parts of Anna's body they could recover are six feet below, as sheltered as can be from the worms and the ruin, resting on satin and in an utter darkness that even I can't contemplate. But I know that's not her. Whatever makes us flew from her with only one witness to the moment, someone who should have never known her at all.

But I told her anyway, pronouncing the word *boyfriend* carefully, like it might break in my mouth, or chip my teeth on its way out. Her stone stared back at me, blank and uncomprehending, which I imagine is exactly what her face would have looked like in real life if I were able to tell her in person.

I laughed at the thought, the sound echoing in the cold evening, bouncing off rocks whose names have been rubbed out by time, silent testament that someone lived and died, but we no longer know who. My laugh came back at me from the snow-covered ground, frozen beneath my feet, the bare trees with black fingers reaching toward the darkening sky.

It echoed back off the stone from a grave behind me, one that I filled, the sound breaking across my shoulder blades accusingly. I stopped laughing, the sound cut short by my throat closing over the fear.

I ran. I bolted from the cemetery and back to my path, my pace bearing nothing of a runner's stride, no calm, measured beat to my steps. I ran like one pursued, with the conviction of my unworthiness fast on my heels.

The conviction that I don't deserve this.

32. **JACK**

Alex Craft is my girlfriend.

This is a statement that has to be examined, turned over carefully, and marveled at even as the days we've been together accumulate into weeks. Alex is my girlfriend, but the word doesn't do justice to what is between us. It's been applied to other girls—okay, lots of other girls—and it's always been appropriate, an indication that this is the female I call or text, the one whose hand I hold in the hallway, and the name that gets tossed around in the locker room when we're talking pussy.

Alex and I are past that. Alex and I have never been there.

I have things to say with her, things I want to share. I call her because I want to hear her voice, especially the cautious way she says *hello*, like she's trying not to care too much that it's me. I liked the guarded way she controlled her enthusiasm at first, unsure about making the leap. But I like even more that it's gone now, the quick uptick in her tone when she answers telling me that her heart just skipped a couple of beats when she saw I was calling, just like my fingers still shake a little when I dial. There is nothing routine about having Alex Craft for a girlfriend, and I'm not just logging my time when we talk.

The guys take their jabs in the locker room, for sure, but they're more careful than they have been in the past. I don't know if it's out of respect for what happened to her older sister, or if enough of them remember what Alex did to Ray Parsons to know better than to pry me for details about getting any.

And I'd be lying if I said it wasn't something that I'd thought about. I'm her first boyfriend. I haven't been somebody's first boyfriend since Branley and I moved on from sharing candy bars to sharing mouths, and even then I don't know exactly what our relationship was. But I know what Alex is to me, and I hope I know what I am to her, and if that means I'm not going to be getting laid for a while, that's okay.

And the best part is that's something I can just say to my girlfriend and she doesn't try to pick apart my

sentence and find an insult in there to get pouty about.
In fact, she laughs.

"I know it's okay," she says back to me.

We're at Park's house. His mom and dad are gone for
the weekend, so he had some people over. Not a ton, a
couple of guys from the basketball team, couple of girls
from their team. Peekay is roaming around, and I know
Branley is here because she squeals somewhere upstairs
and asks who dropped an ice cube down the back of her
shirt.

Her high-pitched yelp pierces right through drywall
and cinder block, right down to the basement, where
I've finally got Alex to myself. We're cozy on a beanbag,
the lights are off, and I told the guys we were going to
watch a movie, which everyone knows means leave us the
fuck alone for at least two hours. And for some reason
I interrupted our heavy makeout session to tell her that
if she's not ready to do it, that's okay.

"I know it's okay," she says again, totally confident in
being a virgin. And damn if it isn't the sexiest thing I've
ever heard her say.

I worried that Anna would be with us whenever we
were alone, a shadowy voice of caution that would put
itself between us anytime I tried to get closer. If Anna is
there, I think she's more in my head than Alex's, because
my girlfriend likes to touch and be touched. But I've

gone slow, still reveling in the fact that this girl, who was an utter mystery to me at the beginning of the year, lets me kiss her now, whenever I want. I know her body, maybe not thoroughly but definitely more than anyone else, and when I touch her I feel how strong she is, yet I can't ignore the voice insisting over and over: *don't hurt her.*

Right now her hands are all over me, and mine on her, and with any other girl it'd be time to bring out the condom, but with Alex I don't even consider reaching for my wallet. Instead I pull back to put some space between us. Because I'm not exactly thinking with my heart right now, and my dick is trying to undo my zipper from the inside.

Another girl might ask me what's wrong, a little bit of a whimper in her voice like she hasn't lived up to something I expected. Instead of that I get Alex's palm, flat against my bare chest, an unspoken question in the amount of pressure she exerts.

"Need a minute," I tell her. Honestly, I need about a year and six feet of bricks in between us to keep myself under control, but I go for the next best thing.

"I think you should meet my parents."

She laughs again, this one coming out in kind of a snort that might embarrass other girls, but not Alex.

"Why is that funny?" I ask her.

"It's not a situation I ever imagined myself in," she says, her own breath still coming a little heavy. There's a naked bulb at the top of the staircase and enough light reaches us that I can see her breasts going up and down, the ridge of her bra pressing against them.

"Well, imagine it," I say, pulling my eyes back up to her face, which is flushed and happy. I made it that way, and that's enough to keep my gaze from wandering.

"Okay, when?"

"There's a home game next week. Maybe after that?"

She nods, her cheek going up and down on my chest. And that little bit of friction gets me riled again, that and the fact that six months ago if you would've told me that a girl agreeing to meet my parents would give me a boner from hell, I would've punched you in the face. But if Alex is willing to do that, Alex who still pieces together her sentences very carefully even when we're alone, it means she's taking this as seriously as I am.

And that's fucking hot.

Once I asked my dad how you know when you're in love. He said you just know, and that if you have to ask the question then you haven't been in love yet. And he's right. Because there aren't words for this. No combination of letters could ever represent what she is to me.

But the flip side is that now I worry about losing her. I worry that I'm going to screw it up, that the Jack who was in the woods the night they found Anna's body is going to reassert himself. That guy was nowhere near classy enough to be with Alex. She is refining me every day, changing me from the person I was into someone better. And I need to be good enough.

Because I'm Alex Craft's boyfriend.

33. JACK

Having Alex in my shitty truck doesn't make me feel good.

When we run we're on the same level; when we end up at parties together we know we're going to find our own corner eventually. We expect to hear from each other every night, each of us checking our phones to see if we missed that moment somehow. But a real date hasn't happened yet, and there's a reason for that.

I can't afford Alex Craft.

Hell, I can't afford any girlfriend, but there's an unspoken agreement that Branley pays my way wherever we go, and I've always managed to string other girls along until I'm bored with them as a hookup and cut them loose. With Alex it's different because I want to take her out on a real date and my big mouth made that happen before my wallet filled me in on how skinny it is.

The truth is we're in my busted-ass truck and she somehow blends in completely yet looks like a million bucks at the same time, and we're headed toward a burger joint because it's either that or a sit-down place the next town over and I don't have enough gas to get us there. And after we've plowed through our five-dollar burger plates I'm going to have to ask her to pay for it, because I am a fucking loser and she'd be flat-out within her rights to call me that.

So that's what I'm thinking about as I pull into the restaurant on our first real date—what a fucking loser I am.

We walk into the place and my mood drops even further because Brian Spurlani yells my name from the back kitchen when he spots us. Three years ago Brian was everything I wanted to be. He was a senior when I came in as a freshman, football two-a-days kicking my ass in ninety-degree weather. We'd lose five pounds in the morning, put it back on when we went home to eat lunch, then lose another seven in the evening. We smelled like ass sweat and our faces were permanently broken out but Brian kept our heads on straight, putting out fires before fights broke out, telling the guys who were about to pass out that they could make it five more steps. And then the five more after that.

Brian is truly a good guy. That's why it kills me a little bit when he comes out of the kitchen to talk to us while we eat and he's wearing a hairnet.

"Hey, man," he says, flipping a chair around backward to sit at the end of our table. "What's up?"

"Just out grabbing something to eat," I say. "Brian, this is Alex."

"Hi," Alex says, and he looks her up and down.

"Alex Craft? I knew your sister. What happened to her was bullshit."

Alex smiles. "Possibly the best description I've heard."

And while she doesn't seem to care that it came up, I hate that Anna is the first thing everybody thinks of when they see Alex, whether it comes out of their mouth or not. Like when people run into me and all they want to talk about is the winning streak of whatever sports season it is, like I'm destined to be only a stat record in their head. Always winning but never moving on. Stuck in this town forever and hauled out in twenty years to hand off a basketball or a football to the kid who breaks my school record, and then that's it. I'm done. Washed up. I'll be like Brian, who is sitting here smiling at me, his pores full of grill grease.

"Didn't you go to Fairmont to play ball?" I ask, and

his smile falters a little.

"More like went to Fairmont to ride the bench," he says. "That and play tackle dummy. Tore my ACL when some big asshole hit me and that was it. Came home over Christmas break and got Tammy pregnant, so . . ." He holds his hands up, like he was totally innocent of any involvement. "So that was that."

I put down my burger, what I have eaten a lead ball in my stomach as I think of all the times Branley was in too much of a hurry and I was too horny to bother with a condom.

"But I'm going back," Brian says, his tone too hopeful, like the way you sound when you talk about your dreams, not your actual plans. "Once little Becca gets into kindergarten, we won't have to pay for day care, and that money can go to Daddy getting his degree."

"Yeah, man, cool," I say, but I know as well as he does that money is going toward putting in a second bathroom, or paying for the next baby.

"So." Brian's eyes wander to Alex. "I heard somebody fucked up Ray Parsons's face—that was you, right?"

Alex takes a sip of her drink. "Yep."

"Right on," Brian says, and fist-bumps her. "Ray used to be a decent guy, but . . . you know." He lays his finger on one side of his nose.

I get it. Decent guys backslide into meth and gang

rape. Good guys knock up their girlfriends and flip burgers.

We get up to leave, my tray still half full because all I can think about is vomiting. Brian refuses to let us pay for our food, so that solves my money problem but doesn't leave me feeling any less of a loser.

"Hey, man." Brian snags my arm at the door as Alex goes ahead. "Just so you know, Ray ain't exactly happy about everyone knowing a chick kicked his ass."

I watch Alex pop open the passenger door of my truck; she has to wrench it a little because it tends to stick.

"Alex can take care of herself," I tell him.

"That's for damn sure, but maybe don't go driving down Central unless you have to, hear me? Ray's mom lives there, and since you kicked them out of the church, Ray and his guys have been holing up there. I don't know, just be careful. Can't ever tell what a tweaker's gonna do."

"Truth." We hug awkwardly before I leave, the smell of hamburger grease sticking to me as I get behind the wheel.

"What was that about?" Alex asks as I pull away.

I should've known I couldn't play it cool with her, act like running into Brian was a casual thing, not a terrifying flash-forward of what my life is going to be if I don't get the fuck out of here and never come back.

And while Alex might know me well enough to get it, starting the conversation means telling her about how I've convinced myself that I can earn it by being a good guy, that getting out and staying out is how karma is going to reward me for not hitting the next joint and turning down every drunk girl who crawls into my lap at a party. And maybe it'll sound crazy to her that every decision I make, every day, is a choice between right and wrong with my future in the balance.

"Jack?"

I don't know how to say these things to her. So I go for the simple version.

"You know how the first day of English class, Miss Hendricks had us write an essay on how we define success?"

Alex nods.

"What did you write?" I ask her.

"What was expected. What did you write?"

"One line—*getting out of this shit hole*. She gave me an A."

"Oh, Jack Fisher," Alex sighs, a teasing smile on her face. "Must be hard when everyone loves you."

I have to laugh at that. Me feeling sorry for myself, with my brain and my looks and my talent. I reach over to put my hand on her knee and she takes it, our fingers entwining as I drive out of town—on Central, because fuck Ray Parsons.

"Define success," I say almost to myself.

"I didn't kill anyone today," Alex says.

I laugh again. "A-plus, babe."

And I think I could probably tell this girl anything, and she would understand.

34. **ALEX**

I'm trying very hard to be normal.

This is not easy for me. Jack helps. Claire helps. When I'm with them I can manage myself a little better, filter my environment so that the little things slide off my new shiny facade. But some things penetrate, and when that happens, I go places I know they can't follow.

We are in the gym. It's negative fifteen outside, and so many of the buses wouldn't start this morning that they put those of us who drive in the gym for now, like a holding pen until the rest of the flock gets here. There aren't enough people for me to fade away, but too many for me to ignore them all. I don't know what to do with myself even though Claire is beside me, chatting about something to her friend Sara.

Sara doesn't like me, and that is fine. It's in the way she watches me from the side, like she doesn't quite trust me. After seeing me rip Ray Parsons's nose and part of his ear off his head, that might be a smart decision on her part.

"Jesus," Sara says as Branley walks past us. "Too cold to show off cleavage, so instead she goes for jeans so tight I can see her thong."

"She looks nice," I say, and she does. Branley always looks put together in a way that tells me she spends hours in front of a mirror before going outside. And while I don't understand that, I can respect it.

Sara looks at Claire like she's waiting for her to jump in, but Claire only shrugs. "Whatever," she says, which earns me a dark look from Sara that I don't understand.

"So you're thirty points from the school record, right?" Claire says, and Sara's face lightens a little bit. They talk on about basketball, which switches over to a party last weekend, and then on to something else that I tune out, their combined voices a pleasant drone.

I watch Claire for a moment. The minimal physical damage she took that night at the church has healed entirely. The emotional damage has left a scar, though, bumpy tissue somewhere deep inside her soul. It's like her naïveté was excised, caution growing back in its place. It's a good thing. I watch her now, this girl who was so close to the unthinkable, now able to laugh and talk about inconsequential things. Part of me wants to ask her how she has done this, but another part of me already knows the answer.

She started from a better place than me. Claire's baseline is closer to normal than mine, her beginning a smooth plane while my life has always been peaks and valleys. Sara has taken me to a valley right now. She knows I don't belong here; something in her senses the wolf in me and would ban it. So I oblige her as much as possible, sinking down into one of the valleys. These are the places my friends can't follow, and I let Claire's voice fade away beside me.

Out on the court Jack is playing a pickup game. Even in jeans he's fluid, his body doing exactly what he wants when he wants it to. I could watch him and find some reassurance, but behind him something else is happening.

There's a boy in the corner humping a basketball and pretending to climax, his face going through a complex series of contortions. It's lewd in its accuracy and I can't stand that I won't be able to get it out of my head now, what this stranger looks like in his most intimate moment. And I hate that he's going back to do it again, egged on by his friends, who seem to find some high cleverness in the fact that now he's behaving as if the basketball is performing oral sex on him.

The teachers see him, I know it. Hendricks looks away and shakes her head; the others roll their eyes when she points it out, but no one stops him. His impropriety has thrown a wall of disgusting around him that no one wants to walk through. And so he keeps doing it.

A few bleachers down, a group of freshmen notice and explode in a chorus of giggles. I don't think it's funny but I can't tear my eyes away. I find myself memorizing his face, my brain cataloging his name when I hear it being tossed around by the girls below me. I shake my head to clear it, finally breaking my line of sight as he *finishes*, as if it's vital that he get to the end of his pretend sexual encounter with sports equipment.

I wonder what would happen if I went down there, took a ball out of the cage, and pretended to have sex with it. I think people would stop and look. I think the whole gym would come to a standstill and teachers would definitely interfere. There would be discussions (again) about what exactly is wrong with me that I would do such a thing. I would definitely log some more hours in the guidance office.

But *boys will be boys*, our favorite phrase that excuses so many things, while the only thing we have for the opposite gender is *women*, said with disdain and punctuated with an eye roll.

The announcements come on and let us know that all

the buses have come in; we can go to class now, resume our daily lives. I'm going to try. I'm going to do my best to get that boy's face out of my head, to ban the distinct expression that signified his pleasure from my mind so that I can open my locker, get my books, smile at Jack when he touches my elbow.

I'm trying to be normal.

But it is so very hard.

35. JACK

There's a dead spot on our gym floor, a place where the padding underneath has fallen away from the wood. When a ball hits a dead spot, it doesn't bounce back right; physics takes over, and talent can't fight science. You're thrown off, the millimeter of pushback you were expecting doesn't come, and from there it's a domino effect. You lose control of your dribble; the fast break that looked so promising collapses into a turnover that makes you look like an asshole. Except that doesn't happen to my team because we know exactly where the dead spot is. It's the definition of home-court advantage, and we've needed every ounce of that tonight.

I'm at the foul line, the entire gym a hurricane of sound as the fans on the visiting bleachers scream at me to fail, while the home side screams equally loud in support, all their words merging into a single wall of sound in which nothing is comprehensible. I glance at the clock even though I know there are only a few seconds left. After I take this shot, there'll be only a tiny sliver of time for the other team to score, our path to the division title easily paved with the passage of one free throw.

If I make it.

My eyes slide off the scoreboard, and in all the waving signs of the bleachers, spinning noisemakers, and screaming people, I spot my Alex, still as a stone, both hands in fists on either side of her face and eyes locked on mine. Around her is chaos, the gym packed with everyone from the point guard's great-grandma to the local bar owner as the best team we've had in a decade closes the books on the regular season. Alex is silent and intense, the exact opposite of everyone around her, yet the only one who has my attention. We could be alone in this moment, and I know before the ball leaves my hands that it's good.

I go straight for her at the buzzer, ignoring the fans who pour out of the bleachers, the pats on the back, the cheerleaders' fingernails sliding off my arms. All I want is Alex, and she stands still, waiting for me to come to her. Her skin soaks up my sweat as I hug her, my jersey as stuck to her as it is to me when we finally separate.

People are still screaming all around me; everyone's got their phones stuck in the air to capture the moment. Kids I don't even know cram their faces next to mine for selfies. And I'm stoked that we won and I made the shot that did it, but right now my mind is somewhere else entirely, my hand in Alex's as I thread through the crowd, leading her over to my mom and dad.

"Alex," I say, pulling her in front of me. "This is my mom and dad. Mom and Dad, this is Alex."

"Hello," she says, nodding at both of them. "It's nice to meet you."

My mom goes in for a hug, which kinda makes me cringe but Alex lets it happen, her hand stiffening in mine a little, but she doesn't drop-kick Mom either so it's not a failure.

"We're so glad to finally meet you," my mom says, her hands still on Alex's shoulders. She actually takes a piece of Alex's hair and tucks it behind her ear, which I totally understand the urge to do because I've done it myself a hundred times, but I shoot her a warning look anyway.

My dad is smart enough to keep his distance, but he smiles at her. "You're the girl—"

And I swear to God if he says *with the dead sister* I will fall right through the dead spot in the floor. But instead he finishes with, "—whose car we pulled out of the ditch, aren't you?"

Alex asks me, "Do you pull a lot of girls' cars out of ditches?"

I squeeze her hand. "Nope."

"Then, yes, that was me," she tells Dad.

"Well, it was worth the effort, then," he says, and she gives him the biggest shit-eating grin I think I've ever seen on her adorable face.

"You two have plans?" Mom asks, her own hand snaking through Dad's. "Or do you want to hang out with the old folks after the game?"

And to be perfectly honest, I was kinda hoping I could park the car out on 27 for a bit before taking her home, but Alex tells Mom she'd love to come over, so I'm roped into at least two hours of euchre and twenty minutes of Mom showing Alex my baby pictures.

And I'm actually kind of looking forward to it.

I squeeze her hand as they walk away, the last few people emptying out of the gym. "You did fine," I say. "I told you not to worry. Just be yourself."

"That is never good advice," she says, and I hug her again. Because I just can't stop touching this girl.

36. PEEKAY

I'm curled into a ball to conserve heat, my pajama-pants-clad knees touching Alex's as our voices blend in the dark, pitched low and secretive so as not to wake my parents.

"Why is it called making out?" she asks.

This is the kind of thing Alex wonders about: instead of talking about making out, she wants to know the origin of the phrase. And I'm totally going to grill her on exactly what she thinks constitutes making out in a minute, but it's actually a decent question, and like everything Alex says, it insists you stop and think about it.

"I don't know," I say. "Because you're definitely not *making* anything yet, and if it's hot and heavy there's

probably more *in* going on than *out*." She giggles a little,
telling me that she knows exactly what I mean, and that
means it's my turn to ask questions.

I know Jack Fisher the same way he knows me—we
grew up together, could identify each other's cars on
the road and even give a casual wave when we meet. But
beyond that I couldn't tell you if he's the kind of guy
who's telling all the others about how far he gets with
Alex, or if he keeps pussy talk on the down low. I don't
know, and I don't know if Alex even understands that
shit like that happens, that it's possible the feel of her
nipples might be public knowledge now, or that the
sounds she makes when she's in the dark alone with him
might get reenacted in locker rooms.

Alex will mutilate people who slip things in my
drinks, and I can't do that for her. But I can protect
her in another way, help her navigate the twisty paths of
her first relationship and try to stop her from getting
played, or at least buffer the blow when it happens.

"So have you guys . . ."

"No," she says, but doesn't offer anything else.

"I haven't either," I tell her. "I was close, with Adam.
But then we broke up."

"As much as I catch Park looking at you, I think you'll
have another opportunity soon."

"Yeah," I tell her. "We've been texting, but nothing's,

you know, happened. Truth is, Adam's the only guy I've ever even kissed. So I'm not going to all-out bang Park the first time he tries anything. But it's not like I don't want to."

"Me either," Alex says. "And it doesn't have anything to do with my sister, either."

We're quiet for a second, letting that settle in before she goes on.

"Do you think you'll be okay with being touched after what happened at the church?"

"I don't know," I say, and it's the truth. "I haven't had a chance to find out yet."

I've had a few nightmares, ones that end with the tweakers getting what they wanted. I wake up rolled in my blankets as if they were a cocoon, layers of cotton protecting me from the real world.

"Sex seems so intense," Alex goes on. "A lot of people are casual about it, like putting part of someone else's body inside of your own isn't that big of a deal. I don't understand that. It's your genitals touching someone else's genitals."

"Only you would describe sex like that," I say.

"Well, that's what it is," she shoots back.

"Yeah, and now I, like, never, ever want to do it."

"Yes, you do," she argues. "And I do too, and there's nothing wrong with that. But it's not something that

I'm going to do with Jack just because I'm his girlfriend and we're supposed to."

"So in other words, you're not Branley Jacobs," I say, going for a joke that falls flat. I hear it not cover the distance between us and immediately wish I hadn't said it.

"You shouldn't be that way about her," Alex says. "I hear what people say and I bet half of it isn't even true. And even if it is—fine. She's no different from you and me; she wants to have sex. So let her."

"Easy to say when it's not your boyfriend she's having sex with."

"Was Adam your boyfriend when it happened, or had you already broken up?"

Technically I don't know, and the burn has faded. My words lack the heat they used to, like I'm saying things out of habit and not because I actually feel that way anymore. I think of Branley that day on her doorstep, and how she's been a little nicer to me in the halls, saying hi sometimes when there's really no reason why she has to.

"I kind of don't think so."

"Me neither," Alex says. "She likes boys, and she can get them. You were hurt by that, but it wasn't Branley who hurt you. It was Adam."

"Fine," I say. "But Branley and Jack used to hook up all the time, Alex. I mean, like, they cut their sexual teeth on each other's crotches and never really stopped even when they were dating other people. So how would you feel if you found out Jack still had Branley on the side?"

"I'd be pissed," she says. "But not at Branley. She doesn't owe me anything."

"Would you, like, rip Jack's face off?"

She laughs, a loud one that she has to muffle with her hands. And part of me is a little bit shocked at that and part of me revels in it.

"No," she says, like maybe she considered it for a second. "But I'd definitely punch him in the dick."

My turn to laugh.

"So hey," I say, finally finding a moment to talk about something that only she and I talk about. "Remember the day I hit Branley?"

"Uh, you only kind of hit Branley," Alex corrects me, and I give her a little shove in the dark.

"You know what I mean."

"Yeah, and I told you the difference between thinking about hurting someone and actually hurting someone is—"

"Is like fucking huge, yeah," I interrupt. "But here's something weird I've been thinking about."

"Oh boy," Alex says, and I shove her again.

"Shut up, I listen to all the weird shit you think about all the time."

Alex makes a *pfft* sound in the dark.

"Okay, so, here's the thing. I realized that yeah, I

think about violence sometimes, but I fantasize about apologizing, too."

"That's fucked up," Alex says—and she hardly ever swears. "Explain."

"Like if I see someone bullying somebody in the hall or whatever, it bothers me and I'll think about it a lot, like *a lot*. To the point where I replay it in my head and create this situation where I'm really nice to them, and tell them I'm sorry that happened or whatever, ask them to sit with us at lunch."

Alex is quiet like she's thinking, so I keep going.

"My mom and dad get all these Christian magazines, right? And when I was little there were always pictures of kids in Africa with cleft palates on the back cover, and if you give five bucks or whatever they can fix this kid's face. There was this one girl who was a big mess, like her face was split in half, and I had this whole thing where I pretended I made Mom and Dad go to Africa and adopt her. She'd come home and live with me and we'd fix her face, but also she'd be my sister because I never had one, and I'd give her half my room and half my toys and half my clothes.

"And it was kind of screwed up because that made me feel better, you know? Like me thinking about doing a good thing took away all my guilt. Kind of like how me imagining hitting Branley helped me take care of wanting to without actually doing it."

"Except in this case it's not a good thing because that girl in Africa benefits in no way from you daydreaming about being her hero," Alex says. "If my dad only considered giving us his money instead of actually doing it, I'd be homeless and eating free lunch."

"And your mom would have to drink bottom-shelf scotch," I add.

Alex fake shudders. "Good thing we're flush."

"Yeah, no shit."

"So did you send in five bucks?" Alex asks.

"No. I asked Mom if we could and she said that it was a stock photo that charity had been using since, like, the eighties and she didn't entirely trust where the money went, anyway."

"That sucks," Alex says.

"Yeah."

The conversation dies, each of us drifting away. Alex's breathing evens out and I know she's asleep, but I can't get there myself. Every time I close my eyes I see that girl's cleft palate. I go ahead and pretend that I went to Africa and got her, that she came to live with me and we were like sisters, even though if Mom's right, that girl is probably twenty years older than me, or even dead by now.

But that's not going to help me sleep, so I pretend.

I pretend that I make the world a better place.

37. **JACK**

Newness wears off.

This is something I've learned about relationships. I've had more than a few run their course, the idiosyncrasies that were once endearing becoming annoying, the jump of my heart into my throat at the sight of her lessening to a skip, then a pause, then the bare recognition that at some point slips into dread, and you know it's time to end it.

It's different with Alex. The newness might have faded, which is inevitable, but it's grown into something better. The panic of not being able to come up with something to say to her has settled into the comfort of companionable silence, my hand resting on her knee, or her head on my chest. The frantic need to be near her and know how she feels has morphed into an almost pleasant ache of missing her when she's not with me, because I know we'll be together again.

We're happily entangled with each other in my basement, a basketball game on the TV that neither one of us is watching, an empty pizza box on the floor that I really need to grab before it's obvious we have a mouse problem. But I don't want to unravel my fingers from her hair, or shift her off my chest.

There are things I haven't talked to her about yet, though. Things I keep wanting to mention, but am afraid to ruin whatever moment we're in. I tug on her hair to make sure she's awake, fully aware it would be my luck to say something important to a girl who's fast asleep. She sits up, and I immediately miss the pressure and warmth of her against me.

"What?" she asks, pulling her hair off her shoulders and into a ponytail.

"Do you remember when we met?" I ask.

It's an odd question to ask someone in a town this small. Chances are there was never a time we weren't in each other's lives, whether we knew it or not. We probably splashed each other in the kiddie area at the public pool, while our soaking-wet swim diapers sagged forever downward. We may have reached for each other from child seats in grocery carts as our mothers passed each other at the store.

But I want to know if she remembers the night Anna was discovered, if she thinks of the version of me who participated in that, the guy with a fog in his brain and his pants around his ankles, a half-naked Branley underneath him. I want her to not remember, but I also want to rectify it if she does, prove to her and to me that's not who I am. Being with her has killed that guy.

"Do you mean in the guidance office?" she asks, and my heart lifts at least three feet out of my stomach.

I could say no and come clean, but she looks so happy right now, and bringing up Anna can't possibly be the start to a good conversation.

"Yeah," I say.

"What about it?"

My mind is still in the woods that night, back when I was still a jackass and she still had normal posture, not always tense.

"Jack?" She taps my leg. "What about it?"

"You said you weren't going to college. Why not?" I blurt the first thing that comes to mind, my initial reaction to her statement months ago that I never got around to asking.

Her face closes immediately, the tiniest shift of muscles making it obvious even in the dim basement that the conversation is over before it even begins.

"I'm just not," she says, the words even and measured.

I sit up and our legs unfold from each other, the heat we'd made evaporating quickly in the cool, dark basement air. "You've got the grades. You're smart as hell. And it's not like tuition would be a problem."

Alex doesn't say anything, her eyes shifting to the ground.

I nudge her leg with mine, trying to reclaim the easy communication we've shared before. "I don't understand."

"It's not for you to understand."

The first stab of annoyance comes fast and hard, painful because it's a mar on the perfection of our relationship. I never wanted to feel this way. Not about Alex.

"Try to explain," I say, my hand finding hers.

"My life isn't like yours," she begins.

"I know," I say too quickly. She closes her eyes and I know she just felt that stab, too. "Sorry," I say. "Go on."

"It's not like yours," she says again. "You're supposed to move out among people, widen your horizons."

"And you're not?"

"No," she says, shaking her head emphatically. "It's better if I don't."

"It's not better," I argue. "What are you going to do? Get a job at the gas station? Waste your life flipping burgers?"

"Not better for me," she says quietly. "It's better for others."

I'm about to tell her that's the dumbest thing I've ever heard when I remember the sound of skin tearing, and Ray Parsons's blood on the church stones.

Her hand pulls away from mine, pointing at the empty pizza box.

"You've got mice."

They scatter as I jump to my feet, receding into the shadows. I grab the box and take it upstairs to the trash, Alex following me and pulling her coat on. We kiss at the door, the conversation unfinished but over.

I lie in bed pondering the wound that the first stab of our relationship left behind, wondering if it's one that can heal or if it will be fatal. I think about the conversation that might have happened if I'd had the balls to ask if she remembered the night they found Anna, and if it would've gone better.

I text Alex and tell her good night, she responds with the same, and I hold my phone tightly, too aware that the present is all we have if I can't mention the past and she won't talk about the future.

38. **ALEX**

I don't like to come home.

Other houses have warmth in them, the lines between the people who live there humming with unspent energy ready to unreel. Conversations from the past still hover in the air, waiting for the threads to be picked up again. The air here is cold, empty to the point of sterility. When I hear my name it's shocking, a word that isn't spoken. Taboo.

It came from the living room, so I follow it, the only light provided from the moon bouncing back off the snow outside. My mother is sitting on the couch, a cut-crystal decanter on the coffee table in front of her, glass in her hand.

"Mom?" I say, which doesn't sound right and never

has. The word carries a history that we don't share, implies picnics and swing sets and trips to the pool.

"Who else?" she asks, and I don't know what to say to that. "Come here," she says. "Have some scotch."

I don't want scotch and I don't want to drink with her, but it's the only olive branch she has to offer, so I take it, the alcohol heavy and hot as it rips down my throat. She throws hers back like water and pours another for both of us.

"You've been out a lot," she says.

I have, and I don't like the guilt that seeps over me with her words. Like maybe I shouldn't be.

"I have a boyfriend," I tell her. That word feels so meaningless here, lacking the fullness it carries at Jack's house, the weight of his mom's hand on my shoulder as we stand side by side in the kitchen, pouring off-brand root beer into plastic cups. I take another drink of scotch, hoping it will make words come more easily. "His name is Jack."

Mom investigates the bottom of her glass like she can't figure out how it became empty so quick. "The boy who brought your car back?"

"Yes."

"He's good-looking."

I know he is, so I don't reply.

She pours herself another and frowns a little when it

overflows onto her fingers, flicking sticky amber drops off into the dark. "Do I need to talk to you about . . ."

"No," I say.

We drink quietly in the dark, each swallow going down more easily than the one before. I feel it in a few minutes, my head floating and the words I need to string together in order to get through this sliding off the surface of my suddenly slick brain.

"Do you have other friends?" Mom asks eventually.

"One," I say. I think about Sara for a second, a person who I spend time with because we both spend time with Claire. "Maybe two."

"Gotta start somewhere," Mom says, her words beginning to slur.

We're quiet again, this unfamiliarity of talking to each other not comfortable but not as painful as I thought it might be, either.

"You're so much like him," Mom says. "It's not easy for me, you know."

I don't say anything because I don't want to talk about this. Not about how my anger builds in my stomach and boils up into my head, venting out through my hands and mouth like steam escaping on the way. Not about how he was the same and I saw that once or twice, how he wanted to throw a punch or break her jaw. But he always stopped himself, and maybe that's something he could've taught me if he'd stayed.

"Once he was gone I hoped the parts of you that are from me would have more room to breathe," Mom says.

"That didn't happen," I say.

"No." She nods. "I wish I could open you up, Alex, unspool everything inside of you and burn out the parts that are from him, put you back together and see my daughter instead of my husband every time I look at you."

I take another drink. If she doesn't instinctively understand that's the same thing, then I can't explain it.

"I've been trying to get him out of my life for ten years," she says, refilling her glass again. "Little things build up when you live with someone. Six months ago I found a vase someone gave us as a wedding gift and I took it outside and broke it. But I can't do that with you. A decade trying to get everything he touched out of this house and I end up raising him instead."

My mom has poetry in her, something I never would have guessed. It must be where my words come from, flowing through me with a power equaled only by the fire in my gut. They're moving now, escaping in a way I didn't mean to or expect.

"I killed Comstock," I say.

"I know," she answers.

And we drink a little more in the dark, that thread hanging in the air. And maybe one of us will reach for it again.

PEEKAY

My dad has some crutch phrases. One of his big ones is
this too shall pass (2 Corinthians 4:17–18, if you're wondering). My mom always tacks her version onto that—*time
heals all wounds*, although I'm not sure she's placed her
trust entirely on the earth continuing to rotate, because
she supplements with chamomile tea. So most of the
crying done in my life has been over steamy mugs with
herbs floating in them, the musty whiff of Dad's big-ass
King James Version flopped open across from me, while
well-meaning pats on the back are supposed to make
everything okay.

This is how my trauma is handled, everything from
Grandma dying to my first kitten tangling with a speeding Jeep to getting my period. I did call Dad out on the

this too shall pass thing on that last one. Then Mom got all loyal and explained menopause and the fact that *technically* Dad was right, it would just take about forty years, and then I cried harder.

So it's understandable that I didn't bring my broken heart to them, dumping the bloody pieces onto the dinner table after we finished our cherry cheesecake. They knew, though. They couldn't *not* notice that suddenly Adam was no longer a fixture in our house, a guy who was so welcome and trusted that he didn't have to knock anymore. But I guess maybe Mom and Dad are smart enough to realize that pointing out the second hand on the clock isn't going to suddenly mend the fissure straight through my aorta.

Here's the thing, though—they were right.

We're deep into winter and I've stopped feeling like there is a spear in my chest every time he's up against Branley in the hallway. To her credit, I actually saw her push him away a couple of times when I came around the corner. It's not like we're friends or anything. We'll give each other a nod in the hallway or cautiously say *excuse me* when we slide past each other in the senior cut line at lunch, but we're not coordinating our clothes every night. Still, the fact that she's trying to not throw it in my face set a warm glow in the black gaping hole where I picture that spear passing through, so many times that the wound keeps getting bigger.

Except I think it closed up when I wasn't paying attention.

The other night I got a text from a number I didn't recognize, an anonymous how r u?

I shot back: who is this? A call came in from the same number two seconds later. I let it go to voice mail, listening immediately after I got the notification. And then Adam's voice, definitely injured: "Seriously, you deleted my number?"

I didn't add him as a contact, but I did keep the voice mail. The righteous indignation buried there amused me.

I texted back: Yeah, I did. What's up?

U talking to Park?

Also amusing. Yes. I am talking to Park, kind of. It started when he texted me to make sure I was okay after what happened at the church, an innocent brotherly text that I didn't read anything into, responding that I was fine and thanks for checking. A couple of days later he asked if I was coming to the basketball game and I answered yes and his response—a simple good—kind of set that glow I mentioned earlier into a spark.

So we've been playing this careful game with each other, one that's fun to play because I know I can't get hurt too badly when all we're doing is texting sometimes. Once we went on an accidental double date when me and Alex and Park and Jack all ended up at the same diner one night. Except when I went to grab my bill I realized that he'd already paid for my grilled cheese. When I said something he smiled at me, so maybe it wasn't an accident that we met up after all.

So when my ex-boyfriend asks, *U talking to Park?* I answer *yes*, and our text conversation out of nowhere ends abruptly.

And I couldn't give less of a shit.

40. **JACK**

I kind of miss Branley.

It's weird. In a lot of ways Branley is my best friend, and suddenly cutting her out made that really clear to me. Yes, sometimes I'd have to plow through piles of shit to get down to the real Branley, the girl who used to sneak up on me in seventh grade and buckle my knee from behind. And it's work to bring that out of her, but it's worth it, always, and I miss that girl even if she's buried inside of a tanned, waxed, lip-glossed, pouty Barbie doll who wants to fuck before starting a conversation.

Because that's what would happen if I tried. I know because she keeps sending me nudes, each a little trashier than the one before since I never respond. She worked up to a video, and I watched it because *duh*, and then I felt kind of terrible. If she just sent me a damn text with words instead of shots of her tits I might actually answer her.

But I can't. Because she's a crowbar in a door I'm trying to shut and she'll wedge her way in and use the leverage to get me in bed and goddammit I don't know if I could tell her no. I miss Branley, but I miss sex too, and I'm trying to be a good guy and why can't the two of those things be separate anyway?

Tonight is not going to be easy. Park wants us to hang out at the church, even though it's ass cold outside. He's got this big idea that if Alex is there with me then Peekay will be with him by default, but the downside is Adam somehow got in on this too and that means Branley will be there. Park's fine with that because it'll just make it even more obvious that this is a couples thing and he's totally into Peekay. And I can't exactly explain to him that Branley sends me palm-worthy vids and that makes the whole thing weird for me, because then he'd want to see it and I'm definitely not doing that.

I tried to communicate my non-interest in this group thing by just making throat noises when he talked to me about it, or responding with texts that just said *meh* or *whatever*. But somehow Alex and I have become an integral part of getting him and Peekay together, and now there will be three couples there. Me and Alex, Adam and Branley, Peekay and Park.

Read as: The Guy Who Used To Bang Branley and His Occasionally Violent Girlfriend Who Doesn't Know Branley Still Sends Nudes To Him, Peekay's Ex-Boyfriend Who She Might Not Be Over and The Girl Who Still Sends Nudes To The Guy Who Used To Bang Her, and The Girl Who Almost Punched Branley In The Face Not That Long Ago and A Pretty Clueless Guy Who Thinks This Is A Good Idea.

It's a small town. There aren't a lot of dating options, but this is still its own special kind of mess.

It's okay because I have my own ideas about how to handle tonight. The six of us all together can only be nonnuclear for so long, so Alex and I are going for a walk after about an hour. We'll be alone, the way we both like it, and I have a surprise for her, and if I said that to Branley she'd think it was my dick even though it's, like, five degrees outside and I am human after all.

Tonight I'm going to tell Alex that I love her. It's been like a pressure inside of me, a combination of words that wants to erupt at the wrong times, sounds that might escape on their own if I'm not concentrating. I swear to God I can feel *I love you* in my throat like a physical thing, and I need to make sure that when it finally gets out there it happens in the right way.

Because this is special, because Alex is special. And I need to make tonight special, too.

It doesn't start out great.

Park is big on planning, but execution is another thing, and lighting a fire with nothing but soaked wood is not easy.

"Son of a bitch," he says, as yet another match flares out before catching.

Alex is watching him with her eyebrows crunched slightly together. I know she's trying not to embarrass him by taking over, but it's freaking cold and our basic needs are going to overcome being polite really soon.

Peekay has her hands jammed into her armpits and starts stomping her feet, which makes her boobs jiggle. Park doesn't even try to act like he's not staring and Alex smoothly takes the matches from his hand while he's distracted.

"Christ, it's cold," Branley says as she walks in, Adam trailing behind her. She's wearing the thinnest jacket possible; it hugs her tiny waist and accents the explosion of her boobs. She looks fantastic, but there's a reason she's freezing.

"I brought body heat," Adam says, and Park makes a gagging noise onto Alex's shoulder. She knocks him onto his ass with her elbow as flames flick to life under her hands.

"Good thing Alex got the fire started then," Branley says, clearly finding her boyfriend as lame as the rest of us do.

Park drags a couple of bigger rocks over to the fire, and I help him with a pew, our combined muscles still not enough to get the damned thing off the ground, so we're making a horrible *screeeech* as oak that hasn't budged in years scratches its way across stone.

It's accomplished eventually. We've got a fire that gives off heat, and seats and beer for everyone. Peekay claims a spot next to Park on the pew so fast that I know this entire thing didn't need to happen in the first place, but we're here now. Branley sits on one of the rocks, her cold hands jammed into her pockets so that the best thing Adam can do is take a rock next to her and put his arm in the crook of her elbow. They look like an awkward prom photo and it's pretty clear if there's dancing she'll be the one taking the lead.

It's kind of funny and my eyes meet Bran's and she somehow finds a way to shrug with one eyebrow and I'm trying not to laugh because secret communication across a fire with a girl who sends you nudes is probably not cool when your girlfriend is right next to you.

Except Alex is not right next to me. She decided

to sit on the ground for some reason, which leaves me sitting on an old aluminum lawn chair that someone dragged here in the nineties and never reclaimed. We're still close. She's by my knee and she does rest her temple against my kneecap for just a second after I sit, which is nice and all, but I like seeing her face and now I don't get to. I settle for running a strand of her hair through my fingers as I crack open a beer.

The fire is hot and the beer is cold enough to have ice chips floating in it, and I'm settling into a comforting haze when Peekay's phone goes off. She jumps, and nobody can miss her face collapsing when she reads her text.

"Sorry," Peekay says, disentangling herself from Park. She's dialing as she walks away from us, her silhouette lost in the shadows. But her words float in the darkness and the ones her voice cracks on might as well be said to our faces they're so loud.

What? . . . I thought he was . . . your parents . . . okay? . . . about you? . . . of a bitch . . . the cops? . . . don't think . . . fucking terrible . . . so sorry . . .

Nothing good is happening here and the rest of us are all looking at one another, not polite enough to pretend we can't hear it and too curious to talk over her so that we actually don't. Peekay comes back to us, flopping down next to Park but not leaning into him, and he looks like a puppy that was told he was being adopted but then someone changed their mind. It's dead quiet and he looks at me because he has no idea what to say or do, and then Branley saves him by being a pushy bitch because that's what she's good at.

"What was that about?"

I expect Peekay to tell her to fuck off, but there are three empty beer cans at her feet and the fire's light only extends so far, making it seem like our faces are the only ones in the world.

So instead Peekay looks up from her phone, dark and silent now in her hands, and says, "You guys know about Sara's uncle, right?"

And we do, so it's not like Peekay really has to say anything else. You can't mow your yard here without someone knowing when you started and how long it took, so if you like kiddie porn we will know. We will know and it won't be talked about openly, but whispered behind hands, texted from one mom to the next, auto-correct not picking up on the words we don't use often because they're too horrible. Kids will be kept a little closer when we're in the same grocery store and smiles will be stretched tighter or dropped entirely. But we will know. And you'll know we know.

Except Alex doesn't, because she's just now crawling out of that black hole of a house to become a part of us.

So when Branley says, "Sara has a little sister, doesn't she?" and Peekay just starts crying and Park says *motherfucker* like he means it, Alex doesn't know what to do. She looks back at me, so very lost, and I don't want to be the one to fill her in but someone has to. So I grab her hand and we take the walk I've been planning, the heat from the fire leaking out of our bodies the second we leave the light, her fingers in mine as cold as naked bones.

It's been snowing a little, so my tracks from earlier are filled in, and this could be the most romantic thing I've ever done except it's not going to be, because I don't think I can very well follow up a conversation that has the word *molester* in it with my first declaration of love.

But the dew has frozen and the moon is so bright it looks like the entire woods is made out of shadows covered in diamonds. So maybe I can salvage this thing after all, and I'm trying to reset my brain when Alex says, "What's that?"

She breaks away from me, her feet punching through the snow.

"Hold up," I call, wanting to be there with her, but she's ahead of me, so when I catch up she's in the little clearing, a solitary Scotch pine standing sentinel in the middle.

I found it last week after work, when Dad told me

Mom said it's time for a tree to go up. Only we can't afford the twenty bucks to go buy one at a lot, so I thought if I could sneak one out of the woods without getting arrested for trespassing that would be all right. And I found this one, the right size, no gaping holes. Like it's auditioning for the role of Christmas tree. So I went to the car and I got my ax, but when I came back I couldn't do it.

There had been a light snow that day, and the branches held on to millions of tiny flakes. Flakes that would be dislodged by the first swing of my ax, then destroyed under my muddy boots as I tore into the trunk, the steel bite ripping through a life lived longer than my own just to die in the living room and be hauled to the street on December twenty-sixth.

I couldn't do it. But I also know it's my last Christmas at home and that's why Mom is insisting on a tree even though everyone knows there won't be many presents under it. So I stayed out until two in the morning and drove to the lot and stole a tree, creeping away with my lights off and the weirdest feeling in my heart. Because what I'd just done was technically wrong, but it felt more right than cutting down the pine in the clearing, and the tree strapped to my car was going to die anyway so I might as well take it.

And I lay in bed all that night and thought about

trees. Dumbest thing in the world. And I wasn't sure what was keeping me up until I realized it wasn't my mom's face (crying; she's that way about holidays) I kept seeing in my head but Alex's, and how she'd told me once she hadn't had a tree since their dad left. And that's when the whole thing came together: the woods, the words *I love you* waiting to be said, and all the things I can't give her because I'm poor and she's not.

I could do this thing, though, and I tried so hard to make it right, and Alex is looking at it now. Ornaments so old that not even my mom can justify using them are transformed by the frozen dew and the moon, every inch screaming with a beauty that will dissolve in the sunlight. Dime-store ribbon tied into bows, razor-sharp with ice, will be wilted trash in a few hours when reality steps in. But this isn't reality and this isn't the morning. It's now and it's my moment and I reclaim Alex's hand and take a deep breath and she says—

"Tell me about Sara's uncle."

41. **ALEX**

It shouldn't be this easy.

There are laws in place that stop us from doing things. This is what we tell ourselves. In truth we stop ourselves; the law is a guideline for how to punish someone who is caught.

Claire's dad likes to say that everything happens for a reason. He must say it a lot because I've been at her house only a handful of times and have heard the phrase at least twice. And if he's right then maybe I'm *supposed* to hear him.

Maybe Claire was supposed to get that text from Sara tonight when I would see her face. Maybe she was supposed to have too much to drink and cry in the car, sharing memories of the times she'd been with Sara at her uncle's house. Maybe she was supposed to point it out as I drove past, choking on words so harsh she can't say them even with beers slicking her throat. *Guess I was lucky*, she says.

I live in a world where not being molested as a child is considered luck.

A fire has been lit inside of me, and if everything happens for a reason, then the kindling has been laid for years, piled nicely as it waited for a spark. And tonight was steel on flint, a heat pulsing within that keeps me warm even in the cold.

Even as I stand outside his home in the dead of night.

After I dropped Claire off, I tried to do the right thing, tried to be normal. I checked my phone for texts. I walked to the side door. I reached for the doorknob and then I was running, my feet punching through snow and leaving a dark path behind me. Now it's his door in front of me, not my own. People don't lock up here. They call it trust but I say it's arrogance, an assumption that nothing bad will happen.

Not to them.

I let myself in.

He's asleep on the couch. The lamp on the side table illuminates his half-eaten dinner, now decorated with a fat winter fly bogged down in the mashed potatoes. It's still struggling a little, threadlike legs pushing against gravy.

He fell asleep with the TV on, the colors flickering across his face as I watch him. The steady rise and fall of his chest, his bare feet on the floor, nails that need to be clipped. The awkward angle of his neck, head resting to the side.

He'll have a crick in the morning. Maybe.

I could leave now. There are reasons why I should. There are reasons to stay, too. I take my time, touching things, moving through the small rooms of his life to see what he keeps. And he does keep things. Things no one should have. I go through pictures, grainy but with enough detail to know what I'm looking at.

Now I can't leave.

He burns wood for warmth, the iron stove in the center room emitting heat like a wall that I move through as I walk toward it. There's a small shovel for cleaning out ash, leaning against the stove, cocked toward me as if in invitation.

It really shouldn't be this easy.

When I dump the embers in his lap, his clothing ignites. His eyes fly open, but he does not see me. There is only confusion, a lack of comprehension so great that it trumps even the pain. The elasticized band of his underwear liquefies and runs across his skin, the tiny hairs on his belly flaming for a brief fiery moment before becoming ash.

His hands go immediately to the pain, wanting to cup it and cover the hurt, but there is no comfort in the movement. Blisters open and break in a moment and his sleeves catch, fire creeping up his arms as he staggers to his feet. He wants to run now—the second instinctive reaction to pain—but he doesn't know where to go and the coffee table is in his way, cracking against his shins hard enough to break skin, but even that does not stop him as he bolts.

He heads for the bedroom, liquid flame lighting the carpet in his wake as parts of his sweater drip to the floor. That room calls to him even as he burns, a black hole that he flies toward, his melting hands providing mutual destruction for the pictures I laid out on the bed. I don't follow, because I don't need to see.

I can hear.

Animals die in the woods all the time. I've heard their screams, startlingly human as they fight something stronger, faster, bigger. But there's a final moment when they know the battle is lost, when the prey goes still and accepts fate, a passive agreement with the predator that they have been bested.

That silence follows the smoke down the hallway, and I know it's over. The small fires that dropped around him have grown, licking up the carpet fibers and now searching for more.

They creep toward me and I've spent too much time watching. I head for the door, my eyes watering against the smoke and my throat tightening against the fumes of the smoldering carpet. Yet I can't move fast because there's an unfamiliar weight in my stomach and I fight against it as I hit the cold, clear air, my feet finally picking up speed as I run down the driveway, to the road, past the woods, places I can't leave footprints.

What was his home is now a pillar of smoke, bits of ash falling from the sky, all that's left of any number of horrific acts. But that's not what puts me on my knees. That's not what makes me vomit, the steam from it rising back up in my face as I retch again and again.

The weight in my gut is gone, leaving behind a dark pit and strained muscles. I lie back in the snow, my body quivering. I don't know what to do, for the first time in a long time. I don't know what I think.

Because that empty space inside me, it feels like guilt.

42. JACK

Sound travels when the air is freezing. Even with the storm windows I can hear a train, though the tracks are so far away I can't see the lights. Its thrum supersedes the constant sound of the breeze moving through the pines near the house, the low grunt of a deer that had been passing through the yard as it sees something it doesn't like. I hear it bolt, hooves breaking through the frozen snow as it flees.

I can't sleep, and it's got nothing to do with noises. I've been hearing these things my whole life, same as I've been staring at this crack in the ceiling my whole life. For some people the constant things are reassurance; they find comfort in the fact that nothing ever changes. But I'm not like that, and right now I hate the crack in my ceiling, I hate the train for existing, and I especially hate the wind for moving the pines outside and reminding me that I'm going to have to go back to the clearing and get all the stupid fucking decorations off that tree.

I curl my fist under my head, fighting the urge to punch the wall. I told Alex that I love her, right after explaining about Sara's uncle. Her eyes did the right thing, lit up as bright as the snow all around us. But her mouth was all wrong, still fused shut with an inexpressible anger. She actually said *thank you*, which was worse than saying nothing at all. We stared at each other for a few seconds after that, another awkward silence like the one after she attacked Ray Parsons descending around us.

I hate not knowing what to say to Alex, and of course here in my bed I've come up with all kinds of great things, words that would've smoothed over my bad timing and loosened some of the muscles around her lips. But those things didn't come to me when I needed them, so we walked back to the church, Alex with her hands in her pockets, eyes on the ground and her face as cold as the wind. Peekay'd had too much to drink and Alex drove her home, giving me a halfhearted wave as she got into the car.

The train is gone, taking its vibrant hum with it. I'm left with the wind and the crack on my ceiling and all the things I could've done differently tonight when there's a tap on my window. I ignore it, focused on the crack, wondering if there's any old caulk out in the garage, and if I can sneak out and get it without my parents wondering what the hell I'm doing fixing my ceiling at four in the morning.

The sound comes again, followed quickly by another, more insistent. I roll over and push the curtain aside to see Alex standing in the driveway, arm pulled back to throw another stone. I wave to her and she drops it, motioning for me.

I know how to dress quickly and quietly, know which spots on the stairs creak loudly, and how to open the screen door just right without making a sound. But I don't know how to do any of these things with my heart beating so hard I can see it in my chest, or with my blood rushing so fast there are dark corners in my vision.

It's the sloppiest sneaking out I've ever done, but I don't care. If Alex is standing in my yard in the middle of the night it means she thinks things were unsaid too, and maybe she couldn't sleep either. Maybe she's been lying on her bed staring at her ceiling thinking about me, and that's exactly what I'll tell Mom and Dad if they wake up.

Some things are too important to wait.

I'm outside, the snow tumbling over the sides of my

shoes and slipping down against my bare skin because I didn't take the time to put on socks. Alex comes toward me, hands out, and I take them, our freezing skin meeting.

"Hey," she says, her voice harsh and scratchy. Her face is streaked with frozen tears, her cheeks stretched and hard underneath them. Her eyelashes are stuck together, dark icicles framing red-rimmed eyes.

"Alex, what are you doing?" I put my hands on her face, rubbing my thumbs over the salt left behind there. It chafes away, blowing into the breeze and leaving redness behind. Her whole face is stiff in my hands and I try to pull her into me for heat but she pushes away.

"I need to talk to you," she says, her voice dark and unfamiliar.

I take a step back. I know this tone; I've seen these movements. Seen them in Mom when we lost Grandpa, in Park when he found out his little sister had cancer. Physical pain we reach for, protect, treat. Pain that comes from the inside we try to push out, working it free in little worrying movements of the hands, eyes that dart everywhere, as if expending all the energy inside will help mine down to the pain, expose it and drag it out into the open, out where someone else can see it and help kill it.

Alex is in pain; it's written everywhere. Every muscle

she has is fluttering. She's like a wild animal ready to bolt, but with nowhere to go. She knows the hurt is inside and running won't help, but she came to me—*to me*—and there's enough pride attached to that that I feel *good*. And that makes me feel terrible, because my girlfriend is having a breakdown.

Alex takes a deep breath, lips working as she searches for words. Finally a calm settles, one that radiates from her eyes and flows outward from there until she's not a panicked animal anymore. She's a frozen statue of my girlfriend, and as she starts to talk, I'm the one who wants to run.

"Jack," she says calmly. "I have reactions to my environment that others wouldn't understand. I follow through on them because I believe in instinct."

I hear a siren, a high-pitched wail as the ambulance comes screaming from town. It digs into my ears, the miles separating me from it turned into nothing by the cold winter air. The fire truck comes next, the one engine that the town owns ripping through the calm that I'd hated only a few minutes ago.

"What are you saying?" I watch her intently, too scared to move, afraid she might bolt if I startle her.

"The other night you asked me about college."

"You said it's better if you don't go."

"Better for *other people*, Jack," she corrects me. "I feel

too much." Her face crumples a little, a thaw creeping in.

"I shouldn't be out," she says, her voice breaking. "It's not safe."

"Alex." I say her name quietly, in between siren pulses. "Alex, what did you do?"

She closes her eyes and exhales, the warmth of her breath pluming all around her. "If I don't let my feelings guide me in my actions, it's the same as not having them at all," she says. Her eyes open and she's scared again, the momentary calm shattered by the noise. "I might as well not exist."

"You exist," I say, and she comes to me, fresh tears filling the tracks left behind by frozen ones. She's in my arms in a moment, but pulls back for one second to lock eyes with me.

"I love you, too," she says.

And my heart slams up into my throat at the same time that my stomach drops into my knees.

Because Alex loves me.

And she smells like smoke.

PEEKAY

Alex is broken, and it's painful to see.

We had this dog at the shelter once, an Irish wolf-hound. Big-ass dog, gorgeous in her own way. We named her Brigit—a good Irish name—cleaned her up and put her on the shelter's Facebook page while we waited to borrow the one scanner all the surrounding counties use to check strays for microchips.

The response was immediate—everyone basically said *What the hell is that?*

People around here have golden retrievers and German shepherds, dogs that make sense, practical pets that others can identify and congratulate you on. There was interest, don't get me wrong. Lots of people stopped by just to see Brigit in the flesh, walk her out of the pity in their hearts and then plop her back in the cage and take home a beagle, saying, "I think we're looking for something a little more . . . normal."

And Brigit, with her long face and distinctive bearing, would curl up in her cage, pride emanating from every muscle. But you could see in her eyes she was hurt. When our turn came to use the scanner I did Brigit myself, my heart skipping a beat when I got a *beep* and a phone number to call. Her family was from New York, which isn't actually all that far from us if you think about it, but everyone around the shelter was so stunned they kept repeating it, as if we found out she was actually *from* Ireland.

Her family came to get her, and not a day too late. Brigit's head had begun to hang, her food dish not emptying at a healthy rate. When she heard their voices in the waiting room, I don't think she believed it. I thought she might go ballistic, tear down the hall dragging me by the leash like a lot of dogs do when they find their people again. But Brigit just looked at me when I clipped her leash on and opened the door, like she suspected this was another opportunity to be dragged out into public to have someone look at her skeptically again.

If that dog had middle fingers I guarantee you she would have flipped off this entire county as she headed home in her family's Hummer.

Someone finally *got* Alex. Someone finally realized that here amid all the regular people and normal lives there was a truly remarkable person, a girl who doesn't look like everyone else or even think like us. Alex is a different breed altogether, but here we just want variations of the same. The safe. The known. Someone finally saw past all that.

Unfortunately that someone was Jack Fisher, and he's the type who takes all the dogs home for an overnight but never actually adopts any.

It's been two weeks since they stopped talking. Two weeks of snow and bitter cold, ice hanging from our windows and freezing up our cars. It's dark when we wake up and getting dark when we head home from school. Some days it's been so cold just going outside can almost kill you. When we do have school, the wind cuts right through us as we walk toward the building, me hunched against it, Alex standing tall, not seeming to care.

Her eyes have been blank, her mouth forming the right words to constitute a response, but there's nothing behind them, no feeling. I've had her over a few times, casually mentioned the names of some boys that I've caught checking her out (because let's face it, once one person tries Irish wolfhound, the others get curious). But she shakes her head, says she's not interested.

She never misses her hours at the shelter and does all her homework, maintaining her path to valedictorian. She moves through all the scheduled events as if each day is a job, and anything more is considered overtime. I position myself in the right place at school, shielding her from Jack as he walks by, hoping my body blunts the chaotic knife of Branley's laughter as she hangs from his arm. But if she's laughing it's not because he said something funny.

Park says Jack doesn't make jokes anymore. We've tried to ask questions, me to Alex, Park to Jack, our words chosen carefully, not like we're digging to figure out why they broke up.

The boys say it's because she wouldn't put out.

The girls say it's because Jack always gets bored eventually.

They're both utterly broken.

And no one knows why.

44. ALEX

I didn't know a living person could hurt you so badly.

When the pain originates with someone who is gone, it's your own memory that hurts you. Walking through the house, touching things they've touched, hearing sounds they heard, wondering what they would've thought of one thing or another. This is pain that I know, pain that I can handle, pain that is so much a part of me that if it were removed I would not be whole.

But when it's someone who's alive who hurts you, the pain can't be escaped. The things they've touched are still warm because they were just there, the sounds they hear reach your ears too—sometimes their own voice, and it's excruciating to bear. I know what he thinks about this, that, or the other because I can hear him saying so.

But not to me. He doesn't talk to me anymore.

I want to take it back.

Not just the words I said in the dark, his face slowly closing against me as the smoke rose from my clothes and the sirens ripped the air. I want to go back further, back to the moment where I stood at my own door. I dream about walking through it instead of spinning and running into the dark. I dream about going to sleep that night to the smell of coconut shampoo, my phone screen glowing with whatever latest text came in from Jack.

I want that instead of what happened, instead of the smoke that I still can't get out of my pillowcase, the dark screen of my phone staring back at me whenever I glance at it. I don't want the memories that I have. The smells and the sounds, and all the small things I did that rounded up to one big thing.

One big thing that I can't take back.

45. **JACK**

It took me a while to be able to go back.

The clearing is frozen solid when I finally get the nerve to sneak up the hill in Dad's truck, the chains on the tires the only thing stopping me from sliding back down. It's been so damn cold nobody has been out in the woods. I can't even find deer tracks. Every living thing is hunkered down, waiting for spring.

I am too, in a way. Every night when I go to bed I'm thankful that there's a streak of eight or nine hours of unconsciousness ahead of me, time in which I don't have to think about Alex and what happened. Sleep is a kind of victory for me, because when I wake up it means there's another day solidly behind, one more step away from that night. I want to pile time on top of itself, years upon years so that I can forget, or at least make what she did a hazy memory. I want to jump ahead a decade to when I'm out of this damn town, and the fresh grave in the cemetery has settled, and Alex is a name that doesn't feel like a slash on my heart.

I kill the engine and listen to it cooling, those small mechanical noises the only sounds out here as the sun sinks. It's easier to think when I'm alone and my brain runs through it all again. Alex's words, the smells that clung to her, the tears on her face and the news about Sara's uncle that tore through the halls the next day. The thing is, I've always been good at logic puzzles, and the only answer that fits says that Alex murdered someone.

It could've been an accident—that's what the cops decided, anyway. It wouldn't have been the first house fire this winter. We've all been freezing in our beds, the cold fingers of wind slipping through the tiny cracks to find us no matter where in the house we are.

But it was the only fatal fire, and the only one where my girlfriend showed up in my driveway immediately afterward, having some kind of nervous breakdown and smelling like smoke. All those damning little things say a lot, and all the pressure that was trying to push the words *I love you* out of my mouth now wants me to scream that Alex is a killer, but I can't do that. Not where people can hear, anyway.

Park wants to know what's wrong. Branley wants to know what's wrong.

Everybody thinks that Alex and I got into some big fight and broke up. I almost wish we had. I wish I'd told her she was crazy, pushed her away from me. But I didn't. I held her and told her everything was going to be okay even as the ash started to drift in from the north, heavier than the snow and darker by far.

What I did was worse. I abandoned her.

It started when her ring tone made me want to vomit instead of answer, the guilt plunging deep into my belly and making me choke. I couldn't read her texts and I couldn't listen to her voice mails, scared of what she might say next. Scared of what she might *do* next. I even stared at the pic I've still got on my phone of Officer Nolan's email and cell once or twice.

But the thing is that I told her everything would be all right. I said that when this girl who I didn't even think could bend was completely broken, sobbing against me and hating herself. And I've been there. I know exactly what it's like to fuck up hard and not be able to fix it, so I couldn't damn her even if what she did was so far above and beyond my own screw-ups we can't even see each other across the gap.

I let that logic have its way with me, and I've waited

so long that if I rat her out now Nolan's going to want to know why I covered for her. Even if I leave an anonymous tip I'm screwed because we—the oh-so-happy new couple—suddenly broke up right when the shit went down, and he'll ask me questions. Questions that tear down the good-guy thing I've got going on and punch holes in any chances I have at a scholarship.

Alex has faded away in the past couple of weeks. Branley is highest on my recent calls list, Alex's number buried somewhere behind some sophomore girl who found the courage to call me in the bottom of a bottle. I couldn't understand anything she said, but I kept the voice mail, hoping I might find it funny eventually.

Branley has been doing her best to cheer me up but I haven't touched her. She's confused and pouty about it, and while I know she could distract me for an hour or two, it would still be Alex on my mind. Because fading or not, she still shines brighter than everyone else, and I have my nights when I want to call her up anyway. Fuck the fire and the smoke and the tears running down her face.

"Goddammit," I yell, punching the horn and sending some birds out of their nests, reprimanding me with harsh voices.

I get out of the truck, snagging the garbage bag I brought along. It billows in the wind behind me like a dark sail. The tree looks like shit: the ribbons I tied on with freezing fingers in anticipation of telling Alex I loved her are ripped to shreds, the ends frayed and brittle. A few of the ornaments have blown off and I step on one accidentally. It breaks with hardly any resistance and a million silver shards scatter across the snow.

I'll never be able to get all the pieces. They'll sink down into the ground with the winter melt, nonbiodegradable witnesses of my failed night that will never rot, just release whatever chemicals they're painted with. I try to scoop everything up, but every time I think I've got it, the sun hits another piece, and soon my gloves are soaking wet, my fingers are painfully crooked, and I've spent a half hour trying to pick up one goddamn ornament and I am pissed.

The part of me that's held on to everything I know is swelling, a bitter anger that inflames my heart and sends my blood pushing through my veins too hard, shooting black spots across my vision as I head back to the truck. Dad's ax is in the back, and it's heavy in my hand as I take my first swing, the tree shuddering under the blow. Ornaments fall and are crushed under my boots but I keep swinging, the pressure in my chest lightening a little with each connection, the head of the ax sticky with sap.

I regret it when I'm halfway through, but it's too late.

The tree leans heavily to one side, the red ribbons now faded to pink dragging on the ground. I stomp down hard on the trunk, right above the deep notch where I killed it, and the *snap* reverberates through the woods.

It's almost dark by the time I get home but I haul the tree out to the woodpile anyway, drag out Dad's chainsaw, and start tearing in. Mom comes out, coat wrapped tight around her body, a question on her face. I wave her away, sawdust flying around me as I take off the limbs, one by one, needles carpeting the ground at my feet. Dad gets home and I see Mom talking to him through the kitchen window, hands moving, as alarmed as the birds in the woods.

By the time Dad comes out the cutting is done. He helps me stack in silence, not commenting on the ornament hooks still clutching in some places, or the strands of wrecked ribbon mixed with the chips on the ground. We finish and he claps a hand on my shoulder.

"Well, that's done," he says. As if cutting down a tree and stacking green wood we won't be able to burn for a year was on the list of things to do today. "Come inside and get some supper."

I nod that I will and he goes without looking back, somehow knowing that the crazy thing I just did was healthier for me than all the normal shit I've been doing every day just to get by. My arms are like lead and my feet drag as I walk to the house. I'll sleep well tonight, solidly. I'll put today behind me, get through tonight.

And maybe tomorrow I won't think of Alex the moment I open my eyes.

"I'm calling it," I say.

"What's that?" Sara asks from the passenger seat.

"It's time for Emergency Girlfriend Pact."

She glances up from her phone. "For who?"

"Alex."

She looks back down at her screen, thumbs flashing. "Hmmm."

I stop at a light, and reach over to knock the phone out of her hands. "Seriously."

Sara sighs. "Fine. But she's your friend, not mine."

"As long as you're in. I may need backup."

I drive to Alex's house and we stand on the doorstep for a few minutes, listening to the knocker echo through the insides. Sara huddles against the cold, hands jammed in her pockets.

"Nobody home," she proclaims.

"Just because nobody's answering doesn't mean nobody's home in this house." I take a chance, twist the knob, and shove my shoulder into the door. It pops open grudgingly and I tumble inside.

"Seriously?" Sara says, but there might be a note of admiration in her voice.

"Alex?" I call out, her name ringing back at me from the pristine walls.

"Claire?" She comes to the top of the stairs, a paperback in her hands. "Why are you here?"

"Girls' night," I declare, climbing toward her, Sara behind me. "Let's go."

"I . . ." Alex glances from me to Sara, unsure.

Sara looks down at Alex's bare feet. "You're going to need shoes," she says. And this simple statement gets Alex moving, bundling into a coat and pulling on a hat as we go out the door.

"You're shotgun," Sara insists as she climbs into the back.

"What's this all about?" Alex asks as I pull out of her driveway.

"We're celebrating," I tell her.

"Celebrating what? My kidnapping?"

"Peekay has enacted Emergency Girlfriend Pact," Sara says.

"We do this anytime one of us goes through a breakup," I explain. "We're celebrating your liberation from having a boyfriend."

"Or in my case, a girlfriend," Sara adds.

"We're going to drink too much and eat too much. Fuck the world," I say.

"She doesn't mean that last one as a verb, does she?" Alex turns in her seat to ask Sara, and I see a twist of a smile on her face in the rearview mirror.

"No," Sara answers. "But the first two are definites. I ordered pizza."

"And I called in Chinese," I say. "Any requests?"

"Um . . . I like cheeseburgers."

"Done." Sara is texting in the back. "Lila is working at the grease palace. And my brother is at the state store tonight, so hooch is covered."

"So where are we going right now?"

"This is the best part," I say as I pull into the dollar store, put the car in park, and give Alex a once-over.

"I think Code Yellow," I say to Sara.

"Absolutely not," she says, leaning forward and protectively cupping her hands around Alex's ponytail. "You're not stripping out these raven tresses. Code Red, all the way."

"Explanation?" Alex asks me, one eyebrow high.

"This is the part where we buy cheap dye, go home,

get drunk, and color each other's hair."

To my surprise, Alex is the first one out of the car.

We have eaten ourselves to the point of physical pain, had too much to drink, and started a fire in the pit in my backyard, which probably wasn't the smartest choice considering our blood alcohol levels and the fresh chemicals in our hair. But it doesn't matter. My mom and dad are at a church retreat for married couples and we're making the most of it.

"You can really pack it in," Sara says to Alex. "You weren't kidding when you said you like cheeseburgers."

"I do." Alex nods, her gaze a little unfocused. "I really do."

"You're staying the night," I inform her, and she nods, the foil wrappers in her hair catching the light from the flames.

"Time?" I ask Sara, who glances at her phone, her own wrappers falling forward into her face.

"We've got ten minutes," she says. "Then we're matchy matchy."

"Somewhat," I say. We decided highlights were best, a little red shot through Alex's black hair that would complement our darker browns as well.

"It'll give your face some lift," Sara explained as she mixed the chemicals, the tang burning the inside of our noses. Alex nodded as if she understood what that meant and I had to smother a smile.

"Thank you," Alex says, leaning toward me now across the fire.

I touch the neck of my bottle to hers and Sara pops a fresh one for herself.

"Are we friends?" Alex asks Sara suddenly.

Sara takes a pull on her cider, touching her own foil and then Alex's. "Looks like it," she says. "Once enacted, Emergency Girlfriend Pact cannot be revoked. We have matching hair now. This is serious shit."

Alex smiles, her gaze going to the fire. "I'm sorry about your uncle," she says. As usual, her words carry more weight than necessary, making it sound like she was personally responsible rather than offering condolences.

Sara freezes for a second, her eyes meeting mine. I nod to let her know that I'd let Alex in on the situation, hoping that was okay.

"Well," Sara sighs heavily. "I know it might sound terrible, but it kind of made some things easier for my family. We didn't have to think about, you know, pressing charges or anything like that. It was just . . . taken care of." Sara snaps her fingers.

Alex nods, as if this makes sense to her.

"But they told us he burned," Sara continues, all

lightness gone from her voice. "Usually it's the smoke that gets them or whatever, but he burned. And I can't even imagine that kind of pain. I don't think anyone should go that way, but it's what happened."

"Yeah," Alex says.

"Hey, good job killing the mood," I tell them.

Sara shrugs. "Sorry."

"It needed to be said," Alex adds.

"I'm officially changing the subject." I reach into the dollar store bag by my side, searching for something I bought while Alex wasn't looking.

Sara's eyes light up, and she claps her hands. "Oh, you're going to love this," she tells Alex.

"What?"

I whip out a plastic tiara, complete with gaudy gemstones, and put it on Alex, hooking the attached barrettes into her hair. "You're wearing that to school on Monday," I tell her. "It's the Breakup Tiara."

She nods as if this makes perfect sense, and it slips down below one eye.

"I definitely will," she says, and we all clink bottles as it starts to snow.

ALEX

I have friends.

There are people who like me, and I have discovered that I like them. Today I am wearing a child's toy on my head, walking around the school as if this were perfectly normal. When I turn my head the tips of my hair fall over my shoulder and I see the faintest shade of red shot through, enough to reflect the light. I touch my hand to it, rubbing my own hair between my fingers and thinking about the fact that somewhere in the school are two other girls with streaks exactly the same color as mine.

I feel a burst of warmth in my gut, like the fire from Claire's backyard didn't go out but was trans-ferred to my insides, a place protected from the wind and snow. A place where I can think about their faces in the fire's light and how they smiled when I talked, and answered me. How they listened and I heard them too and how we all slept on the floor in the living room, perfect trust sending our bodies into a deep unconsciousness.

"Hey, Alex, did you know that you're a slut?" Sara yells at me from the bathroom stall as Peekay checks her makeup in the mirror.

"This is news," I call back.

Sara comes out, buttoning her jeans. "Well, it says so in Branley's handwriting on the back of that door, just FYI."

"Congrats," Claire says, expertly smudging her eyeliner with the tip of her finger. "You've been denounced in the bathroom. You're officially normal."

I take her eyeliner from her and smear out Branley's accusation, telling Claire I'll buy her new makeup. She laughs, and Sara takes the pen, turning my nondescript smudge into a huge piece of shit that is startlingly accurate.

There's a code here that I never knew how to read until now, and it's more than just the high fives other girls are giving me in the hallways when they spot my tiara. Now that I'm out, I am seeing the way some of them talk to one another, not guarded and looking for hurt, but open. The flash of teeth and the upward lilt in a voice when it's spoken by a mouth that's smiling; these are all things that were foreign to me.

I'm learning.

48. **PEEKAY**

Spring means kittens. And we are drowning in them.

It's only April, and Rhonda says things will get worse before they get better, but that seems to be Rhonda's attitude toward everything so I take it with a grain of salt. When Park comes in through the shelter's front door with a box full of mewling babies, I try to tell myself my heart jumped into my throat because I like kittens—and that's all.

We agreed that we're just having fun for now, waiting out the last few months of high school with each other so that we don't have to be alone. Park got a decent base-ball scholarship to a private school in Kentucky, and I'm headed to the Lutheran college, where preachers' kids get a deep discount. So there's already a countdown clock on my new relationship, but I've been telling myself that I'm okay with that.

"Hey," he calls as soon as he sees me, raising the box in the air. "We've got it backward, babe; you're supposed to be the one delivering pussy."

I swat at his arm, but not too hard. "Where'd you find them?"

"Down by Lick Creek."

"You sure there's no mom?"

He shakes his head. "Nope. Whatever asshole dumped them found it in his heart to set out a bowl of milk for them as a going-away present. They—"

"—just crawled through it and got wet, yeah." I take his hand and pull him in the back, where we've set up a kitten room. It's lined with heated beds, and well stocked with bottles and replacer formula. Alex is cross-legged on the ground, a tabby the size of her fist tucked in the crook of her arm while he takes his bottle.

"Someone else is in line for your love," I announce.

"Also, I brought kittens," Park adds. "Hey, Alex."

She glances up. "Hey. How many?"

"Three," he says, and Alex sets aside the tabby she's holding, who screams in protest when she tucks him in with his littermates.

"One for each of us, then," Alex says, reaching into the box and handing me a kitten. Park takes a couple of steps back when she offers him a white one roughly the size of a mouse.

"Uh . . . I don't—"

"They need to get warm," Alex says matter-of-factly, wrapping it in a heated towel and putting it into Park's hands. "Keep it close to your body."

I sink to the floor with my kitten and Park kind of slumps in defeat next to me while Alex mixes fresh formula. I show Park how to hold the bottle at the right angle and pretty soon all three of us are cupping kittens in our elbows, the only sound in the room their frantic suckling as they fill their empty bellies.

I glance up at Park and once again remind myself not to get in too deep. He's adorable with the bottle clenched in his huge hand, eyes locked onto the kitten. I kind of love his hands. They're huge and knuckly, so very male. I was worried that the first time he touched me I would freeze up, only able to think of vomiting in Alex's bathroom and the heavy smell of rubbing alcohol as I dumped a full bottle on my crotch. But it wasn't like that. Ray Parsons doesn't even exist when Park's hands are on me.

But I don't think I'm in love. I don't think I was ever in love with Adam, either. I just had him for so long that the idea of someone else getting him made me feel like I'd been robbed of something that belonged to me, but not something I couldn't live without.

I knew I was really over him when Branley dumped Adam right before prom tickets went on sale, and I didn't think twice before accepting the one that Park bought me. And maybe I imagined it, but I think there might have been a little spark of panic in his eyes when he handed it to me, like our let's-have-fun arrangement might be off now that Adam was available again.

The only reason Adam being free means anything to me is because Branley ditched him the second there was trouble between Alex and Jack, and now she's attached to Jack like a parasite. A really gorgeous parasite, true, but a life-sucker nonetheless. Jack can't get away from her. The day the guidance counselor announced his academic full ride to Hancock, Branley marched straight to the office and got her own application.

I wasn't in love with Adam. I'm pretty sure I'm not in love with Park.

Alex and Jack, they were in love.

I shift my kitten and he lets out a pathetic little noise that breaks the silence.

"He finished?" Alex asks.

"I think so." I lift him up, his belly now round and full. "Time to pee," I tell him.

"Uh . . . ," Park says, glancing between me and Alex.

"You have to make them go to the bathroom," Alex

explains. "They won't do it on their own."

Park's eyes get really big and I laugh at him. "You're excused," I say, taking his kitten from him and pulling a momma cat from the pile of stuffed animals in the corner.

"Holy shit," Park says when he sees it, and I can't help but blush a little.

Rhonda sewed a line of plastic nipples on the stuffed momma cats, explaining to us that kittens will suck for comfort, even if they're not getting any food. And while it's certainly true that the orphans adore their new moms, it does make for some awkward moments in the human world.

"It's a titty kitty," Park says, reaching for it, but I yank it away.

"Time for you to go," I warn him, and glance back at Alex. "You okay on your own for a minute?"

"Yep," she says, eyes still locked on her bottle feeder.

I walk Park out to the front, but he grabs my hand at the door. "Is Alex okay?"

"Doing better," I tell him.

"Is she going to prom?"

"No. She doesn't have a date and she said she doesn't want to third-wheel us or Sara."

"Like it would be hard for her to get one."

I choke back a laugh. "Yeah, you should go mention

that to her; just make sure there aren't any needles nearby."

"Tell her to go anyway," Park says. "What else has she got to do? Sit in a room full of stuffed animals with fake nipples?"

"Fair point," I say. "I'll see what I can do."

49. **ALEX**

In my mind there is a scale.

I do not know how many small lives add up to a big one, or if there is a formula to work it out. How many cats do I have to save? How many dogs? How many injured animals on the road do I have to drag to safety, their blood on my hands, their wild-smelling hair on my clothes?

I think if there is a number then it must be very large, and so I keep my eyes open as I drive, when I run, as I walk through the halls at school. I've scooted spiders out of the path of heavy feet, let a field mouse in through the front door in the middle of winter, swerved on ice to miss raccoons. Everything I can think of, anything I can do to make it better.

I want to tell Jack that I'm doing these things, try to show him that if I don't have regret, exactly, then at least I have guilt. I've put the words together, stitched them into sentences at night, hoping in the morning I will have the courage to spit them out like a string, the others flowing more easily after the first. But Branley is always with him, her normalcy so big and bright that I don't want to put myself next to her, my darkness in stark contrast.

So I let it go. I feed the kittens. I listen to Park and Claire in their happiness and I pick up the next orphan in the box.

And the scale tips a tiny bit more.

50. JACK

My free ride came in, a magic carpet in the shape of a piece of paper that people took pictures of me signing.

Mom and Dad are smiling more, my future solidified by the swipe of a pen, though I know Mom's is bittersweet. And I can't even tell her I'll come home a lot, because I won't. Park is going to Kentucky, Branley is following me because her hooks don't extract easily, and the only other person I'd bother coming back for is Alex, who I can't think of without a wash of guilt and the taste of vomit in my throat.

They made a big announcement at school because we haven't had anybody get a full ride since pocket change could pay tuition. They even had the marching band follow me around playing the fight song during one of the class changes. It was awkward and embarrassing and kind of awesome at the same time, and as I walked past the poster that has the senior countdown on it, I swear I choked up. Which doesn't make any sense because all I've ever wanted to do is leave, and I've got a new fight song to learn anyway.

Then I passed Park and he pretended to punch me in the gut and we wrestled each other down to the ground, and the band circled around us, still playing, because they didn't know what else to do. Which was so goddamn funny Park and I started laughing like idiots and then Peekay called us both assholes, and Park grabbed her ankle and pulled her down with us. She held her instrument in the air as she fell and screamed, "Not my trumpet!" which was equally hilarious.

It was a great fucking day, and I could pretend like there were tears in my eyes because I was laughing so hard. Nobody knew it was really because now that I get to leave there's a part of me that's going to miss this place, and nobody knew that when I passed Alex our eyes met, and I saw tears sitting in hers, too.

PEEKAY

You do not just tell Alex Craft she is going to prom.

I'm pretty sure Alex has never done a single thing in her life that she didn't want to do, so finding a way to get her to prom is like casually suggesting to my dad that maybe he should consider Islam instead, just for variety.

Sara still needs a dress, so I told her we were taking Alex with us, hoping that somehow racks of dresses will have the same effect on her that depressed dogs in cages do. But Alex sits silently in the store, watching without comment as Sara parades around in a bunch of dresses. Open torso, slit to the hip, cut to the breastbone, skirt so short you can see the curve of her ass. Finally she puts on a deep purple one with an open back and Alex speaks up.

"That's the one," she says.

They're the first words out of her mouth since she got in the car, so Sara actually listens. I've been spouting out compliments and advice for the better part of an hour. My arms are weighed down with a magenta "maybe" and a flamingo-pink "possibly," but it's Alex's solitary comment that gets Sara's attention.

"Why?" she asks, brow furrowed skeptically as she glances over her shoulder at Alex.

"You've got great back muscles," Alex says.

"I do, don't I?" Sara agrees, checking herself out in the three-way mirror. "So what about you?"

"What about me?"

"Let's see those back muscles, girl."

Alex actually laughs, but she waves Sara off. "I'm not trying on dresses."

"Why not?"

"She *claims* she's not going to prom," I say.

Sara stops admiring herself and turns to glare at Alex. "Don't even tell me it's because of Jack Effing Fisher."

"Not entirely," Alex says. "I just don't want to go."

Sara crosses her arms, and I'm very glad I'm still half-hidden behind a pile of dresses in my arms. "Because of Jack Effing Fisher."

"I—"

"Listen." Sara comes down the three steps from the

elevated mirror to stand in front of Alex, skirt swishing as she walks. "Last year when Alice told me I was just her experiment before she left for college, I wanted to crawl into a hole and die. Like, totally and actually die. But did I do that?"

Alex looks her up and down slowly. "Apparently not."

"I didn't want to go to school because she'd be there. I didn't want to go to practice because she'd be there. I didn't want to be a camp counselor, because she'd be there, too. So I had a choice: I could either not do *any-thing* for the rest of my life, or I could suck it up and act like it didn't bother me. And you know what? If you pretend long enough that it doesn't bother you, pretty soon it actually doesn't."

"She's right," I say, craning my neck over the pile of silk and satin in my arms. "Remember how I was about Adam?"

"Yeah," Sara agrees, hands on her hips. "Pathetic."

"Thanks a lot," I shoot back.

Sara reaches over blindly and pulls a dress out of my arms, the flamingo-pink one with slashes in the torso. "So you're going to put on a dress, Alex Craft, and on Monday you're going to buy a prom ticket."

"I don't think that's my color," Alex says.

"Then pick your own damn dress," Sara says, and punches her in the arm.

Alex punches her back, and I bet anything they're both going to have bruises, but it doesn't matter because Alex is going through the racks, sliding hangers aside to give each dress a once-over before moving on.

"Thanks," I say to Sara.

"For what?"

"I've been racking my brains trying to think of a way to talk her into going to prom. I never considered just yelling and punching her till she caved."

"Well, if nothing else works, we'll just leave a trail of cheeseburgers up to the country club," Sara says.

"I heard that," Alex's voice soars out from the racks.

"Don't tell me it wouldn't work," Sara calls back.

Alex emerges with a few choices and we riffle through them, Sara sending her into the dressing room with firm instructions to make sure we see *all* of them, no cheating. I lean back in my chair while Sara tells me about the girl she's bringing from Waterloo, and I'm not thinking about Adam or Park or anything.

And it's really, really nice.

52. **JACK**

Shit. Shower. Shave. This is how a guy gets ready for prom.

Branley has been getting ready for two days. Yesterday was phase one, which involved a very long salon appointment that she informed me consisted mostly of waxing, and made a big deal out of telling me they had to order more wax ahead of time because she was *very thorough*. Today is phase two. Phase two is pedicure, manicure, hair, and makeup. She fills me in on the brand of makeup that, again, the salon had to order because the one place in town that will do facials doesn't carry the high-end stuff. And I couldn't give less of a fuck, but senior prom is going to be her crowning achievement, and there's a part I'm supposed to play.

I know I'll end up in bed with her. Tonight I'm going to get drunk, probably be an asshole to a few people, and then I'm going to screw Branley because she wants me to. And if I'm being honest, the bottom half of me is into it, even if the top—where my brain and my heart are—knows that it's all wrong and I shouldn't go to the lodge that a whole bunch of us went in on together for after prom.

I shouldn't go because if I do I'm the same Jack Fisher who started senior year, the guy who was led around by his dick and drank too much. The guy who hadn't ever been in love or had his heart broken. A guy who never knew Alex Craft. But that guy was also happier in a lot of ways. He didn't know things that I know.

I wipe the rest of the shaving cream off my chin, let Mom snap a couple of pictures of me in my tux, and then I head out the door. At Branley's house there's a whole process involved. Her parents make me wait in the living room and she actually comes down the stairs to me, like we're getting married or something. They video my reaction, and I don't have to fake it. She looks amazing. Stunning. Absolutely gorgeous.

I tell her that, and I mean it, and she actually blushes a little. I can see it under all the makeup and it makes me want to tell her to wash her face, put on a pair of jeans, and we'll go up to the lodge early, wade in the stream like we used to when we were kids. But her mom is pinning a boutonniere on me (tinted to perfectly match Branley's dress—sea-foam green—I know this because I've been informed many, many times), and if I said let's drop the shit and just be ourselves there'd be hundreds of dollars thrown away.

So I put on my fake smile and her parents take about a thousand pictures and tell us what a beautiful couple we make, and I bite down on my lip because I don't know if we are a couple or ever have been. Branley laughs and smiles, rests her head on my shoulder, leaving behind a smudge of makeup on my jacket that I really hope will come off because I can't afford to pay any kind of cleaning fee.

Then we're in the car and I'm trying to drive but Branley keeps putting her hand on my leg, her head on my arm, touching me so much that it's distracting more than erotic and all I can think about is that this is what college will be like. She'll follow me around and her hands will be on me all the time, feeling, touching, needing, and I'll give her whatever she wants because I always have and that'll just make it worse. My grades will slip and I'll lose my scholarship and have to drop out, and Branley will follow me home and *fuck* I probably will end up marrying her and we'll have kids and they'll go up to the church to make out with the kids of the people we're going to see at prom tonight.

"Stop touching me," I say, my voice so hollow she actually listens.

I glance over and I can tell she's hurt but I can't let it bother me, not after the thoughts that just chased through my brain, an endless loop that I can't stop picturing.

Prom is a sea of colors, all of them vying for attention, much like the girls wearing them. Red, green, blue, a few brave souls in yellow, a couple of colors I'm pretty sure don't even have names and definitely don't occur in nature. What I see the most of, though, is flesh, everywhere. Technically prom is supposed to follow dress code, but the teachers know that if they toss some kid who spent hundreds of bucks on a prom dress they'll have to deal with a pissed-off parent, whether it shows her areolae or not.

So there's legs and tits everywhere, quite a few midriffs. Shiny white teeth flashing out from behind lips coated with gloss, shining unnaturally beneath the lights. I brought a flask and I've been helping myself a little more than is probably smart, but I don't know how else to deal with this night. I tell Branley I need to sit a song out, that if I keep moving I might lose the chicken cordon bleu I paid thirty bucks for all over her dress. It's a threat to her perfection, so she allows me to go.

I'm sitting at our table, fishing in my jacket pocket for the flask, when I see the hole in the brightness, a spot of darkness that stands out among the chaos. Alex is weaving through the crowd in a brown dress that probably looked like a bag on the hanger but looks better than sex on her. It covers everything it should but hugs close, giving you an outline of what's underneath that is way hotter than just going ahead and showing it.

Branley looks fantastic, no doubt. She looks like the perfect teenage prom date, a little kid playing dress-up. Alex looks like a *woman*, like an adult who has already seen it all and doesn't need to prove shit. She heads for a table on the far side, where I see Sara and her date in matching dresses.

Branley's watching me over the shoulder of her dance partner, eyes slit like a cat ready to pounce. I grab my punch glass and tip the flask into it under the table, almost dumping half the drink when Peekay flops into the chair next to me.

"Hey, asshole, dance with me," she says.

It's not the most flattering invitation I've ever had, but I know Park brought his own flask and it looks like Peekay got in on that action early. She drags me onto the floor so hard I'm tripping to avoid stepping on the back of her dress, which drags even though she has on heels. Even with the shoes her face just hits my chest, so I'm looking down into her fairly flushed cheeks as we start to dance.

"You see Alex?" she asks.

"Yeah."

"She looks good, right?"

There's no harm in my admitting that, so I nod, trying to steer us away from Branley so she can't overhear our conversation.

"So what's up with that?" Peekay pushes on.

"What do you mean?"

Peekay rolls her eyes, and suddenly one very pointy, nicely painted fingernail is digging into my chest. "You listen to me, Jack Effing Fisher," she says. "Branley's run-of-the-mill. She's a golden retriever, you got me? Alex is an Irish wolfhound." The nail pushes in a little farther.

"An *Irish wolfhound*," she repeats, red-rimmed eyes daring me to contradict her. "And you can't just walk away from that."

She's so mad at me I don't know if I'm going to get the chance to explain that I just came to that realization—or something like it that didn't include dog breeds—a few minutes ago. I pick her up by her elbows and lift her so that we're face-to-face, which at least gets the digging nail out from my skin. She's so surprised she stops talking.

"I know," I say, and the depths of how well I know it

must show because Peekay suddenly smiles, transforming her whole face. I put her back down and she barrel hugs me, little arms stronger than I expected.

"If Branley is a golden retriever and Alex is an Irish wolfhound, then you're a pissed-off cocker spaniel," I say.

"With rabies," she adds. "And don't you forget it." She bares her teeth at me and disappears into the crowd.

I'm at the edge of the dance floor, Alex's table only a few feet away, the doubts of the past few months reduced to nothing. My mind is trying to piece together an argument against it, but my heart knows what it wants and my feet are already moving in her direction. It's not a decision so much as instinct, and I'm beside her, my hand on hers as I say her name.

She looks at me, her eyes even bigger with a dash of eyeliner around them.

"Can we talk?" I ask.

She nods, takes my hand, and leads me out of the room, out to the balcony where the fresh air and Alex beside me is the most sobering thing I've ever experienced. I don't want to say stupid things. I don't want to tell her she looks nice or say I didn't expect to see her. I only want to talk about the things that matter, the things that have been rolling around in my brain for months, knocking into all the normal things I'm trying to concentrate on and throwing them off course. But the only thing that comes out is the truth, simple and impossible at the same time.

"I want you," I say.

Her face lights up, the lingering shadows I've noticed from afar for the past few months thrown aside as she smiles, her expression the only answer I need. And somehow that was the most important part. Now that it's been said, I feel like everything else, no matter how horrible, is manageable.

"You're sure?" she says, her eyes searching my face.

"I need to ask you some things first," I say. "Are you coming to the lodge after?"

"Claire and Park are, but I don't think I'm invited."

"I'm inviting you."

She raises an eyebrow. "Is that okay?"

"There'll be so many people there no one will know either way. We can't talk here. Branley will be on me any second and she might throw her drink in your face."

Alex shrugs. "Then I'll kill her."

I almost laugh, but the sound gets stuck in my throat. Alex watches me for a second in silence. "Kidding," she adds. "I have criteria."

And then I do laugh, an expulsion of all the darkness that's been inside me since I was with her last, confusion pouring out of me into this bright moment of clarity.

She slips away from me, back into the swirl of chaotic color that we just escaped, and I rest my head in my hands.

I know there's a wrongness encapsulating everything, that Alex has done something terrible—maybe more than I know. But buried underneath all the questions and answers I might not want to hear is a very hard kernel of truth.

I'm in love with this girl.

And that's what I'm holding on to right now, in this moment.

I carry that peace with me to the lodge. Nothing penetrates the buoyancy that's filled me since I locked eyes with Alex, said the words that have built up for so long.

Branley separates from me at the door, trailing a finger down the front of my chest and telling me it's time for her to move to phase three of getting ready. I nod, well aware that I'm about to disappoint her. She disappears into a bathroom and I take a beer from the fridge, wind my way through groups of people.

There's a decent pool game going. Some of the guys already managed to alienate their dates by paying more attention to the Xbox than them. Peekay and Park are curled up on the couch together, involved in each other and not their beers. Everyone says hi to me. A couple of girls ask where Branley is, but I fend them off, eyes roaming the crowd for the one person who matters.

I spot her on the deck, back turned to the house. She switched out the dress for a dark green hoodie and jeans, but her hair is still up in a knot. I slip out the back door and she turns with a half smile, hand out to me.

"Ready?" she asks.

My phone goes off and I've got a pic from Branley. She's sprawled on a bed, wearing a little red nothing, rose petals strewn on the sheets around her. She's seductive, gorgeous, amazing. The wet dream of 99 percent of the male population.

I'm ready. Are you coming?

I text back a simple answer—no—aware it's going to land me in a shitstorm later. Then I turn off my phone.

"Ready," I say, and I take Alex's hand.

I walk away from the lodge, the heat, the people, the light.

I walk into the dark with Alex.

My spine is vibrating as if it would erupt from my back, singing in the night air as we find a downed log to sit on, the moon lighting our path.

"Tell me," he says. "Tell me everything."

So I talk.

"After Anna, I was numb. It started in my heart, like a defense mechanism so that I wouldn't feel all the pain. But it pumped through my veins, flowing into my head. I couldn't feel anything, ever. I wasn't even sad. My entire body, my mind, everything was like scar tissue. Insensitive. Dead. Protective."

He nods. I've seen his body, know it well. Scar tissue is something he understands.

"I felt the first thing in a long time when they let

Comstock get away with it," I say. Jack's head drops, a groan escaping, trailed by the fog of his breath.

"You were just a freshman," he says.

"The only thing stopping us is ourselves," I say, and he covers his face with his hands. I don't know what he's thinking, but it's been said and can't be taken back. Like so many other things.

So I tell him.

I tell Jack about Comstock's drunkenness and the baseball bat, the metallic ring of metal against skull, and how he slid to the ground like a bag of water. I talk about my strength as I lifted him onto the chair, the hammer and the nails, the sucking sound of his lung trying to re-inflate, the flow of everything I needed being provided to me in the moment. The easiness of it all convincing me that everything was as it should be.

I tell him and he listens, his head still in his hands as the frogs begin to sing around us as they grow accustomed to my voice. I go on.

"I was a scar, inside and out. Claire came along and started picking at the edges, her fingers finding a way to open me a little. And then you. You tore me apart and now I'm a fresh wound, open to the air and the infection all around me. Everything gets in and everything hurts. I'm this raw, bleeding thing feeling everything for the first time, the joy and the pain. When Sara called Claire that night at the church—"

His fingers are on my lips. "Stop."

"I thought you should know," I say.

"I do know. I know and I'm still here, right next to you."

I'm crying and so is he, the heat from our faces evaporating into the night. I fall into him and we just hold each other, arms wrapped so tightly I don't know where he ends and I begin and it doesn't matter anyway. We pull apart and he puts his hands on either side of my face, tears sliding away under his thumbs.

"Can you stop?" he asks.

I don't know. I've wondered myself, had so many moments when the words were in my mouth, the necessary sounds to both damn and save me unable to find their way out under the grim stare of my mother.

"I don't know," I tell him.

"Can you try? For me?"

"Yes," I say, and his eyes catch all the light of the moon as he smiles.

"We can do this," he says, hands dropping to mine to squeeze tight. "I've got a good scholarship to Hancock. Come with me. You've got the grades. Pay the late application fee and just fucking leave. We'll go together, get you some help."

His hands leave mine to spin in the air, helping to

weave this tale of hope and the future. Something that might actually happen now that this weight is not on my heart, every beat a struggle.

"Yes," I say.

"Maybe we can get an apartment, live off campus," he goes on, now that I've confirmed this daydream could become a reality. "I don't have a lot of money but I'll get a job, do whatever it takes."

"We'll get a dog," I say.

"An Irish wolfhound," he says emphatically.

And I'm laughing. Laughing at his optimism, his absolute conviction that everything is going to be okay.

But maybe he's right.

Maybe it will be.

54. PEEKAY

Branley's shit is so lost it wouldn't matter if it was microchipped.

I nearly jump out of my skin when she busts out of an upstairs bedroom, the door hitting the wall so loudly it stops the party dead. She's nearly naked and fisting a wine bottle that looks to be empty, all her eye makeup now streaking down her face in a multicolored river of tears.

"Where the fuck is Jack?" she screams, and Park and I immediately shrink into each other a little bit.

Everyone is staring for different reasons. The girls because witnessing the top of the pyramid take a tumble is a spectator sport, and the guys because Branley is on a balcony and not wearing any underwear.

"Where?" she screams again, raising the wine bottle as if she's about to throw it on the head of anyone who withholds information.

"Branley, honey . . . ," Lila says cautiously, climbing the steps toward what can only be her utter annihilation.

"Don't you *honey* me," Branley yells, scanning the downstairs for a target. Her eyes catch mine and I will her to be drunk enough not to recognize me.

"Is Alex here?" she demands. "Did she fucking come *here*?"

My tongue feels like it's glued to the roof of my mouth, but I don't need to answer because Branley is already coming down, bare feet slipping on the last few steps. Lila catches her but she jerks her arm away, gaze still locked on mine.

"Bran, I think maybe—" Park begins.

"I'm not talking to you," Branley interrupts. "I'm talking to Peekay." She points at me, her finger a bare inch from my face.

It's the nails that get me. I know Branley, like it or not, and she aims for nothing less than perfection. Earlier tonight those nails were glossy, buffed, manicured, the pearlescent hue accenting the blue of her dress in tiny complementary ways that only someone who spent a few hours poring over colors would appreciate.

And now those nails are gone. Ragged. Bitten to the quick. Even the tender skin alongside the nail beds has been chewed. I don't know how long Branley has been upstairs alone, but she drained a bottle of wine and gnawed at herself before the anger drove her down here.

She tried. That's what I'm seeing in the damaged hand sticking in my face, the tracks of ruined eye makeup running down her cheeks. Branley tried to keep her abandonment to herself, tried to not make a scene, tried to retain some dignity.

And it's leaking away, right now, right in front of me. The girls are using one hand to cover sly smiles and the guys aren't even trying to hide the fact that they're taking pics of Branley in her lingerie.

"C'mon," I say, dragging a blanket off the back of the couch and throwing it around her shoulders. A little sigh escapes her and she sort of collapses forward into me, all her energy gone now that the anger has been spent. I lead her to the bathroom and she slumps into a corner, tanned legs now riddled with goose bumps.

I wet a washcloth and start working on her face, wiping away the layers of makeup that she painstakingly applied before, all of it for Jack. I wash away the remnants of lipstick, now feathered and cracked instead of decorating his body the way she'd planned. I clean her face while she sobs, her shoulders going up and down in a silent dance of bottomless sadness that I'm only too familiar with.

Branley's heart is broken and it's Jack Fisher who's done it to her.

I can't help but comfort her, wrapping the blanket around her tightly while she searches for words, telling me things that I'm not meant to hear. There are a couple of hesitant knocks, quiet questions whispered through the door by girls who *only want to help*, but Branley tells them all to go away. It's me she wants, me she's pouring herself into. And as Alex's friend, I'm the worst possible choice.

"Does he love her?" Branley asks, her fist tight around a tissue.

"I don't know," I tell her, glad I can answer honestly. "If he said so, she never told me."

"But what do you *think*?"

I wish I could say *I don't know* again, but I saw Jack's face when he spotted Alex tonight at prom, have watched him try to move through every day that they've been apart as if he wasn't being torn in two.

"Yeah, he loves her," I say. "And I'm pretty sure she loves him."

I thought Branley would break down again when I said it, but she just nods as if I've confirmed the inevitable and blows her nose.

"It's all I've got, you know," she says.

"What?"

"This." She indicates her drop-dead body with a casual wave. "I'm not smart or funny or mysterious."

"Uh, you're hot," I tell her. "That goes a long way."

"Nope," she says, shaking her head. "What have I got left? Ten years? Fifteen? How long before my tits sag and my hair goes gray and I get wrinkles? How much makeup will I have to wear to compete with the other women who are interesting so people listen to them, who got good jobs because they're smart, who got Jack because they're mysterious? How long before my husband gets bored and bangs a younger version of me because I don't have it anymore?"

Branley just asked me a long line of really depressing questions and I don't have answers for any of them. I think she's selling herself short because I've glanced at her papers when they come back and she pulls Cs. She might not be Ivy League, but she's not a dumbass, and being nice might go a long way if she, you know . . . tried practicing it a little bit more. I don't tell her these things because she's drunk as shit and barreling on and probably wouldn't remember anyway.

"This is what I am," she says. "And I've only got so much time to use it in, so that's what I've done and it wasn't always the right thing and maybe it didn't even make me feel good sometimes."

She blows her nose again, and wads up the tissue. I hand her a fresh.

"I'm sorry about Adam," she says.

I've put him so far behind me that it takes a second for me to put it together, like maybe he died in the past couple of days and no one told me and Branley is offering her condolences.

I start giggling.

"Why is that funny?" Branley asks.

I explain and she actually cracks a smile, the skin around her swollen eyes crinkling with the effort. "You know what I mean," she says.

"Yeah, I know. Don't worry about it."

"Seriously. I made you feel the way I do right now," she says, tears welling again. "And I wouldn't wish it on anybody."

I look at the water leaking from her eyes, the new flush creeping up her cheeks. "Me neither," I say.

And I hold Branley's hand as she cries.

55. **JACK**

The world is new and I am reborn in it.

Sure, spring always feels this way. It's like we forget how to live over the winter. Our lungs do the job of pushing the stale cooped-up-in-the-house air in and out to keep us alive. We move from building to car to the next building as fast as possible, backs hunched against the wind, faces hid in hoods and hats, eyes on the ground as we go. Joy leaks out of your body in the winter and whatever isn't sheltered is frozen solid.

But it's more than the thaw that's in my system and I'm not very good at hiding it. Even Park has told me to get that fucking grin off my face more than once. I'm stupid in love, and broadcasting it onto everything I see. The grass is greener, the air warmer, the baseballs a brighter shade of white.

The senior countdown is in the single digits, Alex and me neck-and-neck for the valedictorian spot and loving every second of goading each other. I try to delay her in the halls with a long kiss, telling her that she doesn't need to study, and she responds by biting my lip just enough to let me know it won't be that easy.

"Get a room," Park yells as he passes, arm slung around Peekay's neck.

I throw a pen at him but he snatches it out of midair and I spot Branley ducking into a classroom down the hall, the bright sheen of her hair unmistakable. I can't deny there's a stab in my gut when I see her, a trailing wound left behind that smacks of guilt. I ignore it, focusing instead on Alex's freckles, darker now that she's been coming to my baseball games.

"See you tonight?" I ask.

"Girls' night," Alex says, shaking her head.

"You can see Peekay anytime," I counter.

"I can see *you* anytime."

I can't argue with that. With Alex officially accepted into Hancock and Peekay going to the Lutheran school, it'd be selfish to keep her to myself now when I'll see her as much as I want later.

"Okay," I say. "I'll figure out something else."

Park's been on my ass about going hunting with him

before turkey season is over, even though I know we'll probably just end up drinking in the woods. And I'm cool with that, but my phone vibrates in my pocket before the bell rings at the end of the day. It's a text from Branley, which hasn't happened in weeks. We had it out over the phone the day after prom, her hysterics rising and swelling so much I put her on speaker because I couldn't stand it right next to my ear. But I deserved it and I knew it, so I let her anger break over me in waves and never argued with anything she said.

And she said some pretty terrible things. I was just using her for sex (I could claim the same), I never cared about her at all (I almost wish that were true), I was a player and a liar and a son of a bitch. And I have been those things, all of them. So I let her say them, and hoped this was how I paid my dues.

I'm expecting more of the same now, a last volley of hate that she needs to get out of her system before we can move past it. Instead it's simple.

can we talk?

I don't know. Can we? The truth is that I want to. Branley might have fallen in love with me slowly without my knowing it, but when she fell out, it was a firestorm from hell that eradicated our friendship.

Alex is in my blood and fills my mind. I'd like to say that my whole heart is hers as well, but there's a

corner of it that belongs to Branley by right. A part
filled with firecrackers and crawdads and my childhood.
My thumbs move across the keypad.

what's up?

Wnt to tell u I'm stl going 2 Hancock. Nvr wuz 4 u. They've got
a gd RN prgm.

They do have a good RN program, and Branley would
make an excellent nurse. But I don't know how much I'm
supposed to say right now.

cool

Apparently that wasn't enough, because my phone
rings two seconds later. I hesitate for a moment before
answering, but as usual Branley gets her way.

"Hey."

"Hey," she says back, her voice the version I like,
pitched low and normal. It's not the Branley who wants
something, high and pouty.

"It's no big deal about Hancock. I never thought you
were going there just because of me anyway," I say.

"Other people did," she says, and I can't argue with
that. I open my mouth to tell her that Alex will be at
Hancock just in case she hadn't heard, but she keeps
going.

"I've got some of your stuff," she says, which isn't a
huge surprise. I've dumped shit in her locker more than
once, so I didn't have to walk all the way to mine before
lunch. We've carpooled for years. She probably has more

of my own stuff than I do.

"Like what?"

"I don't know, all kinds of shit," she says. "There's, like, a pile. Couple of shirts, a jump drive, some hats. Um . . . at least one pair of boxers."

"Just the one?" I ask before I can help it, a smile twisting my lips.

She giggles. "I washed everything."

"Thank God," I shoot back, and we're both laughing.

"Anyway . . . I wanted to get it all back to you," Branley says. "Can you meet me out at the church in about half an hour?"

"I'll swing by and pick it up."

"That's not a good idea," she says. "I . . . I said some pretty not-nice things about you to Mom and Dad. They're not very happy with you right now."

I sigh. Branley's mom and dad have been my second parents my whole life. Having them *not very happy* with me makes me feel like shit.

"Give it time," she says. "It'll blow over."

"Yeah, I'll meet you in thirty," I say.

"Cool."

She's about to hang up when I stop her. "Hey, Bran?"

"Yeah?"

"We good?"

"Oh yeah," she says, and I can hear the smile. "You and me, we're going to be all right."

A girls' night with Alex is never normal, mostly because she's one girl who hates to be indoors.

Even in the dead of winter, she'd drag me into the backyard and start a fire in the pit, our fronts too hot and our backs too cold as we passed a bottle back and forth. More than once she took me out to the state park, indifferent to my complaining as I trudged behind her on trails so steep wildlife were the only ones using them. But a girls' night with Alex always brought peace with it too, and that's something I've been looking for lately.

All anybody wants to talk about right now is endings. School is almost *out*. *Last* day of senior year. A phase of our lives is almost *over*. An era is drawing to a *close*. I'm really sick of well-meaning advice from people who like to remind me that they were teens *not that long ago.*

Everybody else sees a finish line ahead and I'm stuck on beginnings. My heart tells me that I like Park a little more than we agreed upon when we started seeing each other, and as I glance at Alex as she drives I feel an even deeper sting.

It's hard to believe we've been friends for only a year. This girl knows everything about me, has seen me at my best and worst. We're at the point in our friendship where we can be quiet together and it's not awkward, but we can also both sing in the car very loudly and not be embarrassed because we both sound like shit.

It's like that. And I'm suddenly very aware that it's as temporary as Park and me. She's headed halfway across the state to Hancock, and I'm going halfway the other direction to the Lutheran school. Sure, we can text and email, make promises to *try to get togethe*r soon or when we're home on break. Then when we do go out it'll just be an update, like a folded letter in a Christmas card— *this is what I did since I talked to you last time; now you know.* Then we'll do it again the year after that, each meeting a bullet-point conversation to keep each other informed, but never intimate.

I'm afraid of that happening with all my friends, but Alex the most. She's the one most likely to call bullshit on even perfunctory get-togethers, unhappy with the

charade of being friends when we aren't actually anymore. I want to find a way to say these things, and have
been plowing through a couple of beers to make the
whole thing less awkward while she drives out to a bea-
ver dam she wants to show me (yes, really). She's got her
eyes on the road, humming something that I'm pretty
sure she's making up as she goes, when I blurt out what's
on my mind.

"I wish I had you longer," I say, then blush up to my
ears. "Wait—that sounded weird. What I mean is . . .
never mind. Screw it."

Alex's eyebrows go together and she brakes, pulling
off the road into the shade of a little turnaround in the
woods. "I get it," she says.

My head is humming a little so I just nod, too aware
that I don't have a way with words like she does.

"Claire, listen to me," Alex says, using the tone that
makes dogs sit even when she didn't give the command.
So I listen.

"I didn't have anything for a long time," she says.
"All I knew was my house and school. There was a path
in between the two I never left, like a sleepwalker. You
woke me up, Claire. Pushed me off it and made me see
other paths, other people. Do you realize I wouldn't
even be going to college if it wasn't for you?"

"Really?" I ask, voice small as I pick at a hangnail.

"Yes," Alex says. "After graduation I wouldn't have even had that path anymore. No school. Just home."

"That's no good." I shudder, thinking of Alex stuck at home with her mom, two shadows passing each other without speaking until they both forget how.

"Definitely not," she says, putting the car back in gear and us on the road again. "So don't think that college changes—"

In the cup holder, her phone goes off as a text message comes in.

"Want me to get it?" I ask.

"Sure."

"What the fuck? It's from Branley."

Alex shrugs. "What's it say?"

"Just that she wants to talk to you and can you meet her at the church in half an hour."

Alex doesn't say anything, but takes a left at the next crossroads, which makes my head sing with alarm bells on top of the beer buzz.

"We're not seriously going?"

"Why not?"

"Uh, because she's like your archenemy or something."

"She's not."

"Alex, seriously—"

"Branley's not a bad person. If she wants to talk to

me so she can get some closure, I'm not going to deny her that."

I'm about to say that closure is overrated, but she's already switched back to the conversation before we were interrupted by Branley's text.

"College won't change anything between us, Claire," she says. "The kind of friendship we have doesn't just stop."

I don't want to argue about going to see Branley, so I crack another beer as we head toward the church, the shadows of the woods around us lengthening in the dying light.

57. JACK

I'm the world's biggest idiot.

An idiot for thinking Branley would let me go so easily, for not reading more into her parting shot over the phone, for not questioning why she wanted to meet out at the church and not at her parents' house. I'm an idiot for not taking everything I know about Branley and realizing the equation didn't add up. Branley who doesn't give in. Branley who always gets what she wants. Branley who is sprawled across the altar when I walk in, push-up bra obvious under her cheerleading uniform, lacy panties flashing in my face.

The worst part is, I'm an idiot with a dick, and that part of me is dead curious about what she's got planned.

"Jack," she says, trailing circles with one finger in the

dust on the altar. "I'm glad you came."

"What the fuck are you doing, Branley?" I say, trying to keep my voice even. When she sent me a pic after prom, all I had to do was turn off my phone so I didn't have to see. Now she's right in front of me, and I can't look away.

"How many times, Jack? You and me, right here on this altar . . ." She pitches her voice low and sexy, and I tell myself I'm walking toward her so I can hear and that's the only reason why. "How many times?" she asks again.

A lot. The answer is a lot. Her hair hanging down the side, brushing in the dirt. Our noises echoing back at us from the stone walls. I clear my throat.

"Where's my stuff?" I say.

Her eyes go big and wide, fake surprised. One finger goes to her lipsticked mouth in mock confusion. "Shoot. I forgot it at my house."

"Goddammit, Branley," I say under my breath, but she's smiling at me, the perfect mix of the girl I know so well and one every straight guy in the world wants to fuck. "Get down," I tell her.

She shakes her head. "Come up here with me."

"You know I can't."

"Bullshit, Jack," she says, temper poking through the bedroom act. "You've been mine for years. She can't just take you away, and you can't act like I was nothing."

"You weren't nothing," I say immediately, even though I hate myself for it, especially because it's true.

Her face softens. "Then c'mere," she says. "One more time."

And I'm considering it. What would it really hurt, to say good-bye to Branley in the way she likes best? Alex would never know and goddammit *I want to*. Those are the only reasons why I should, against a million better reasons why I shouldn't. But the wants are louder and more immediate, filling my head as she leans into me, perfumed hair against my cheek.

"Jack," she says into my ear, and my whole body is humming. I think I hear a car outside and I pull away, but her hand is on the front of my pants and I don't move far.

"What was that?" I ask.

"Nothing," she says, hand against me. She's going in for a kiss, but the half second of space between us cleared my head, disrupting everything I want to do and reminding me of what I should.

"Bran," I say, and put my hands on her shoulders. "This isn't happening."

"Dammit, Jack," she hisses. "All I want you to do is fuck me."

"If you won't, I sure as hell will" comes a deep voice from the front of the church.

I spin around, broken glass sliding under my feet,

arms out in front of Branley like somehow I can keep the two guys who just walked in from seeing her. They're hunters, locked and loaded for turkey season, shotguns in hand and a wave of whiskey breath preceding them that tells me bagging a bird wasn't their only goal.

"What you two doing?" the guy out front asks, a twisted smile that says he already knows. He gets closer and I see why the smile goes past a leer and into something worse. It's because he's missing some of his nose.

We recognize each other at the same moment, and Ray Parsons turns back to his buddy, the one Alex never touched because she didn't have to. "Well look who the fuck it is, Billy."

"We're just leaving," I say as I feel Branley's knees poking into my back, her fingers tight on my shoulders. She's breathing fast and shallow, little puckers of air hitting my neck.

"Fuck you are," Ray says. "We've been looking forward to running into you for a long time. Where's your girlfriend, huh? Got a new one? This one ain't so scary, is she, Billy?"

Billy's bloodshot eyes skip right over my shoulder to latch onto Branley. "She ain't scary at all," he says. "Bet you could bend her over in two seconds, Ray."

"Get out of here," Branley says, her voice shaky. "Leave us alone."

"We're not gonna hurt you," Ray says, ignoring me and talking to Branley. He leans his shotgun against the wall next to the door; Billy does the same. "See?" He spreads both hands in front of him but he's still coming toward us, his smile too wide and empty, and Branley knows it.

"I said get the *fuck* out of here," she yells.

"Listen to the mouth on her, Ray," Billy says, following his friend.

Branley's curled into a ball behind me and I've still got my arms out but I don't know what to do with them. If these guys have got more than fucking with us on their minds we're screwed and I know it.

"We don't want any trouble," I say.

"Neither do we," Ray says, and now his chest is inches from mine, the stink of his breath in my face. "But some pussy'll do," he says to Branley.

"Back the fuck off." I shove him, but he barely moves. It doesn't even knock the smile off his face as he reaches around me to grab at Branley's leg.

She yells and kicks, her bare foot striking out to hit him square in the face and splitting his lip open. I take a swing but his friend is on me and the punch hits him in the shoulder instead, not hard enough to do anything other than throw us both off balance as we land on the ground and roll in the dirt, hands grabbing for a hold.

I hear Branley screaming but all I can do is struggle. Billy is stronger than he looks. I get my feet under me but he's on his too and gets my arms pinned behind my back. I buck and kick, swearing a blue streak as I see Ray drag Branley toward him across the altar, her skirt pulling up to show a tiny red thong that covers absolutely nothing.

He smacks her bare ass, leaving a welt. "You came up here looking for something, girl," he says. "And you're getting it."

I'm fighting and twisting, anything I can do to get free, but Billy's got a grip I can't break.

"Ray gets his mind set on something, not much you can do to stop him," Billy says, his tone weirdly conversational. "He's had a bit to drink too. Let him have his fun and nobody'll get hurt. It won't take five minutes."

Five minutes. Like the fucking problem is that we're on a schedule and not that Branley is about to be raped right in front of me. She's kicking and screaming but he's already got her panties off and is going for his belt when I hear the sound of a shotgun being pumped.

There's a moment when I lock eyes with Alex, calm and collected, gun in her hands. I've got the space of a breath to tell her not to.

And I don't.

58. ALEX

This is how I kill someone, the cold steel of a gun unfamiliar in my hand but easy to decipher.

When I pull the trigger he is blown clear off the altar, a spray of blood arcing across Branley's screaming face as he goes. There's another yell, this one low and guttural. I hear someone coming for me, but I don't know how to reload the gun and I always knew it would end this way, regardless. Violence begets violence, and if I want to be a cog in that wheel, I have to accept when it stops on me.

His shoulder hits me right in the sternum and I'm flying, my back arched as I sail over a pew, the first of the stars popping in the night sky trailing across my vision as I land so hard some teeth are knocked loose, slipping down my throat before I have a chance to spit them out.

I hear Jack screaming and Branley crying and a vacuum of silence where Peekay's voice should be, as blood flows down my shoulders so thick it feels like hair, wet and heavy.

This is how I die.

And I am not surprised.

Branley is hysterical, blood running down her face as she slides off the altar and crumples to her knees. She's crawling for her underwear and saying my name over and over, but I go right past her to the other side of the pew. The guy who tackled Alex is leaning against the wall, mouth agape. "Shit," he says, looking up at me. "Shit, shit, shit."

Alex is half on, half off a pile of rubble—the same one we sat on a few months ago when she gave me her number. There's bone sticking out of her arm and her shoulders don't look quite right, but it's what's above that rips a sound from my throat as I go down beside her, hand clutching hers. The back of her head is caved in and blood flows down the rocks, bright red contrasting with the light pink of her brain.

"Alex?" I say, hands on her face, fingers on her open mouth. "Alex?"

Her eyes flutter and a ridiculous hope blooms in my chest. "It's okay," I tell her. "It's okay. You're going to be okay. We're going to fix you."

And I want to, right now with her mind out in front of me. I want to reach inside and pluck out the darkness, find the parts of her that aren't supposed to be there and let the medics sort out the rest. Her fingers tighten on mine, but barely, and I know I'm bullshitting myself.

"Alex." I say her name loudly, needing to say at least one thing. "I wasn't with her, I wasn't with Branley. I wouldn't do that to you." I'm yelling in her face, and the ghost of a smile spreads on her lips.

"I know," she says, her words barely closing the distance between us even though I'm right on top of her. "You're a good person."

And then she's gone, the inches between us nothing as she slips away and I'm only holding what's left behind.

60. PEEKAY

My life is a list of things I didn't do.

I didn't send five bucks to a girl in Africa.

I didn't call the cops after Ray Parsons tried to rape me, so he tried again on someone else.

I didn't tell Branley she's more than tits and ass and legs, so she still believed it.

I didn't stop Alex from coming to the church even though I knew it was a bad idea, so now I'm standing here, empty hands at my side, looking at the blood spattered on the wall. Red trailing fingers point accusingly downward at a body hidden behind the altar.

Branley is on her butt in the dirt rocking back and forth and crying, her underwear in a ball in her hands, tears running down her face. A guy is against the wall saying *shit, shit, shit*, over and over again, like it's the only word he knows. I can see the top of Jack's head over the pew, but Alex isn't getting up and I don't want to know why.

My head is still ringing from the shotgun blast as I make my way over to Branley, but I'm barely lifting my feet and I trip over a beer bottle, the sound of it rolling away empty and hollow. Branley looks up at me but doesn't stop rocking. I sit down next to her, peeling the thong from her hands.

"I'm sorry," she says, words barely seeping out between tears. "I'm sorry, I'm sorry, I'm sorry."

"You should put on your underwear," I tell her. I don't know what else to say and it seems to be the most sensible thing at the moment.

The guy in the corner is still saying *shit shit shit*. Between him and Branley's *I'm sorry*s filling the air I can't make my own words. Jack isn't saying anything either, just leaning over an unmoving Alex, holding her hand against his face. It's limp and loose in his hold, and I try not to look at her blood pooling around our shoes as I crouch next to him.

There are no questions, but I want to ask them anyway. I want to say, *Is she dead? Is she gone? Is she going to be okay?* so that Jack can tell me no, no, and yes. But the words won't come because I know speaking them is useless, even as I reach out and press my warm skin against hers, now cooling.

The litany of *shit shit shit* has stopped, and the guy against the wall looks at me. "Hey, I know you," he says. And I think my own mother could be in front of me right now and I wouldn't recognize her.

"I don't think so," I say, but he's saying *shit shit shit* again.

Tonight I have been too stupid, too slow, too still. I have not done things I should have. My hand goes for my phone but my fingers are too shaky to dial.

"What are you doing?" he asks.

"Calling the cops," I say. Like I should've fucking done months ago when I was right in this very place but I didn't, and now Alex killed someone and I don't know what happened to Branley, and there's blood pooling on the floor and fuck I just figured out where that guy knows me from.

Now all I can say is *fuck fuck fuck*, and he takes it from me, making the call himself. I slump next to him, rock cold against my back.

"Here." He hands me a stick of gum. "You don't want to smell like beer when the cops come." I take it, balling up the wad of paper and throwing it on the floor with the rest of the trash.

"I wouldn't have done it," he says. "To you that night,

or to that girl now. You gotta know that."

And I don't know if it's guilt or fear or shock making his voice quiver, or maybe it's the actual truth and he wants so badly to believe it himself he's got to tell me, of all people. But I don't want his words, because I can't forgive him right now. Not when the spreading pool of Alex's blood has almost reached me.

"It's just Ray, man," he says. "He's like a bulldozer. You're along for the ride or you're crushed underneath."

And I think, yeah, he would've raped me, and Branley too, because who wants to be crushed when you can do the crushing? But when he gives me my phone back his hands are shaking worse than mine, and we can hardly make the exchange.

So I don't say it. I don't tell him that he's an asshole who would rather rape girls than stand up to his friend because I couldn't even make a fucking phone call to report my own assault because I was worried my friends who were drinking would be pissed at me, so what the fuck do I know?

"What do we tell them?" I ask. "What do we tell the cops when they get here?"

"The truth," he says. "Ain't no way around it. We tell them the truth."

The truth is that I saw my best friend kill someone with no hesitation. The truth is that I stood still and did nothing while the life was knocked out of her. The truth is that Alex had just told me we had the kind of friendship that doesn't end.

The truth is she had no way of knowing she was wrong.

61. JACK

I tell the truth. All of it.

Officer Nolan comes to my hospital room and writes until his pen is out of ink, holds up a finger to let me know he'll be right back, and returns with one from the nurse's desk, an advertisement for an antidepressant stamped across it.

He hasn't said a word and I have no idea if he believes me or not, but when he asked me what happened I wanted to answer, and not just about tonight. Because maybe if I talk about Alex—the Alex from before I even knew her—she won't be able to leave me yet. I'm keeping her alive with words, telling what happened years ago right up until now.

The town will explode, I know. Alex's name will

be everywhere, yearbooks cracked open so people can point and say they knew her. Her name and mine will be linked together forever, our names and faces the first thing that come to mind when the other is mentioned. And that's exactly what I want.

I'm dead calm as I talk, piling the words on top of one another so I don't have to hear my parents' voices in the hall, demanding to see me. I told Nolan to keep the door closed so I could tell the factual version, the one that has dates and times, conversations and locations. I'll tell Mom and Dad the story from my heart, the one with Branley and blood, the smell of smoke in the night and tears sliding over freckles.

The nurse told me I'm in shock and that's why I don't feel anything yet. I'm okay with that, because I know when it hits it's going to be a freight train that flattens me, knocking the wind out and leaving me on my knees, mouth open in a perpetual inhale before the racking sob breaks out.

Branley is already there. She's having a complete breakdown in the next room. I can hear her through the wall, the rise and fall of her voice as familiar as my own but breaking with emotion, whipping everyone along in a tide that floods through the whole hallway. She started screaming when they separated us, feet kicking, swear words flying. It took two orderlies to get her under control but they must have lost their grip at some point because now I can hear them yelling at her to get down off the bed and stop swinging the IV tree.

"Your friend isn't cooperating," Nolan says, putting the final period on my statement and slapping his notebook shut.

"Don't expect that to start anytime soon," I say.

"Okay for your parents to come in?"

I nod and they're through the door in a second, a nurse on their heels. My mom is a mess of tears, her face a mask folding under the mixed pressures of anger and grief, Alex's name a word her lips can't form yet. She just says *your girlfriend* with a question mark at the end of it, and I shake my head no. Dad's more like me, a brick wall that I know I'll have to run smack into as soon as I get home, all the questions and repercussions stopping me short the second I walk in the door.

"We want to keep him overnight because of the shock," the nurse tells my parents. They try to argue that I'm better off at home, but the truth is I'd rather stay here, and not just because I'm not ready to tell them everything. The sooner I'm home in my bed staring at the crack in my ceiling, the closer I'll be to returning to everyday life; the sooner I'll have to stare at the Hancock pennant my mom hung over my bed and admit that the fantasy Alex and I spun together about apartments and part-time jobs and Irish wolfhounds was exactly that—a fantasy. One that evaporated right in front of me in a spray of blood.

I know that the seconds are ticking by, making minutes, turning into hours, becoming days that will stretch into weeks and years. And with every sunset Alex will be a little farther from me, her face a bit fuzzier, her voice an echo, our time a memory. And I'm not letting go just yet. Right now life is on pause and I want it that way, because she can't slip away from me entirely until I start moving on.

Branley comes to me in the night, smelling like hospital soap and tears. I heard her shower running through the wall and her skin is still hot from it. Some of the red fades as she lies next to me, her body cooling. But there are spots where she scrubbed herself raw and they stay bright, peeking from under the sleeves of her hospital robe, the hem that stops right above her knees.

"I'm sorry," she says again, her throat raw.

I wrap my arms around her and she settles into me, her nose fitting in the spot between my collarbones, my chin resting on her head. We've been like this so often, as friends and as more, that it's second nature. Our breathing finds a rhythm together and I feel her soft movements beneath the blanket. I put my hand on hers to still it, where she's rubbing her upper arm. Her breath hisses out in pain as my fingers pass over three bumps just under the skin, embedded shot.

"I wouldn't let them take them out," she says, her lips moving against my chest.

I nod my understanding as her hand goes back to them, rubbing up and down in a hypnotic movement that draws us both down into exhaustion. And while she came to me out of habit, I know there's more comfort for her in those wounds than I can ever give.

62. **PEEKAY**

I'm somewhere I should never have to be.

Alex's grave has already settled, the dirt sinking a little lower with each rain. The grass all around her stone is trampled and muddy, pockmarked from the high heels and camera tripods. But the news crews aren't the only ones coming. I've been here every day in the week since her burial clearing away the debris.

There are the expected flowers, which I've been taking home and putting in vases until Mom said our house smelled like a funeral home, then clapped her hand over her mouth like she wished she could force the words back in. The plastic flowers I took to Goodwill until the girl at the donation center told me they didn't want any more. Now I just throw them in the Dumpster.

There are other things I don't know what to do with. Notes with names and dates, pages of diaries ripped out and weighed down with stones. Some of them have been folded tightly, some wide open, edges flapping in the wind. They're for Alex, not me. I read only a few at first, the open ones that were begging for someone to finally know. I wanted to stop because I couldn't stand the hot weight of all their knowledge in my stomach. Still, I read them. I read them until I understood Alex and what she did.

Her tombstone has become a shrine, the pilgrims coming under cover of darkness to unburden their secrets. The notes I clear away, sending their accusations to the sky with flames and smoke while I sit at the fire pit, across from the empty chair where Alex should be. Some things take longer to burn: a broken necklace, a frayed bra clasp, a pair of underwear with *I was fourteen* written on them in permanent marker.

My father presided over her funeral, not meeting my eyes when he quoted Romans 12:19 (*Do not take revenge, my friends, but leave room for God's wrath, for it is written, "Vengeance is mine, I will repay," says the Lord*), but he looked right at me when he hit on Micah 7:19 (*And all our sins are cast into the depths of the sea*). I don't know if he meant Alex's sins or everyone else's. Or maybe my own.

I hadn't talked to Jack about what he told the cops until we crossed paths at her grave one evening, me hauling away an armload of wilted flowers, him carrying a fresh batch. When he tried to talk to me about it, I punched him in the chest and he let me, crushing petals against him and driving thorns into his skin.

"You really didn't know?" he asked, eyes pinning mine in a way he must've picked up from Alex. I couldn't find words so I shook my head and walked away, but his question stuck with me.

No, I didn't know. Everyone else wants to talk about the Alex who tore Ray Parsons's nose off when he tried to hurt me, the Alex who tortured the man who killed her sister, the Alex who burned a child molester alive and blew a rapist away with a shotgun blast. Nobody wants to talk about the girl who held kittens in the palm of her hand, humming to them while they fed, or the girl who would pick fleas off a dog for hours. Because nobody else knew her.

I'm left to mourn someone alone, someone who I can't square with the one they put in the ground, the one the camera crews want to interview me about. I don't know how to say good-bye to someone who shared only half of herself with me.

Going back to school is the hardest part. The principal makes a big announcement about how we still have jobs to do even though there's only two days of school left, and we can't let *recent events interrupt our education.* The halls are filled with Alex's name even though she's not here anymore, and the whispers are so loud I almost don't hear Branley's gasp from the next locker down.

Somebody drew a dick on her locker. Anonymous. Erect. Demanding.

"Seriously?" Sara stops when she sees it.

Branley just stands there, a flush rising in her cheeks. I dig in my locker for a pencil, finally finding one with a decent eraser. Sara opens her backpack to find her own and between the two of us there's nothing left but smudge marks in a matter of minutes. But there are still tears in Branley's eyes when she thanks us and walks away as the bell rings.

Sara shakes her head. "Motherfuckers," she says under her breath.

"Yep," I agree.

"Dick," Sara says.

"What?" I ask, eyebrows shooting up.

"Dick." She points with her pencil at another drawing, this one on the wall down by the science room. The tardy bell goes off and we exchange glances.

"We're gonna need a bigger eraser," I say.

"I'm happy to let recent events interfere with my education if you are," she says.

We spend the rest of the period scavenging the halls, rubbing our erasers down to nubs and going to our lockers for fresh ones. I laugh for the first time in a while when Sara tells some other girls about what she dubs Penis Patrol.

"I don't get it," Marilee Nolan says. "It's not like I doodle pussy everywhere."

"Maybe you should start," somebody says, and Sara's eyes meet mine, her fork paused halfway to her mouth.

The next day the front entrance is covered in peach-colored window paint, the only way in or out of the school through a massive vagina. I almost choke in the parking lot, I'm laughing so hard. Sara joins me at my car.

"What do you think?"

"Don't they have security cameras?"

"Yeah, but it's worth it. I bet half the guys won't even walk through."

And she's right. The principal has to force a whole herd of sullen males through the doors, yelling at them that they're all late. Sara is called to the office halfway through the morning and I'm surprised to see her sitting in the cafeteria at lunch.

"I thought for sure you'd get suspended," I tell her, setting down my tray.

"Nah, the art teacher told the principal it was for my

final and that it was a peach and if he saw something else that was his fault, not mine. Then she gave me a book on Georgia O'Keeffe."

I let the fake smile I've been wearing in public slip away when I go to the bathroom. The grief sneaks up on me when I'm alone, cracking its way through the little walls I've built up to keep it away. Alex is gone but she's very much still here, and not only in my mind. I've seen her in Sara's willingness to skip class and erase dicks with me; in a loud complaint from a freshman instead of just rolling her eyes when a senior smacks her ass; in a *not cool, man* from Park when one of his friends made a rape joke. And she's here in the bathroom stall with me, her hand behind the writing on the wall even if it wasn't her fingers holding the marker.

stay away from Blake C.—date rape 3/26

me too—2/4

chad will roofie you don't party with him

There's other stuff there too: *Branley Jacobs is a whore* and *Alaina's a man-stealing bitch*, but they're faded like someone tried to wipe them away, the one about Branley half blacked out.

There are tears pooling in my eyes as I sneak into the janitor's closet. I'm armed with bottles of Windex, paper towels, and a Sharpie when I slip into the boys' bathroom in between classes, half expecting to be high as a kite before I get out of there. The motion-sensor lights kick in and even though it's the boys' bathroom, all I can see is Alex leaning against the sink as I wash my face, telling me why punching Branley isn't going to do any good.

I'm crying by the time I go into the first stall, the door clicking shut behind me as I pump the Windex, ready to wipe away anything that pisses me off. Instead I end up sitting on the toilet, reading things I never expected.

I love Jessica

Yr mom blew me, followed by

My mom's dead

Then—*Sorry, dude. My bad.*

Peekay won't put out

My fingers tighten into a fist, but underneath it I recognize Adam's handwriting: *U don't deserve it.*

And on the back of the stall door graffitied in letters as high as my arm:

REST IN PEACE ALEX

I pop the cap off my Sharpie, the smell filling the stall and stinging my eyes as I add underneath, *Amen.* The motion lights flicker off, but I can still see the message imprinted on my eyelids.

And I think maybe, just maybe, she can.

ACKNOWLEDGMENTS

All my books have taken me to dark places, but this one had special corners where the shadows were quite deep. As per my usual I dragged others there with me. Extensive thanks first need to go to my critique partners and fellow authors R. C. Lewis, Kate Karyus Quinn, Demitria Lunetta, and S. L. Duncan for reading without flinching . . . mostly.

I had many questions as I dove into this manuscript, many of them relating to the decomposition of dead bodies and the specific manner of the damage I would be inflicting on living ones. Special thanks to Scott Blough and Lydia Kang for assisting with the dead and the living, respectively.

This was my first attempt at writing from a male perspective, and I must thank Geoffrey Girard and Jordan Nelson for answering my man questions, including how to make a proper fist and not being alarmed when I abruptly text, "Tell me where the thumb goes again?" with zero context whatsoever.

Always, thanks to my amazing team at Katherine Tegen—Katherine, Ben Rosenthal, Stephanie Hoover, and Erin Fitzsimmons—and the lovely Margot Wood of Epic Reads. Publishing is a business, but they make it feel like a friendly one. Extra commendation to my unflappable agent, Adriann Ranta, who reacted well when I told her I had a manuscript in my closet from fifteen years ago that might be worth dusting off.

Lastly, my long-suffering family, especially my mother, who worries what the people at church will think of my books. And my boyfriend, who patiently cooks dinner and nods while on the receiving end of a manic creative burst coming from the floor, where I'm usually located at those times.

Turn the page for a sneak peek of Mindy McGinnis's
new psychological thriller

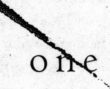

o ne

I'm digging splinters out of my gums again.

The closest music store carries only cheap reeds, and Mom and Dad won't pay shipping for something that weighs practically nothing. The end result is me leaning over the girls' bathroom sink with Brooke's tweezers, trying to focus on the sliver by my canine rather than my best friend's morbid fascination with the process.

"Some space?" I ask, pulling back from the mirror. It's hard enough to do this without her shoulder rubbing against mine.

"Sorry, Sasha," she says. "It's just so gross."

Which is exactly why she's leaning in. That's the kind of girl Brooke is. She'll pop the zits you can't reach and offer to skin everyone else's cat in bio, but the downside of having that for a friend is that she's also intensely interested in any open wounds you might have. I'm back up against the mirror, my breath fogging exactly where I need to see before she speaks again.

"I've never even heard of people getting reed splinters in their gums. . . ." She lets her sentence die out, like I'm supposed to provide a more likely explanation for the slivers of bone-white wood that work their way out of my gums.

"Reeds break." I shrug. "And no one else practices as much as I do."

Brooke nods in the mirror, because there's no point arguing about that. I arch an eyebrow at her and she nods, letting me know she won't interrupt again.

I pull down my lower lip, resting the tweezers on the callus that's developed on the inside. The latest splinter is barely poking through, a hard white tip in a sea of soft pink. Getting a good grip on them is always the worst part. Each near miss creates a scraping noise I can feel as well as hear, a tiny vibration that passes through the roots of my teeth. But leaving it there isn't an option. The last time I ignored one I got an infection and couldn't play for a week, after which Charity Newell challenged me for first chair. I retained my seat, but she looked oddly hopeful afterward—so I hadn't crushed her.

I pinch down on the tweezers at the right moment, the tip of the splinter flattening under the pressure. Behind me I hear Brooke taking a deep breath as I pull, the end finally coming free, the tiny round hole in my gum filling with a dot of blood. I run my tongue over it, the tang of copper fading quickly. Brooke takes her tweezers back from me, inspecting the tiny fleck of wood still stuck on the end.

"Does it hurt?" she asks.

I rinse my mouth out with water and do a quick check to see if there are more. "No," I tell her, which is sort of true.

Like a lot of things, it only hurts if you let it.

Brooke keeps an eye on me throughout lunch, like she thinks I'm going to cough up a femur or something. We're at our normal table, tucked into a corner where the band geeks and literal drama queens find a measure of peace. We can talk about wet versus dry embouchure without any unwanted sexual innuendo from idiots, and the word *thespian* gets by without giggles. Which is not to say that we don't have our own brand of shortcomings. If I hear one more joke about Heath's trombone . . .

"God, take a shower, Harver," Lilly says, but her eyes show something less than disgust as they follow Isaac Harver across the cafeteria. Brooke's too.

"That's easily three days no-wash, maybe five,"

Brooke says.

"You would know," Lilly says, rubbing the tips of her squeaky-clean blond curls between her fingers.

"Two weeks, baby." Brooke flips double V's for victory toward the football players' table. She hasn't let them live down the eighth-grade bet to see who could go the longest without showering. They ignore her, so she decides to pester Lilly instead.

"Like you'd pass up the chance to shower with Isaac," she says.

Lilly's narrowed eyes are still on him as he flops into his seat at the table by the window, the one that all the stoners claimed at the beginning of the year and no one had the guts to oust them from.

"Is there a prerinse involved?" Lilly asks, and Brooke busts out laughing.

"Omigod, you whore."

I smack down my spoon, not caring that chili splatters across Brooke's sweater. "Do you mind?"

"What?" Her eyes are wide and confused, but Brooke can't quite pull off total innocence. She knows exactly what she did.

"You should watch your language," I tell her. "One day it's going to bite you in the butt."

"I think you mean ass," Brooke says, and Lilly ducks her head so I can't see her smiling. But I know she is.

"Seriously, Brooke. Remember when Miss Upton dropped the f-bomb at band camp?"

"That one time?" Brooke adds, and Lilly can't smother her laugh.

That joke needs to die already.

"She was almost fired over it," I remind them.

Summer band camp doesn't exactly bring out the best in people, especially by midweek. Hauling heavy instruments in hundred-degree weather, blowing every breath you've got into music you haven't learned yet, and fresh breakouts around your lips as your mouthpiece jams every drop of sweat right back into your pores makes you cranky. It's not ideal, but it still wasn't okay for the flag instructor to toss out the big no-no when a girl lost her pole grip and Miss Upton took one in the face.

"I think you'd swear if your nose was broken too," Lilly says. She sneaks a glance at me and adds, "Maybe."

"Yeah, and anyway, she didn't actually say *fuck*," Brooke goes on, ignoring my wince. "It was more like—" She dumps some milk into her palm, huffs it up her nose, covers her face with her hands, and makes an inarticulate noise that might or might not be a swear. I can't tell because I'm already pushing back from the table to avoid the white froth Brooke is spewing everywhere.

"What?" she asks. "Too much?"

"No wonder you don't have a boyfriend," Lilly says.

Brooke waves her off as she wipes her face with a napkin. "Who cares? Unlike Sasha, I can survive without Heath's trom . . . boner."

And there it is. At least once a week. Why couldn't I date a drummer?

I wad up my own napkin, tossing it into my chili, where it immediately starts to soak up grease and sink.

"Seriously. Why are we even friends?"

Brooke stops laughing, managing to look dignified even with twin rivers of milk flowing from her nostrils. "I really don't know," she says.

And somehow, I feel like I didn't win that one.

There is nothing as beautiful as silver against black.

My clarinet rests in its case, but not for long. It's time to practice, time to smell wet cork and my own breath, time for my brain to disconnect and my fingers to move of their own volition, music seeping out from under my bedroom door until Mom calls me down to dinner. And maybe even after that, if I play softly enough that they can't hear.

Six years ago Mr. Hunter brought us into the high school band room, our little sixth-grade bodies small enough to fit into the instrument cages. He showed us every instrument, played a B flat major scale on each one, sent little slips home to our parents explaining financing options and the pros and cons of new versus used.

I knew what I wanted, even then. An unswerving dedication fired in my soul at the sight of the clarinet. I'm not like Lilly, who started out on trumpet, said it hurt her lips too much and tried a sax, flaked out and switched over to the flute, which she's stayed with for two years—but I've seen her casting looks at the oboes lately. I'm not like Brooke either, happy to stand in the back and hit bells, drums, timpani, freshmen, anything that gets close to her mallets.

They chose music because we always did things together, from dressing up like triplet bunnies at Halloween to making a pact that our boyfriends always had to get along with one another or it was a deal breaker. Lilly's talents extended from the orchestra pit to the stage, even if she had yet to snag a lead role, while Brooke had transposed her penchant for hitting things into a decent softball career.

Me, I live by one thing. And I do it well.

I snap the joints together and tighten the ligature, ignoring the slight scream in my wrist as I do. My hands have crackled since seventh grade, the tendons forever swollen and stiff. Mom keeps warning me that I'm doing permanent damage. Dad doesn't comment because he always has earplugs in.

It's together now, resting on my lap; the last rays of the evening sun slipping through my window and bouncing off the keys. I love how it looks so complicated, spikes of silver flaring, empty holes of nothingness, a mass of wood and metal that almost seems vicious until you hear its voice. Low. Melodic. Lulling. It can convince you of anything if you listen to it long enough. My hands find their place and do their work. They must want Brahms tonight because that's what my ears get.

There's nothing better than letting your brain go dead. I use it so much, taxing it to the limit with facts, theories, definitions—whatever I need to regurgitate for the next test. Then I push everything I dedicated my mind to for the week out the back door to make room for the next batch, the next test, a red A+ bleeding onto the white of whatever paper I wrote last.

It's my hands that know the clarinet, not my brain. It unclenches, resting lightly in a fluid bed as Brahms rocks it to sleep, the curtains of my eyelids drawing shut to give it peace from the daylight.

My phone goes off.

I jolt, knocking my teeth against the mouthpiece. The reed cracks and I suck back a word that I'd yell at Brooke for saying. I settle for growling deep in my throat as I dig through the mass of covers on my bed for the phone. It dings at me again, lighting up enough for me to see it under the pillow where it slipped when I tossed it on the bed.

There's a text from an unfamiliar number, with a monosyllabic message.

hey

I don't hesitate with my response. A few years ago Kate Gulland accidentally sexted with her boyfriend's dad because of a single-digit mix-up. She said it made Christmas dinner incredibly awkward.

Who is this?

There's no answer. I stare at the screen until the opening bars of Beethoven's Eighth that I use as my background begin to blur into each other. I roll onto my belly, phone still in hand but composure shattered. Full-on practice mode is my favorite place to be, but it's not an easy one to get to. Recapturing the semiconscious state that I prefer will take a full ten minutes, only to be interrupted again as soon as dinner is ready.

The phone vibrates in my hand, light bouncing off my palm.

Isaac

I roll my eyes.

Whatever, B. Give your little bro his phone back.

Brooke's time would be better spent perfecting the new cadence on her quads than screwing with me over text, or next week the woodwinds are going to march right into the brass when we try to pregame. I turn off my phone as Mom's voice sails up the stairs.

Dad likes to say the only things you can count on in life are death and taxes, but I'll add our seating arrangement at dinner to that. Dad at the head, Mom at the foot, me to his right. There are scuff marks on the wall behind me where I've shoved away from the table too hard, the back of my chair scraping away slivers of wallpaper and digging into the drywall underneath. Seventeen years' worth of minor arguments and a few dashes for the bathroom are imprinted there, marking my place.

I've charted the conversation while staring at the empty chair across from me. I know what to expect the moment my butt is in my spot, so I have my answers preloaded, my mouth ready to convince them I'm present and accounted for while my hands work through some fingering, tapping on the dead silence of fork and spoon.

"How was school today?" from Mom is a middle E, simple and sweet, a good warm-up for more complicated things to come.

"Fine. We played *insert current band piece here* and Brooke said, '*fill in with best friend's witticism of the day.*'" One note up, the F, all throat, which is fitting, since this is the most I'll say in the dinner hour.

Mom says, "How was work?" This is my cue to launch into the A flat major scale, because I'm not needed here. Dad will talk about foreign and domestic taxes, 529 payouts and offshore banking, then complain about people who don't understand these things. He fills his plate while he talks, making sure none of his food touches.

Much like the chairs around the table, safe distance is always assured.

He'll ask how her day was next, and Mom will talk about a long phone call with a friend, reiterating it almost word for word. I once made it through all twelve major scales while she informed us about someone's spinal fusion. I don't remember whose.

Sometimes I wonder what Mom's day is like once Dad and I are gone, if she's relieved to see our backs or if the house feels empty without us. Her coffee cups have permanent rings on the inside, her levels of determination rising as they drop. I imagine her day, starting with getting everyone else moving, ending with turning out bedroom lights. Though she always has something to say at dinner, I've noticed that Mom's stories are never about her.

My fingers have stopped moving, a spoonful of mashed potatoes paused halfway to my mouth.

"Sasha?" Mom asks. "Everything okay?"

"My day was fine," I say, and a line of worry forms

between her eyebrows. I've interrupted the flow of dinner, said a line from the beginning here at the end, where it doesn't belong.

"How are you?" I ask, and the line deepens into confusion. Dad always asks how her day was, which is something else entirely.

"I'm . . ." Mom shakes her head, not able to improvise an answer to an unscripted question. "I'm fine," she says. But her voice goes up at the end, turning it into an uncertainty.

Dad clears his throat. "Sasha."

"I'm fine too," I say.

And my chair smacks the wall as I leave.

Homework waits for me, reliable as ever. I turn on my phone so that I can have some Pachelbel in the background while I work. Everyone else in the world might prefer the Canon, but his Ciaccona in F minor blows it out of the water. Brooke says I only listen to it to be elitist.

I smirk while my phone powers up, thinking about Brooke. I'm sure I've got either an apology or a long line of texts from her still trying to convince me she's Isaac. Instead I get this:

WTF you gave me your #

U want me to txt you or not?

A new one comes in just as I'm about to crack some sass.

Whatever

Brooke may be my best friend, but she knows better than to whatever me, over text or otherwise. My phone shakes in my hands as I consider the alternatives. There aren't many. Either someone who doesn't like me is screwing with me—and I'll admit, that list is long—or, this actually is Isaac. Which puts me in an odd place because I have nothing to say to him. I settle for

I think you have the wrong number

Then I mute my phone and fire up the Pachelbel.

Brooke says life is easier in the key of F.

Of course she always adds "you."

Two stories of survival
from MINDY McGINNIS
"A brutally beautiful debut, not to be missed."
—MICHAEL GRANT, New York Times bestselling author of the Gone series
NOT A DROP TO DRINK
Mindy McGinnis
IN A HANDFUL OF DUST
Mindy McGinnis
"This writer is for real."
—New York Times bestselling author Michael Grant
KT
KATHERINE TEGEN BOOKS
An Imprint of HarperCollinsPublishers
www.epicreads.com

JOIN THE

Epic Reads

COMMUNITY

THE ULTIMATE YA DESTINATION

◀ **DISCOVER** ▶
your next favorite read

◀ **MEET** ▶
new authors to love

◀ **WIN** ▶
free books

◀ **SHARE** ▶
infographics, playlists, quizzes, and more

◀ **WATCH** ▶
the latest videos

www.epicreads.com